MW00772119

grotesquerie

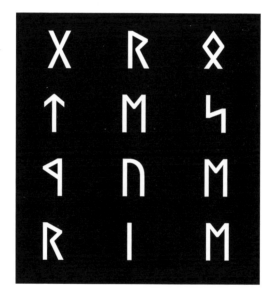

Advance Praise for *grotesquerie*

"Richard Gavin is an important figure in the contemporary horror/weird fiction field. Influenced by masters such as Blackwood and Ligotti, Gavin is cerebral, yet empathetic. He reconfigures classical tropes to suit his own unique perspective. *grotesquerie* is a major event."
- Laird Barron, author of *Swift to Chase*

"*grotesquerie* contains the latest records of Richard Gavin's continuing explorations of the intersection between the mundane and the numinous, the earthly and the spectral, the pastoral and the horrific. Drawing on and in dialogue with such writers of the visionary weird as Aickman, Ligotti, and Machen, Gavin's fictions extend the tradition into bold new territory. Original, idiosyncratic, Richard Gavin is like no one else."
- John Langan, author of *The Fisherman* and *Children of the Fang and Other Genealogies*.

"In *grotesquerie*, Richard Gavin summons ancient gods and vengeful ghosts. He nods knowingly to the horror/weird fiction greats, but forges a singularly unique vision."
- Priya Sharma, author of *Ormeshadow*

"...richly articulated nightmares that will delight horror fans [...] will put readers in mind of both classic weird fiction and the supernatural mysteries of the 1970s."
- Publishers Weekly

Other Books by Richard Gavin

Fiction Collections

Charnel Wine
Omens
The Darkly Splendid Realm
At Fear's Altar
Sylvan Dread: Tales of Pastoral Darkness

Esotericism

*The Benighted Path: Primeval Gnosis & The
Monstrous Soul*
*The Moribund Portal: Spectral Resonance and the
Numen of the Gallows*

As Editor

Penumbrae: An Occult Fiction Anthology (co-
edited with Daniel A. Schulke & Patricia Cram)

grotesquerie

richard gavin

UNDERTOW
PUBLICATIONS

grotesquerie
© 2020 Richard Gavin
Cover art © 2020 Mike Davis
Cover design © 2020 Vince Haig
Interior design, typesetting, and layout by Courtney Kelly
Interior decoration designed by Alvaro Cabrera|Freepik
Proof-reader: Carolyn Macdonell-Kelly

First Edition All Rights Reserved

TRADE ISBN: 978-1-988964-22-5
LIMITED HARDCOVER ISBN: 978-1-988964-23-2

This book is a work of fiction. Any resemblance to actual events or persons—living, dead, or undead—is entirely coincidental.

Undertow Publications Pickering, ON Canada
undertowpublications.com

Publication history appears at the back of this book.

'To the everlasting spirit of Rosaleen Norton, this lot of shadows & masques is offered.'

"If the objects of horror, in which the terrible grotesque finds its materials, were contemplated in their true light, and with the entire energy of the soul, they would cease to be grotesque, and become altogether sublime."

— John Ruskin, *The Stones of Venice* (1853)

Contents

Banishments

T he storm had swollen the creek and infused it with sludge. The brothers had come to the bank to take in some of the elements' power, perhaps even to feel rinsed and purged by these forces. But the sight of the muddied current gushing past caused Will to think that the tired cliché was untrue, for this brackish water did indeed seem thicker than the blood that supposedly bonded him to the man standing beside him.

Mutely they watched the parade of bobbing wreckage; a porch rocker, a bicycle tire, the tattered remnants of a tarp. These and more seemed to be flaunted by the roaring current, like a victor showcasing the spoils of battle; trophies from the homes this hurricane had pummeled.

Will sighed melodramatically; a wordless urging for them to be moving on. The pair stood under a dull sky. Will was secretly counting the seconds until this ritual of contrived grief over the fate of Dylan's neighbours, most of whom had been strangers to Will since childhood, could be tastefully concluded. He opened his mouth to speak, to remind Dylan that his house had been scarcely grazed by the storm, when they witnessed Death encroaching.

It came shimmying along the bends, using the current as its pallbearer. Under a sky whose grey conveyed a celestial exhaustion, Death swam swiftly.

It came in the form of an oblong box of tarnished iron. A fat padlock in the shape of a spade bounced upon its latch, clunking against the angled side; a lone drumbeat that provided this funeral its dirge. The coffin bobbed, spun in an eddy, then jutted toward the bank behind Dylan's home. Its motion was so forthright that for an instant Will believed the box was meant to reach them. It quickly became entangled in the low-looming branches and thickets that bearded the muddy bank.

Will watched as his brother charged down the embankment and entered the creek until its rushing waters rimmed his waist. Dylan managed to grip the end of the case just before it drifted out of reach. Dragging it toward him, Dylan nearly lost his footing, the sight of which inspired Will to leap to the water's edge.

Both of Dylan's hands were now clutching the oblong box. His movements were unnervingly jerky.

"Heavy!" he shouted. Will reached out to keep his brother righted.

The case struck the bank with a thump, which was soon followed by a faint sucking sound as the clay began to dutifully inter it. Will concluded that it must have been a struggle for the creek to keep this weighty thing afloat.

Dylan stood shivering. His pants sat slick upon his legs and his boots were weighted with frigid water. The brothers took a moment to study their treasure, which was, they discovered, more akin to a basket than a box. It was composed of iron bands, each approximately ten centimetres wide. The bands were woven together as one might do with wicker. The knit was airtight. Not a speck of the interior was visible. Will used the heel of his hand to wipe away some of the moisture from the lid. Two of the bands—one vertical, the other horizontal—felt rougher than the rest. Kneeling, squinting, Will surveyed the engravings.

If they were words, they were in a language of which

Will knew nothing. If symbols, Will had neither faith nor imagination enough to decipher them. The markings were crude. Their asymmetry and jagged texture suggested that the engraver was rushed, or possibly enraged. The wedges, gashes, and curlicues formed a decorated cross that stood out from the rest of the iron weave.

Will was suddenly seized by a divergent memory: he hearkened back to Dylan's and his parochial education. He envisioned the two of them now as being Pharaoh's daughters, rescuing a floating ark from its reedy doom.

"Let's get it inside," Dylan said, breaking his brother's reverie. "I'm freezing to death."

They returned to the house. Will entered first, snapping on the chandelier as a defense against the gloom. The light made the dining room inappropriately cozy. It also illuminated Julie's letter, which had been left on the walnut table; two tiny islands of white upon a sea of black wood. When Will had first arrived he'd found his younger sibling locked in a toxic fixation with this missive. Dylan had not merely studied it to the point of being able to recite both pages from memory but had begun to autopsy its script in search of hidden truths. Like a cryptographer, he'd started compiling lists that twisted the Dear John note into anagrams, into weird insect-looking hybrids of letters, not unlike the iron basket's engravings in fact.

Will hurried to the table and swept away the handwritten leaves and the handsome envelope that had held them.

Dylan approached the table.

The foul runoff from the iron case made a brown stippling pattern on the carpet. Dylan grunted as he set down the box.

Will held out his hands dramatically. "What now?"

Dylan, breathing heavily, tapped the heart-shaped padlock and then exited the room. For Will the wait seemed vast. When his brother returned, he came bearing a small tool chest. Silent with focus, Dylan went about unlocking the oblong box.

A squeeze of bolt-cutters made short work of the heart-shaped lock, which fell uselessly to the floor. Will studied this heart, which, despite being made of iron, could evidently be broken as readily as any other.

"Ready?" asked Dylan. Will shrugged. He truly was unsure.

The clasps that held the lid in place made a shrill peeping noise as Dylan peeled them back. He asked for his brother's assistance in lifting off the lid.

One glimpse of what the box contained caused Will to lose his grip. The lid crashed against the dining table, knocking over one of the high-backed chairs in its descent. Dylan brought a hand to his mouth.

The infant corpse was hideously well preserved. Its flesh, which looked as though it had been doused in powdered azure, still sat plump upon the bones. Its eyes were shut but its mouth was mangled wide, its final mewl trapped silently in time. Naked as the day it was born—if born it had been—the babe's body glistened under the electric chandelier's clinical light. Will, who was unable to bring himself to study the thing closely, assumed this sheen was creek water, but he made no effort to confirm this.

The creature's head was horrible. Will was unsure whether it was supposed to be a canine or a swine. Either way it was misshapen, like a hammer-forged sculpture by an unskilled artist. It also looked like it had been skinned. Its anatomy was terribly apparent.

"Look," urged Dylan, "come see. This figure. It's just so…"

"Gruesome?" offered Will.

"…so real…"

He was touching it now, his fingers passing in a reverential pattern over arms, belly, and tortured face. "Feels like it's made of wax."

This process ended with a hiss. Will looked at his brother,

whose fingers were welling up with blood.

"Its eyes are filled with pins."

Will's brow furrowed. He leaned into the coffin. His brother's blood droplets sat as miniscule gems upon the infant's livid brow, shimmering like beads of a sanguine rosary. Dylan was correct; what had been inlaid into the waxen eyelids were not lashes but rows of keen pins. The tongue appeared to be some form of curved blade. Will was also able to see the strange studded rows that lined the baby's wrists, shoulders, waist. They were nails; rugged and angular, the kind an old-world blacksmith might have wrought with hammer and flame. Some of the nails had been welded to the coffin itself. These held the figure in place, bound it. (Though he hadn't meant to, Will accidentally observed that the infant was sexless.)

"There's salt in its mouth," Will added.

Radiating from the casket's interior was the stench of musty vegetation, the decay one smells just before winter buries autumn's rot. Shielding his nose, Will stared down at the collection of waterlogged roots, leaves and petals that clung to the bottom of the box. This strange potpourri had formed a bed for the idol of crib death. The underside of several iron bands also bore the same mad engravings as the cross on the lid.

"We should call someone," suggested Will.

"Like who, the police? There's been no crime here."

"Maybe not, but this isn't right."

Dylan replaced the iron lid. "We don't even know what this is. It could be valuable. A work of art, maybe even a relic. I'll do some online research later." Dylan lifted the casket with a grunt.

"Where are you taking it?"

"Downstairs. I'm going to towel it off so I can get some clear pictures of those engravings. Somebody has to know what they mean."

Will stood listening to the clunks and puttering noises

coming from the basement. His brother then began to whistle some cheery, improvised tune.

※

For supper Will prepared them pork chops and steamed greens. They ate at the tiny kitchen table, for Will was unable to bear eating where the casket had been.

The only soundtrack to their meal was the sound of their own chewing. Dylan scarcely lifted his gaze from his phone, which sat next to his plate. He scrolled through photo after photo of the infant effigy, of each incised character upon the iron coffin.

"How many pictures of that thing did you take?" Will finally asked, uncapping a fresh beer. He did not take his eyes off his brother as he drank.

Dylan merely shrugged.

"Why don't you put that thing away so we can talk about what's really going on?"

The wooden chair creaked as Dylan leaned back. "What's there to say? Julie left. End of story."

"There's a whole lot to say," replied Will. "For starters, why don't you tell me how it reached this point? As far as I knew, you and Julie had the perfect marriage. Not to mention a free house with no mortgage to carry." Will could hear the edge creeping into his voice but did not care. "No kids to take your money or your time, and then two days ago I read this panicky social media post from you telling all your friends that she's gone. When I phoned, you sounded like a shattered man. You were barely coherent. I tell you I'm coming home to see you, and now you expect me to believe that after just one day you're fine?"

"I'm getting there."

"Well that's something, I suppose." Will rubbed his chin, sighed. "Can you tell me what happened at least? I mean, not every detail, just what led to Julie walking out?"

Dylan coughed into his fist. "Two days ago, she left me that letter telling me that we've drifted apart," he explained. "She said she didn't love me anymore, so I called her cell and left a voicemail saying that if that was true I want her to stay away for good. End of story." Coolly, he then took up his phone. "So it looks like those engravings are a mix of all sorts of different languages; Coptic, Germanic runes, ancient Greek."

Though he didn't fancy talking about their grotesque find, Will resigned himself to the fact that the topic of conversation had irretrievably shifted. "Did you find out what any of them mean?" he asked. He was given a simple 'yes' as an answer but received no elaboration. After a few frustrating moments had passed Will rose and hastily collected the plates.

Later in the evening he went down to their father's old workroom, where the casket sat upon the antiquated workbench. Dylan had already settled onto a wooden stool and had resumed his study of the etchings, referencing them against various websites on his phone.

"Where do you suppose it came from?" Dylan's tone was so wistful it rendered his question rhetorical. "Upstream obviously, but from where?"

"What, are you planning on returning it somehow?"

"I want to see if there's more. I want to know."

"Know *what*? Dylan, you'd better start giving me some straight answers. I came all the way back here to help you, so the least you can do is be honest with me."

Unable to bear being ignored, Will retreated upstairs in a manner both childish and melodramatic. Storming off to the bedroom he'd occupied until he left home at sixteen felt surreal, but surreal in an ugly, off-putting way, as though he was willingly stepping back into the very cell from which he'd managed to escape years earlier. The original wardens might have perished, but the prison was still being maintained by the heir apparent.

He stood listening to a house that had grown too still. Stepping into the hall, he found it vacant and dim. Descending the stairs, Will's nose was affronted by the scent of smoke.

"Dylan?" he called. When no reply came, Will hurried to the basement, where the smoke was thickest and its fragrance was chokingly strong. His eyes stinging, he made his way to the workbench, where faint embers spat upwards like tiny fireflies.

The floor suddenly went unstable beneath him. Will was hurled forward. Peering through the billowing plumes, he could just discern the dozens of woodscrews that carpeted the concrete and had tripped him up. Turning his gaze to the workbench, he saw the last of the embers fluttering down in grey husks to the open Mason jar that sat half-filled with the black remnants of burned paper. The jar was one of dozens their late father had used to store screws, nuts, bolts. This one had been set atop the casket.

Among the jar's blackened leavings was a scrap of paper that had not succumbed to the flames. Will recognized Julie's handwriting.

Again, he called his brother's name. The only response was the patter of rain that was beginning to strike the windows.

※

Will hadn't intended on falling asleep. He'd only retired to the living room sofa because there seemed to be little else he *could* do. He'd tried to watch television, but the storm had knocked out the satellite signal. The day's paper was a jumble of meaningless words. There had been no sign of Dylan.

He'd closed his eyes and had felt a soothing numbness passing through him. He'd watched distorted memories of his own boyhood in this very house pass across his mind's eye.

Had he always felt this way about his brother, he wondered? Always brimming with such jealousy over the ease and comfort with which Dylan's life seemed to have been blessed? Had it not been his own decision to leave home at sixteen and allow himself to grow estranged from his kin? Not even the successive deaths of both his parents was enough to lure Will back. It took discovering that Dylan had inherited the house and was now enjoying a happy marriage.

Will had learned of this turn of events through his obsessive, covert searches on social media. He was grateful for the technology that allowed him to keep tabs on Dylan cheaply and easily. It was this same medium that had allowed Will to watch Dylan's life dissolving. Ever a sponge sopping up attention, Dylan posted regular updates about his crumbling marriage, which gave Will the privilege of watching his brother's life crumble in real time. Only after a particularly fatalistic-sounding post about how Julie had left for good did Will finally attempt to reach out. Dylan had positively gushed over his brother's first communication in two decades. He'd immediately invited him back to the old house. Little did he suspect that what was driving Will's actions was not empathy but *schadenfreude*.

His sadistic pleasure was short-lived. Within hours of arriving home Will found his brother's state of mind…disquieting. Whatever heartsickness Dylan had been detailing for his online friends seemed to have been replaced by a form of mania. Will had even wondered if the whole drama had been nothing more than a ploy to bait him back to this suburban trap. But to what end?

Will's reverie was violently disrupted by a phone ringing. Blindly he fished out his cell from his shirt pocket. It was turned off.

Across the room, Dylan's cell phone rattled upon the dining room table. Will rose and shuffled toward it.

The caller I.D. consisted of a smiling selfie of Julie, along with her name and a tiny heart icon glowing beside it. Will took up the phone and wrestled with the idea of answering it.

It went still and silent before he could decide.

Will turned and began to search the house for his brother, but his efforts were in vain. Only after he'd stepped outside to check the backyard did he spot Dylan. He was stepping through the gate at the far end of the yard. From the vantage of the back deck, Will could see beyond the wooden fence to the elegiac creek that rushed ahead in search of eventual immersion into Baintree Lake.

Dylan crossed the yard. He was soaked to the skin. His shoes were slathered with mud. As his brother climbed the deck stairs, Will was able to see that Dylan's eyes were glassy, were fey.

"Where were you?" he asked.

Dylan pressed past him. His passage through the house left earthen footprints on the carpet. Stopping in the living room, Dylan began to peel away his dripping clothes. They plopped onto the floor. Stripped, Dylan shuffled down the hall toward the bathroom. Will heard the door click shut, then the telltale sound of running water.

Dylan finished showering and returned to the living room, dressed in socks and a terrycloth robe. He toweled his hair absentmindedly, staring at the wet stains on the carpet.

"I hung your clothes on the rack downstairs," Will explained, "and I tried to scrub the footprints out of the carpet as best I could. Mind telling me where you were all night?"

Dylan's mouth hitched into an unsettling half-smile. "What, you taking over for mom now that you're back?"

"I'm *not* back. And I'm not resurrecting mom. I'm just worried about you."

"There's nothing to worry about, truly *nothing*." Dylan chortled weirdly.

"Julie called your cell just before you came in."

These words choked off Dylan's meandering laughter. They also drained the blood from his face.

"*What?*"

Nonplussed, Will reached for Dylan's cell phone and displayed it, like the bearer of proof in some grand epistemology. "Looks like she left you a voicemail."

With a quaking hand Dylan slid the phone free. He had noticeable difficulty manipulating the keypad, but eventually he held the phone to his ear.

From where he stood, Will could just discern the mousy rasps of a shrill voice.

Dylan's arm dropped. His phone clunked against the floor.

"What is it?" asked Will frantically, "what'd she say?" He scooped up Dylan's dropped phone and slid it into the pocket of his trousers.

Wordlessly, Dylan advanced to the master bedroom. Will followed, spitting out a string of brief and frantic questions, none of which were answered.

Now dressed, Dylan stepped back into the hall. He was breathing heavily. "We have to return it," was all he said before charging downstairs.

He resurfaced bearing the iron casket. Will wrested on his shoes and tried to keep pace with his brother, who was already unlatching the gate at the rear of the yard. The creek was positively roaring as Will struggled to stay at Dylan's heels. The rain was intensifying, portending another storm.

"Where are we going?" he cried.

"Not far," Dylan replied. "I'll put it back. I'll make it right."

Together they traipsed the back of Baintree Common. In boyhood Will had played endlessly along these leafy banks, both with friends and with his brother. Though the housing complex had not appreciably changed over the years, its present aura seemed threatening.

"Here it is!" declared Dylan. "Help me with the fence."

"Whose house is this?" Will rasped as he gripped one of the fence boards. He watched his brother reverentially slip the woven coffin through the gap and then painfully wriggle himself through. Will followed. It was obvious that quizzing Dylan was futile.

The backyard of this home was far better maintained than that of his boyhood home. Will halted when he saw Dylan approach the sliding glass door. He waited to see who would answer his brother's rapping.

But Dylan did not knock; instead he set the casket down on the lawn and yanked at the door, throwing his weight into the task until the lock gave.

Aghast, Will began to feel as though he was watching a movie rather than experiencing the present. He saw his brother calmly take up the casket and slip past the ruined door. Panicked that he might be spotted, Will found himself following.

The strange house was immaculate in both upkeep and solitude. Standing in the kitchen, staring at the stainless-steel appliances and the polished floor, caused Will to suddenly become heartsick for his mother.

Dylan was noisily moving through the lower chambers. Will rushed to the descending stairwell. Once there he made note of a trio of framed photographs that hung in the main landing. Wedding photos, enlarged and richly coloured. The groom was a stout man with a crew-cut hairstyle and slender glasses balanced on a slightly bent nose. The bride was blonde and rather pretty.

Will's hand felt for the stair's railing. He gripped it and forced himself to breathe.

The bride in the photographs was Julie.

Will hissed his brother's name, for his throat allowed for nothing louder.

"I think it came from here," Dylan called back. "Come see."

Will's every step was reticent. His heart was thudding loudly. His saliva tasted of metal.

The chamber in which Dylan stood was scarcely broader

than a storage closet. An old-fashioned laundry tub stood against a wall built of cinderblocks with yellowing mortar. A cold draft lifted tufts of cobwebs from the grey brickwork. They lapped at the air like spectral tongues. The tiny room was uncharacteristically neglected and decayed compared to the rest of the house.

"Look!" cried Dylan. He pressed the chisel forward so that his brother might inspect it. The chisel's blade was caked with bluish wax. "This is what they used to sculpt it! And look down there!" Dylan pointed to the concrete floor, which had been stained barn-red. The paint was bubbled and peeling. Moving nearer, Will smelled flowers and something like old potatoes. There was a drain grill set into the floor. "I'll bet you they just lifted this grate and sent that thing downstream toward our house. Listen! You can hear the current through the grate. I watched this house all night from the banks, just waiting for them to leave for work. I knew it must have come from them. I *knew* it!"

"From *who?*" Will managed. "Dylan, whose house is this?" He lifted his hand. "Up there. Up there I saw..." He swallowed. "Dylan...what happened to Julie?"

Dylan was already crouching down to pry the grill from its nest. He looked up at his brother. His expression was one of shock. "There is no Julie," he said, as though it was the dullest of facts. "I made her up."

"But her pictures...upstairs there are..."

"I know. I copied all her photos from her social media account. Her real name is Chantal. She and her husband have lived in Baintree for a few years now. I've never met her, I just like the way she looks, so I made her my wife."

Will shook his head. "But there are all those photos of the two of you on your profile," he protested. "And with other people as well."

Dylan shrugged. "Photoshop. None of those people exist. The names of all my friends on social media? They're all fake accounts that I created. In fact, you're the only real person out of any of my online friends. The others are just stolen pictures and fabricated names."

Will bent over. It was as if his brother's revelation had struck him in the solar plexus. "Why?" he whispered. "Why, Dylan?"

"It wasn't supposed to go this far. I never thought you'd actually come, even if I did post news about my wife leaving me. You shouldn't have come back here."

"Neither of us should be *here*, not this house. This is crazy! Now let's go. Let's go home. We'll talk about it there, not here."

"Not until I see if this is how they sent it downriver. Help me lift this grate up."

Will was stock-still. A revelation had caused him to seize up. It took a great deal of willpower just to bring his hand to his pocket and free his brother's cell phone.

"What is it?" Dylan spat.

"She called you. Julie called you. You heard her voice. Let me hear her message. Dylan? I want to hear that message."

When his brother refused to yield from jimmying the grate in the floor, Will began frantically thumbing and scrolling about Dylan's phone.

"What are you doing?" Dylan shouted. He stood and lunged for the phone. The grate slipped from his fingers and clanged down viciously upon its frame. Before Dylan was able to yank the phone away Will had managed to bring up 'Julie's' number from the call history. He pressed the Dial icon. A purling noise leaked through the phone's speaker.

A beat later this noise was overpowered by a hideous buzzing that seemed to be emanating from inside the iron coffin.

The brothers were paralyzed. They stared into one another's fear-widened eyes. Neither of them could bring themselves to face the buzzing casket. Again and again the phone rang.

Even after Will dashed his brother's device against that decaying red floor and saw it splinter, the casket continued to hum.

Dylan eventually gripped the coffin lid. It hit the floor noisily.

The bluish thing was wriggling. Dylan took up the homeowner's chisel and began to tear the thing to pieces.

"No!" screamed Will, though he was unsure exactly why. Rushing up alongside his brother, he peered over the rim with its arcane etchings and looked at the pristine mutilation.

The livid wax curled back in ugly whitish rinds and rained down in clumps as Dylan continued to slash and twist and gouge. Though merely an effigy, its autopsy made Will's stomach flip. He watched the torso part and smear as his brother fished out the vibrating phone, which went still and silent the very instant it was freed from its host.

Now it was Will who began wresting free the floor grate. Dylan simply shuffled past him. Though he averted his eyes from the carnage, Will dutifully collected phone, carcass, and casket, dropping each in turn into the pipe. He heard them splash when they struck the watery base that was churning somewhere below.

He then ran as he had never run before. Outside the rain flailed and swept like great shapeless wings. Will wended the length of the raging creek, his feet puncturing the sucking clay that seemed to be slipping into the moving current moment by moment.

His relief at spotting Dylan up ahead was immense. He shouted his brother's name, but the storm swirled his voice into its cacophony, muzzling it. Dylan was leisurely sauntering along the bank, whereas he was running full measure. Will could not seem to close the gap between them. Time and again he cried out for Dylan but received not even a backward glance.

His frustration and fear ascending, Will took up a rock and hurled it at his brother's back. But before the stone could strike him, Dylan veered dramatically to his left.

The gate to their yard was still hanging open by the time Will reached it. He passed through and made his way toward the back deck.

He was stunned by the sight of figures, just merely visible through the glass doors, milling about their dining room. A peek into the kitchen window, which was veiled by mother's handmade curtains, revealed similarly obscure shapes shifting, gesturing, talking. Some of the figures were familiar to Will, having seen their photoshopped life moments many times on Dylan's social media page. The pattern of the lace curtains seemed to pixelate their faces.

The din of this unbidden gathering was audible even through the storm. The wan afternoon reduced the house's interior to a cave, but Will guessed that these guests numbered in the dozens. He scaled the steps of the deck. He wanted nothing more than to see his brother.

Moving to the glass door, Will suddenly stumbled. He looked down to see Dylan's shoes sitting tidily side-by-side. The downpour had already rinsed away much of the river mud. Will reached down to collect the shoes but discovered that they had been nailed to the wooden deck. The spikes that pinioned them were chunky and black, akin to the ones that pinioned the effigy to its casket.

The glass door slid back on its own. The susurrus was instantly silenced.

Something whimpered from the recesses of the house, something that sounded pained.

One of the figures stepped into the half-light and reached a flickering, blurry hand through the open doorway.

Will attempted to flee but found that he too had been rooted.

Fragile Masks

"**W**oolf."

The word caused Paige to flinch in the passenger seat. She scanned the leaf-carpeted banks of the road, looking for signs of movement.

"It was Virginia Woolf who took her life that way, not Brontë," Jon explained, "my mistake. Wait, did you think I saw an actual..."

"You gave me a start," she said brusquely.

Jon's mouth hitched into a grin, which made him look more pained than amused. "Maybe you have some Halloween spirit after all."

Paige made a noise with her throat, then stared out at the drabness that surrounded them. The road was all clay and ugly stones, and the trees that flanked it had lost their foliage. They passed a pumpkin patch, a cornfield, both of which had been gleaned of their growth. Even the sunlight was filtered through strips of gray clouds that reduced it to a vague glimmer, the way the features of the dead grow indistinct beneath the shroud.

"Any of this look familiar?" asked Jon.

"The country all looks the same to me."

"Oh. Well, according to my phone we're less than three miles from the bed-and-breakfast."

The final bend was riddled with potholes, forcing Jon to slow the car to a crawl. The phone app instructed him to turn left.

"Hmm," he muttered, "that doesn't seem correct."

"Why not?"

"Take a look down there, honey. That lane looks like a footpath. I doubt I could even get the car down there without getting the sides all scratched up by those trees. I'd hate to damage my new present." He patted the dashboard gently, then touched Paige's hair. "I know you said these places all look the same to you, but do you remember turning down a little lane like this when you were last here?"

"Teddy and I didn't stay at this particular place," Paige explained, "but it was near here."

Jon rubbed the back of his neck. The rush of blood had made him feel hot. "*Teddy...*" he mumbled, though not so softly as to go unheard.

She reached to the steering wheel, placed her hand over his. "This can be *our* place."

They made the turn.

He'd been correct about the narrowness of the lane but had underestimated its length, for by the time they came upon the white two-storey house, the main road was no longer visible. It was obvious that the photos they'd seen of the establishment online had been taken in fairer weather and during better times. The sloping lawn that had appeared so rich and manicured was now a sparse, brownish mat, interspersed with mud puddles and a birdbath of broken stone. Jon did his best to mask his feelings of having been swindled.

"I guess we just park over there." He indicated an oval patch of the yard that was inlaid with white gravel. They drove up alongside the beige jeep that was parked there, and then Jon switched off the engine.

He stepped out and immediately gave the car, which Paige had given him as a spontaneous gift over the summer, an inspection for scratches.

"The paint is fine," said Paige.

Jon nodded, collected their bags.

The only detail that distinguished the house as a business was a small placard beside the doorframe: GUESTS—PLEASE RING DOORBELL FOR SERVICE.

"This doesn't look very..."

"Very what?" Paige asked.

Jon shrugged. "All I mean is, you can afford to holiday in places much nicer than this."

"I think it's perfect."

Paige obeyed the sign and pressed the button. They stood in wait on the covered porch and Jon whispered to her that he hoped they would have enough privacy.

The woman who drew back the inner door was genial, energetic, and, Jon felt, very well put together for someone her age. Her hair, obviously dyed, was the colour of rusted tin. She extended her hand, introduced herself as Imogene, and then plucked both suitcases from Jon's hands.

"Oh, that's not necessary," he said.

"Nonsense," replied Imogene, "come, come."

The couple followed a wake of perfume that smelled of clean linen. Imogene led them to a handsome Edwardian desk and bade them to sit. Stationing herself behind the desk, she deftly collected file folders and confirmed the details of their stay.

"Just one night it is then?"

"Yes," Paige said.

"It's refreshing to have guests here on a Tuesday, especially during the off-season. Both of my rooms are booked for tonight in fact. Are you here for the Halloween Ball over in Durham?"

"There's a Ball?" Jon asked.

At this same instant Paige uttered, "No."

"Oh, that's too bad," said Imogene. "The other couple

that's here said they're not going either. You really should reconsider. It's a good deal of fun. I'm going there myself after supper tonight. You did know that here we offer both dinner and breakfast to all guests?"

"Yes, that's excellent, thank you," said Paige.

"Can I ask if that scent from the kitchen is tonight's dinner?" Jon said.

"It is—Irish stew and homemade bread."

"Good Celtic fare. That's fitting."

Imogene looked confused.

Jon felt himself blushing. "Halloween…it was a Celtic festival…way back, I mean."

"A fountain of information, this one," she said, winking at Paige.

They signed the registration forms and were shown to their room, which was slight but stylish.

"The tub is really something," Paige said as she emerged from the washroom, "I could practically swim in it." She found Jon standing between the bed and the nightstand. He had a finger pressed to his mouth. Warbled voices, one deep and the other bright, were audible from the adjoining room.

"Just as I'd feared," grumbled Jon as he maneuvered out of the awkward space. "These walls are like tissue paper. We'll not have any privacy at all. I can practically hear them breathing next door."

"Well there's nothing we can do about it now."

"I suppose. Why don't we go for a walk before dinner?"

"I'd rather not."

The woman beyond the wall laughed shrilly.

Jon sighed. "What *would* you like to do?"

"I think I'm going to soak in that tub for a while."

He was hoping for some indication that Paige wanted company. When none came, he proceeded to unpack and then went to appreciate the view, such as it was, from the upper storey window. The landscape that surrounded them looked as dull as the piled clouds. Their room was facing the lane, yet even from this higher vantage the main road remained obscured by bends in the lane and by the unkempt verge.

"Pretty?"

Paige's voice startled him. He spun around and asked, "How was your bath?"

"Lovely, but now I'm famished. I'll get dressed and we can go downstairs."

Soon after, they were about to venture down when Paige decided to change shoes. While Jon was waiting in the hallway, the other couple emerged from their room. Jon experienced a pang of social anxiety. The three of them nodded and offered vague greetings.

The other man then said, "Hello, Paige."

Jon snapped his head back to the doorway of his room.

"Teddy."

"Did you say?" Jon uttered hoarsely.

"I'd like you to meet Alicia, my fiancée. Alicia, this is Paige and...?"

Jon shook hands but did not think to introduce himself. The four of them casually forged a circle. Three of them conversed. Jon, however, scarcely spoke and heard even less of the discussion. His brain was oscillating between disbelief and rage.

"Well," Teddy said, checking his watch, "shall we go down?"

He wrapped his arm around Alicia's waist and the two of them descended the stairs. Paige was about to follow when Jon gripped her wrist.

"I need to talk to you," he rasped. "In here." He opened the door to their room. Paige was reluctant to close it once she saw the expression on her lover's face. "What do you take me for?"

"I'm sorry?" she said.

"Is this your idea of a sick joke, dragging me here to spend the night with your ex-husband? What, are you two comparing your new paramours?"

"I didn't know he would be here!"

"Right."

"I *didn't*. Last year we stayed near here, yes, but how could I have known that he would pick this exact place on the same night as we did?"

"An amazing coincidence, no?"

"That's just what it is." She pressed herself against him, kissed his neck. "I swear. I'm not thrilled with this either, but let's not let it ruin our trip. Let's just go have some dinner, be civil for an hour or so, and then I'm going to prove to you that I'm yours and only yours."

Paige's whispered words and the gestures that followed caused Jon's anatomy to reflexively awaken even though his take on the situation hadn't changed. Paige took his hand and together they slipped down to the dining room.

Four settings had been placed upon a large tortoise-shell table that sat beneath a hanging lamp with a golden dome. Teddy and Alicia were already seated, their hands clasped in a churlish show of their bond. Jon forewent his habit of pulling out Paige's chair. One wall of the dining room was covered in gold-veined mirror panels. Jon moved in front of this and sat down heavily. He poured himself some ice water from the crystal pitcher. He could feel Teddy seeking eye contact, perhaps to start a conversation, perhaps to assess how deeply his presence was troubling him. Jon refused to look up from his glass, at least until the kitchen door swung open and he caught sight of Imogene wheeling in a serving cart. It took all his resolve to keep from laughing in the woman's face.

Imogene's costume, if it was that, was a hybrid of Hollywood witch and low-rate prostitute. Her reddish hair was now capped with a conical hat and her eyes were heavily laden with kohl. The dress she wore revealed too much of her flesh, which in turn betrayed far too much of her age, or so Jon felt. Her breasts, plumped by a push-up bra, were creased and freckled, and her legs sat lumpy inside their stockings.

Jon's sense of disgust was suddenly replaced by a powerful lash of shame. Had his inner self always been this judgmental, this ugly, he wondered?

The other guests proceeded to heap praise on their hostess's appearance, which only increased Jon's self-loathing.

"I'm off to the dance just as soon as I get you good people fed," said Imogene. "Now, please don't even trouble yourself once you're finished. I'll clean everything once I'm back, and then the dining room will be all ready for your breakfast feast tomorrow."

As she ladled out the stew, Teddy questioned her about it containing eye of newt. Other jokes, equally dreadful, were offered. With the main course served, Imogene then made several trips back to the kitchen, returning each time with a platter of desserts, which she laid out in a row on a stout hutch that stood against the dining room wall.

"Here is my cell phone number," she said, snapping a business card onto the table. "Don't hesitate to call if you need anything, but I won't be late at all. Happy Halloween!"

Her heels click-clacked along the hardwood floor and she was gone.

Jon spooned up more of the stew, which was nowhere as succulent as its aroma. Teddy, Alicia, and Paige had no difficulty finding topics of conversation. When Jon emptied the last drop from the pitcher, Teddy clapped his hands and announced that he'd brought something much finer than ice water. He rose from the table and darted upstairs, returning a moment later with a bottle of twenty-year-old scotch. Glasses were filled, including Jon's. They drank and chatted and switched off the overhead light to bask in the cold moonlight.

Jon cleared his throat. "Alicia, can I ask you something?"

In the bluish light, her startled expression appeared ghastly. "I...suppose so."

"Did you know that Teddy here was once married to Paige?"

Alicia's eyes fell to her finger of scotch. "Yes, of course I did. Teddy told me."

"*When* did Teddy tell you? Before you came up here? After?"

Paige gripped Jon's forearm, mouthed the word 'stop'.

Alicia shrugged and said, "I think the important thing is that we all managed to get away, tonight especially."

"Why? Because of Halloween?" asked Jon.

"Because of Paige's father," Teddy said in a steely, final-sounding tone.

Jon felt his brow furrowing.

"This is the anniversary of his passing."

The fact that it was Paige who provided this information refreshed Jon's overall annoyance. The fact that he was ignorant of today's underlying significance to Paige made him feel wilted. Alicia reached over and began to rub her paramour's back. Teddy's eyes were fixed on Jon. Shadows obscured the nature of his gaze, but Jon could sense that it was withering.

"I'm sorry, I didn't realize." Jon was overcome with regret the instant he uttered the apology. Why should he offer comfort to a man who should by all rights be a relic in his lover's past? But Teddy was no memory, no skeleton in Paige's closet. He was here, right alongside them, shadowing their every moment together.

"I take it that you were close to your late and former father-in-law?" asked Jon.

"Teddy and I tended to him during his last year," Paige explained. "It was an awful time. Daddy was so sick, so frail. He required around-the-clock care."

Jon didn't care at all for the way Paige's expression changed while she recalled this ordeal, of which he had known nothing. Her face had become a mask of admiration, respect.

"If he was so sick," Jon began, "his death must have been

something of a blessing then, yes?"

"I'm sure it was no less painful." This time it was Alicia doing the judging.

Jon had to resist the urge to let out a primal scream.

"That's why Paige and I, together or separately, always try to get away every October 31st and go somewhere new."

"Somewhere we've never been."

This last phrase was uttered by Paige and Teddy in unison. Jon turned to her, saw the tears sparkling beneath her black lashes. Alicia reached across the table and handed Paige a napkin.

"I'll be in the room," Jon said plainly. His ascent of the stairs was noiseless. Once inside their room he found he was without energy. He flopped onto the bed and switched on the television, which was ludicrously large for a room of this size.

A news station was recapping its main stories. Jon gazed absentmindedly at this for a few minutes before deciding that discussions of the Dow Jones and fuel-tax hikes were much too vulgar. A changing of the channel flung him into a séance. The Classic Movie channel, like most stations, was marking the holiday with a horror marathon. This particular scene was unfamiliar to Jon, which did not surprise him as he'd never been much of a film buff. It was in black-and-white. A lone violin provided the reedy, spectral score. A foursome of well-to-do-looking adults was seated around a circular table. They appeared to be meeting in a seaside mansion. A single white candle guttered in the foreground. The camera was positioned to give the viewer the impression that they too were part of this circle.

One of the women at the table began to groan. The camera spun to face her. "*…Laughing Lady, is that you?*" gasped one of the others at the table. "*Laughing Lady, come back. Join us in this circle, gathered here in your honour. In life, your powers condemned you to the bedlam. In death, you found freedom. Share your wisdom with us!*"

Cackling suddenly blasted from the speakers. Jon was surprised to feel the hair on his arms lifting. A howling wind extinguished the on-screen candle. Jon took up the remote and pressed the Information button:

HAUNT OF THE LAUGHING LADY/1958
CAST: JAYNE VANCE, CYRIL DONNELLY. DIR.
JACQUES PEPPET.

Jon had never so much as heard of the film or any of its talents. He switched off the set and reposed for a few moments in the unlit stillness.

His trance was broken when a pair of headlights brightened his window. He listened intently but heard no car moving down the lane. The lights dimmed then dissipated. Jon went to the pane and peered out. The moon was now masked by clouds, so only hints of the environment were visible: the skeletal trees, the vague lay of the path, his and Teddy's vehicles reposing side-by-side. Had Teddy's jeep also been a gift from Paige, Jon wondered?

"We need to talk."

He hadn't even noticed Paige entering the room, so her voice startled him. He had to squint just to pick up her reflection in the glass.

"I don't feel like talking."

He returned to the bed and lay down again. Paige continued to speak, even lecture, but Jon did not listen.

What he did listen to were Teddy's and Alicia's voices as they leaked through the wall that divided their quarters from his and Paige's. The exact words were instantly interred in the dividing wall, but Jon could tell that their conversation was, if not heated, then certainly emotional. At one point he heard their door close, then heavy footsteps on the stairs. He strained to pick up any further sounds; hopefully the closing of the house's main door, the sound of Teddy's jeep engine. But the only noises were those of Paige readying herself for bed and, later, the faint rumble of her snore. Jon knew that for him sleep was far off, if not altogether impossible.

Another pair of lights suddenly brightened the window. Though these lights were somewhat murkier than the first, their hue was unusual—red-tinged, like two signal-lanterns glowing wanly by some rustic stretch of railway. Again, these lights arrived noiselessly, but this time they lingered.

Jon rose and moved to the glass.

The light radiated from two small orbs the size and hue of fresh embers. Jon watched them as they bobbed before the main floor window. The sensation that overcame him as he studied the orbs was something Jon could not identify. Though the lights dazzled him, he felt no joy. While their sheer strangeness frightened him, he would not have called this feeling terror.

The lights began to waver, brightening and fading in turn.

It was crucial that he fully see them, that he bask in their presence as intimately and for as long as possible. He mustn't let them vanish. Even the act of closing the door behind him felt like an interminable delay.

Jon took the stairs two at a time, but by the time his feet hit the foyer, the glowing orbs were gone.

Disappointment weighted him like a millstone. He imagined himself as the figure in some Expressionist painting—all shadow and low-hanging head, stewing in his own ennui.

"Is she taking care of you?"

Jon spun around and saw that he was not the sole figure in this grim setting. Teddy was seated at the dining table. The bottle of scotch before him was visibly emptier than it had been at dinner. Judging by the slur of his speech, much of it had gone down Teddy's throat.

"Did you see them," Jon asked, "the lights?"

"I'm sure she is," Teddy continued. "Paige takes care

of all her men. For a while. That's the way it goes…Paige's father took care of her, then we took care of him… That long final year…we took care…we just had to add a little bit in his food…just a touch…meal after meal after meal…even the coroner couldn't tell…Paige saw to everything… And then the windfall was all hers…she told me it'd be ours…but it was hers…or hers and yours now maybe…"

"What are you saying?"

Teddy refilled his glass. The silence that hung between the two men was made even more tedious by the grandfather clock whose ticking emphasized the interminable length of this pause.

"I don't like this place." Teddy's voice had now assumed the grating whine of the self-pitying drunk. "Don't like it at all…too close to last year's…we should have gone farther away…you should have gone farther, too…"

The light returned. Or perhaps this was the emergence of a different light altogether, for its colour and its intensity were different. No longer the scarlet orbs, this new light was bluish and painfully bright. It pressed in on the entire front of the house, brightening the foyer like some close, ferocious moon. Jon hurried to the living room's picture window.

Without, the entire property was awash in the livid shimmer. All shadow had been purged.

This queer new illumination made the figure that was moving down the lane plainly visible. It was human, or had once been, but its form was devious in shape, and each shambling step it took toward the house looked painful. The figure's right arm swung wildly as it moved, yet its left seemed almost fossilized in place. The head was cocked at an impossible angle. Jon hoped that it was merely the wind pressing against the boards, for he could hear the unmistakable sound of moaning.

"What is it?" Teddy had moved up behind Jon and was squinting through the hanging sheers. "…Why…" This was the only word Teddy managed before his breathing was reduced to a series of sharp, frantic gasps. He backed away from the window, moving into the dining room where he upset one of the high-backed chairs before crumpling down onto to the carpet. "We didn't hide well enough...*he's found us...he's found...*"

Teddy's voice was muted. What silenced it was the presence that had miraculously managed to go from shambling down the winding lane to standing inside the foyer of the house.

Jon stood in the living room, staring at the apparition. It was the first time he'd ever doubted his mind and all his senses. For even though he was wholly present, his every sense engaged by what was now before him, his rational brain refused to accept it. Like a spoiled child, his reason ranted against the sight of this crooked guest.

The interior of the house had become stilled, as if the hands of time were being held in place by some greater force. Everything seemed to be stretching, crackling with the cold, stifling power of impossibility.

The figure was that of an old man. Jon's nostrils were impacted by a waxy stench of illness and unwashed skin.

For an instant Jon thought of bursting through the picture window and tearing down the lane. What prevented him from doing this was a genuine uncertainty that he would even find a world out there, at the lane's end.

The figure advanced to the staircase. It appeared to be using the banister to pull its frame up the steps. When it was halfway up, Jon discovered that the revenant was footless.

By now the bluish glow had faded, leaving the main floor in a terrible darkness. Paige's face flashed in Jon's mind, breaking his trance. He took a step forward and was instantly overwhelmed with vertigo. Swallowing back the bile in this throat, he staggered to the stairs.

Teddy was visible in his periphery, huddled like a puppy

under the dining room table, his large frame quaking, his sobs sounding like cat mewls.

Jon found himself no better equipped to scale the stairs than the spectre had been. Even the idea of touching that banister repulsed him. Instead of using it, he crawled up the carpeted steps before frantically moving down the hall. He turned the handle to their room, tumbled inside, and immediately shut and locked the door.

"*Paige!*" he hissed, again and again. Her snoring was louder now. Not even his violent shaking of her body managed to rouse Paige from sleep.

The walls here were so very thin, every sound seeped through from the opposite room. Jon sat on the floor beside the bed. He listened helplessly, or, if he was being honest, feebly, to every awful noise that stabbed at his psyche; the thuds, the feminine screams muted by, what? A pillow? A foul hand? There was low grunting and creaking springs. The headboard thumped against the wall again and again, in a rhythm that should only ever be made by lovers. One of the room's hanging pictures was knocked from its hook.

When Jon heard Alicia struggling to call out Teddy's name, he dragged himself into the bathroom and shut the door. Not daring to switch on the light, or even to breathe too loudly, he crawled into the tub that was still damp from Paige's luxurious bath.

✳

Jon shifted, his limbs aching. Though he was sure he hadn't slept, he was groggy nonetheless. He sat up in the tub and, against his better judgment, he strained to listen.

There were noises in the house, but not the kind he was expecting. Through the floor he could hear the chink of dishes and women's voices. He recognized Paige's laugh.

He climbed out of the tub and, with breath held, pulled

back the door. Clear autumnal sunlight filled the bedroom. His and Paige's suitcases were sitting atop the made bed.

Stepping into the upper hall, Jon had no trouble avoiding the closed door to Teddy's and Alicia's room. He descended the stairs, keeping his hands in his pockets.

Paige was the only guest in the dining room. When she saw Jon in the foyer, her only greeting was a lift of her eyebrows. She bit into a pastry, then reached for her coffee-cup.

The hutch by the mirrored wall was heaped with a variety of cakes and pastries. The silver coffee-urn needed polishing.

Imogene entered through the swinging kitchen door. Her outfit was in such contrast to yesterday's attire that it took Jon a moment to identify her.

"Good morning," she said. She was dressed in slacks and an oversized cable-knit sweater that was the colour of yellow sugar. Imogene placed another tray of delicacies on the serving table.

Jon pulled out a chair and sat down.

"Imogene was telling me that she's thinking of only staying open for the summer from now on," Paige said.

"I'm considering it," said Imogene. "It would be nice to just let people see the place in full-bloom. I might just close it up once the leaves begin to turn." She was not wearing any makeup.

The sound of movement drew Jon's eyes from his hostess to the foyer. Teddy was patiently leading Alicia down the stairs, whispering lovingly to her the entire time. When Jon saw Alicia's appearance, last night's potent vertigo once again pressed through him. Her flesh was as bloodless as the revenant's. Jon couldn't help but wonder if she was now somehow infected, if she shared in whatever affliction kept creatures like that in their half-life. Her manner was catatonic.

The couple exited the house without a word. Through the picture window Jon watched their jeep driving down the sunlit lane.

Imogene went back into the kitchen, at which time Paige expressed how disappointed she would be if the bed-and-breakfast wasn't open next fall. She said this could be the beginning of a new Halloween tradition for the two of them.

Jon was unsure which two she meant. He stared at his reflection in the mirrored wall, whose gold veins marred his face like cracks in a fragile mask. This image bored into him, caused his hands to tremble. Halloween's masquerade was now over and fate, it seemed, was forcing him out of his cherished disguise. The last twenty-four hours, with all their ugly spite, antagonism, and above all cowardice, raced through Jon's mind. Everything was coming undone. His precious mask was slipping. Jon lowered his head, partly in shame and partly to avoid looking at the marbled glass. He knew it was only a question of time before he'd have to look upon the long-hidden face of his true self.

Neithernor

1.

Vera was my only cousin and was a distant one in more than the usual way; genetically, yes, but also geographically, emotionally, and, I now see, in the character of what one might call spirit or soul. We had never shared any sort of kinship, or truly any acquaintanceship, to speak of. Best as my holey memory serves, Vera and I had met only a single time, at a stuffy family reunion that had taken place during my tenth Thanksgiving.

To suggest that any sort of foreshadowing had taken place during that soporific feast day would be prevarication of the highest order. I recall only that Vera had worn a plaid skirt and that her hair was very dark and very straight and rather short; not quite as short as I'd worn mine, but nearly. It is dubious that we exchanged any words beyond asking for a condiment to be slung down the chain of hands that lined the long banquet table.

Forearmed with this knowledge, I hope you might appreciate the dazed reaction I experienced when, on assignment, I came upon her name in conjunction with a tiny art gallery on the outskirts of the city.

"Yes, they're very interesting, aren't they? Very interesting indeed. They're made by a local woman; each piece is done by hand and each is one-of-a-kind." This was the voice of the older man who was perched behind the tiny counter. His was the physique of an overfed pigeon and his eyes were large and rheumy. The wooden stool that braced him groaned woefully each time he fidgeted, which was often. His teeth were the grey of cooked mushrooms and they shimmered with saliva when he smiled, which, thankfully, he did but once.

"Unique," I said, hoping that the proprietor would retort with something like 'Oh, yes, very unique' or 'truly unique' so that I could then correct him by saying that the word 'unique' implicitly means something singular and without equal and thus requires no modifiers to enhance it. I enjoy giving these sorts of lessons to my public. Language is so very important, dying though it may be.

But the droopy man's only response was a wet-sounding sneeze. I moved further down the gallery's aisle, pausing to study an especially complex and delicate-looking piece that sat beneath the smudgy glass of a display case.

"That the carousel you're looking at?" the proprietor asked, returning his hanky to the inside of his vest. "A keen eye you've got, sir. I'm fond of that one myself."

I nodded. "Yes...yes I suppose it is a carousel at that. Truth be told, I thought it was a scorpion at first."

He chortled. "That's the rub of it. That's Ms. Elan's gift, you see? Your eye's sharper than most, I daresay. She calls this series 'Neithernor,' because they are neither one thing nor the other. One sees two things at once, you might say. Take that one, for example..."

He leaned forward on his stool and for a moment I feared he might try to rise, but he merely pointed to the case at the end of the show floor. I moved to it to save him further exertion. I studied the biggish piece featured there.

"For the longest time I thought that one represented a handheld mirror, then a young lady from one of the universities nearby told me that it was most definitely an Egyptian ankh. Now I don't know which it is. I tell you, the funny thing is, when I leave here at night I will often think about Ms. Elan's work, while I'm cooking my supper or lying in bed about to sleep. I think of it, but I can never remember exactly what these pieces look like. Isn't that a puzzler? I sit here five days a week and I study them, trying to memorize every curl and bend, but once I leave this room, my memories change. The pieces become something different than what they were. Neithernor..." the old man's mind was drifting.

"Maybe it's like the Hindus with their *neti neti*, 'not this, not that,'" he continued. "Talented artist, she is. I'd like to show you my favourite of her creations, a sofa with teeth, but it sold in August."

It was on the tip of my tongue to boast about my relation to the artist, but I didn't.

"It's clear she's been successful, given that this gallery showing is all hers."

The man's head drooped as if ashamed. "We're a consignment gallery, sir. We'd pay our artists if we could though. Surely we would."

"She lives locally you said?" I returned, changing the subject.

"Well, her representatives do at the very least. They deliver me new pieces every few weeks or so."

"Her works do sell then?"

"Occasionally. To tourists mostly. Slow time right now, being the off-season."

"Could I trouble you for Ms. Elan's contact information? I'm the arts and culture writer for the Mirror and I'm always looking to educate my readers on the more unique goings-on outside of the city."

"A writer! Well, well, well. But you have me at a disadvantage, sir. Vera is a very private woman."

I nodded. "That's fine. Might I leave you my information so that Vera or her representatives can contact me if they wish?"

"Yes, yes."

I produced my card then made my way to the door.

Prior to exiting, I posed one last question to the owner.

"Yes," the man confirmed, "yes, every piece is, sir. Copper wire and human hair, that's Ms. Elan's medium. As I said, sir, you've a keen eye. Very keen."

2.

After I returned to the city and to the echo-heavy building that is the Mirror's headquarters and to my tidy desk that is stationed within it, I had every intention of drafting an official proposal concerning a local interest column on my cousin Vera. But two enmeshed events intervened to keep me from forwarding the idea to my editor. The foremost of these was an electrical fire in the annex beside mine, which resulted in irreparable smoke damage to a number of my belongings, including the entirety of my music collection and a suede armchair that was very nearly a favourite. The next event was my becoming engaged to a woman named Cara.

I am to blame entirely for this romance. Cara was a clerk at the music shop that sat between the Mirror office and my smoke-damaged home. For a period of a month, perhaps longer, I incorporated a stop at the music store into my lunch hour routine. Cara was not the reason for my frequent visits (though she would likely say otherwise). I was simply trying to not merely replenish but actually improve my lamented record collection and the shop's location was convenient. My guilt in this crime of the heart was ordering Tchaikovsky, which women almost always equate with sensitivity. He is my own concession to the delicate, and it cost me. I have always theorized that women like men who like Tchaikovsky. I have become living proof of this theory.

What shall I say about our courtship? We talked and Cara made recommendations of records I did not buy. Somehow, we ended up at a café and later in her bed and much later in a townhouse that we shared. As to who proposed to whom, my recollection is foggy, but Cara insists that I asked her in a manner that was "endearingly shy." This is the version she tells her friends and her mother, at whose apartment we have lunch every Sunday. I suppose this version is accurate enough.

There were and are obvious advantages to my relationship with Cara. Companionship always puts one more at ease with one's own eccentricities. Alone, one's compulsions can become forces of anguish and alienation. Betrothed, they twist into endearing quirks in the eye of one's lover. This of course is so much easier than the futile quest to entirely remake one's self to fit an ideal.

Also, Cara received an employee discount on any records she purchased, so I was able to rebuild my collection much more quickly and at less expense than I'd initially thought.

One Tuesday in November, a most unexpected thing happened. Cara walked through the door shortly after six, smiled, and then handed me a parcel. Its shape and thinness were obvious enough to render the brown paper wrapping superfluous. But then the real question was, exactly *which* record had she gotten me?

I set my magazine aside and said, "Thank you, my dove," and pecked her cheek.

The peeled wrapping revealed a cream album jacket. A slate-grey circle with a straight line underneath, akin to an underline used for emphasis, was its only adornment.

"Dear?" I said.

"Scelsi," Cara replied, turning from me to remove her coat. "Put it on."

I broke the seal and heeded.

What came leaking through the speakers was a warbled and creeping harmonic of brass, of strings being tediously bowed. I stood holding the record sleeve. Something cold and shapeless raised the hair on the back of my neck.

"This music," I began.

"Do you like it?"

"It sounds as though it's...melting."

"It's called *Anahit*. Scelsi wrote it for Venus. That's why I bought it for you."

I must have been visibly confused, for Cara explained that this music, which I found remote and coldly firm as a headstone, seemed to her to illustrate a kinship between myself and the composer.

"In what way?" I asked, feeling the edge creeping into my voice.

"Just listen. Scelsi felt the same about women as you do."

"Did he?" I asked, now spinning in one of Cara's eddies of insinuation.

"Did he?" she repeated before regressing into the unlit kitchen.

A few moments later the scream of a kettle was added to the Italian's razor-wire concerto.

Cara then told me something about Scelsi that I have never forgotten.

It was only natural that I felt impelled to reciprocate her gift, but after a few fruitless hours gazing through boutique windows and pacing the airless labyrinths of antique shop after antique shop I began to question exactly how well I knew my fiancée. Of all the curios I'd spotted, none seemed to represent her. But then, how well did the Scelsi recording represent me? Rather poorly in my candid opinion.

I then began down a lane of thought that I admit I'm less than proud of taking. I started to suspect that Cara's motive was less about gifting and more about challenging. The outré concerto was a gauntlet of sorts, a distorted mirror that was designed to disconcert me about not only her but also myself.

As I said, I am not proud of the way I searched for Cara's motives in dark corners.

I'm even less proud of the fact that I decided to best her at this game of malice that I projected upon her. But it was as it was. Far be it from me to burnish reality. If the game was to be Presents Beyond the Pale, I knew just the bauble to use for my next play.

3.

I sought the phone number of the little gallery in the little town where Cousin Vera's little creations could be had. I found no listing. My editor had long ago eliminated my off-the-beaten-path travelogues, but the gallery keeper didn't know that. On a Friday I left the office after only a half day and drove north, hoping all the while that the gallery would be open.

I found it closed, permanently. A cold autumn rain began to fall as I stood on the sidewalk, peering into the showroom as though this would somehow alter its condition. Was I expecting the cold potted lamps to suddenly brighten, the showcases to fling back their dustcovers and once again be filled with Vera's fetishes?

Like a petulant child I gripped the entrance handle and shook the door with violence enough to cause the little bell to rattle inside. Then I returned to my post on the sidewalk and tried to think of alternatives.

Had the day not been so gloomy I would likely never have noticed the light that went on in the second-storey window. But notice it I did, beaming like a small amber moon just above me. I took a few paces back and looked upward. The silhouette's frame suggested that it was the gallery clerk. I waved and called "Hello!" and prattled something about being the newspaper writer.

The shape disappeared from the window. A few moments later it was standing in the little alley that divided the gallery from the organic bakery next door. My suspicion had been correct; it was the gallery owner. He was dressed in saggy pyjamas, a housecoat and tattered plaid slippers. The umbrella in his dirty fist was designed for a child.

"I wanted to ask you about Vera," I told him after he showed no inclination toward speaking. "She's my cousin, you know."

He was unfazed. "The gallery is no more, I regret to say. I've nothing to sell you."

I wiped the rain from my face and approached him. "Yes, I can see that. But I'm hoping you can call Vera's representatives for me. It's important."

"No way to call *them*," he said. He gave me a beckoning wave and started back down the alley from which he'd emerged. I followed him to a flimsy wooden door, which he pulled back. I squeezed into the tiny landing, holding my breath as the man latched the sad-looking door. "This way," he said. I didn't need to be told this, for the landing only had two exits: the alley door or the bowing stairs of wood so worn they were ice-slick. I climbed with care, for there was no handrail to aid me.

My host unlocked and pressed the black-stained door open at the head of the stairs. I followed him into an L-shaped apartment that smelled of old cooking and cat urine. The room had but two sources of illumination: a skylight of clouded plastic and, unnervingly, a nightlight in the shape of an antique streetlamp that glowed from a wall plug.

"Sit, sit," urged the man. I was reluctant. In way of furnishings there was a tan sofa and a wooden glider chair. The sofa's upholstery was bearded in long cat hair, so I chose the wooden glider. I never did spy the cat. He settled into the sofa and immediately lit a cigarette, producing an ashtray brimming with mangled butts. "What do you fancy?"

I cleared my throat. "I'm looking for a present for my fiancée. One of Vera's sculptures...because they are so...highly unique."

He nodded and nodded, reclining his head to spout smoke into the already cloying atmosphere. This caused his pyjama top to part at the seam. His breastbone was uncannily large and knotty. The sight of it distressed me.

"We was hoping for a newspaper story from you," he returned, rather brashly. I noted that his accent, which had previously suggested the posh air of Knightsbridge, suddenly clanged with an antagonizing cockney lilt.

"Ah, yes. Well, I'm sure you can imagine how it is; editorial bureaucracy and the like. I pitched the idea, but my superiors turned me down." I wondered why I felt the need to explain myself to him. "But I'd still like to purchase a piece, and to be put in touch with my cousin if that's also possible."

"The first bit is, aye. But as to Cousin Vera..."

"Nothing's happened to her I hope."

"Why do you say that, eh?"

I couldn't answer. "Um...would you happen to have any of Vera's pieces left here?"

The man kept his eyes on me as he extinguished his cigarette.

"Cuppa first, yeah?"

"That's not necessary."

"I'm afraid I must insist, 'tis nearly four after all."

"Well in that case."

I scanned the room while my host put the kettle on. The sight of the myriad smudges and smears on the walls gave birth to imagined bugs crawling coldly across my skin. As I scrambled for a way to politely refuse any food or drink from the whistling man in the kitchenette, my eyes happened upon a plaque that was affixed to the moulding above another door, one that led perhaps to the bedroom or lavatory. The plaque was carved from a wood that was cayenne-red and was so thickly varnished it appeared wet. The word NEITHER-NOR had been scorched into the wood by someone skilled in the art of pyrography. Each of the ten characters was modelled in Blackletter script. Given this, regardless of Neithernor's meaning, I obviously couldn't help but hearken back to

Alighieri at the Gates of Hell.

"Milk and honey?"

I'd grown so lost in my contemplation that I first mistook my host's query as an offering from Paradiso. Glancing side-long, I discovered that my host was holding a tray upon which both these condiments were standing. I took my tea straight. It was bitter and the cup smelled as though it had been wiped with a dirty rag.

I held my breath while I drank. I might have spewed out some banal chatter, I cannot recall. My next memory was of asking to be directed to the lavatory. I was peculiarly hopeful that it existed behind the Neithernor door, but it was at the end of a stout hallway.

Closing the door behind me, I splashed some cold water on my face, and panicked over what my next move would be, for I now felt nothing at all like a visitor and more like a double agent on some life-or-death mission. Using the room for its true purpose, I stepped back into the living room in time to see a bird-like woman pressing the NEITHERNOR door shut behind her.

"Vera?" I was surprised at how breathless my voice sounded. She turned to me.

How time had ransacked my cousin. She stood before me dressed in a soiled white smock, her hair concealed beneath a knitted cap like a patient in the thick of her battle with cancer. Her face had slid from delicate to skullish. Of her complexion and the state of her teeth I shall not speak.

"Come join us for tea, Vera dear," called my host, rising to collect another stinking cup. Only then did it strike me that I did not know his name. The question leapt to the tip of my tongue but died there. The last thing our motley gathering needed was gaucherie.

We sat and sipped and inhaled second-hand tobacco smoke. Vera gave me a lone glance. Furtive and fearful at first, she rectified it, or rather attempted to, by hitching the corner of her chapped mouth into a kind of grin.

Distressed, I asked her bluntly if she was well.

"Oh, yes. Just tired, I suspect."

The response came from the man, touching off my suspicions of a Svengali-like command over my cousin.

"Have you been working on new art, Vera?" I put a heavy emphasis on her name to indicate that I wanted her reply.

"Endlessly," she said. Her voice sounded as I'd feared it might.

"Is that your studio beyond the door there?"

She looked at the man in the sleepwear.

"I should very much like to see it if I may," I added, rising. I moved swiftly so as to carve the bearded man off before he could stop me. Vera did not even attempt to.

NEITHERNOR was not a studio, nor even a room, but rather a closet.

Shallow, lightless, and fragrant with old wood, the recess contained a stout metal stool and, upon the dust-studded floorboards, a spool of gleaming copper wire. Shelves lined either side of the closet and each was stacked with pastry boxes of thin white cardstock, all lidded and bound like caskets awaiting interment. A hatch door was set into the centre of the back wall. It was secured with a latch and padlock, both of which had also been slathered in the same eggshell primer.

A hand reached in front of me and pressed the door shut.

"Neither a studio nor a closet," I said with deliberate impertinence to the bearded man. He stood regarding me with a diamond-hard gaze. His face began to redden and twist. I've no shame in admitting my fear. You too would have been afraid.

"I would like to call on you again, Vera," I called as I reached for my coat. "I am still interested in one of your pieces."

She sat on the sofa like one adrift in dementia. Her mouth moved but I did not hear what she'd uttered.

"We'll have something for you," the man said. I closed the apartment door and took the stairs at a hare's pace. Outside I clung to the street door with one hand while collecting the narrowest wooden slat I could find from amidst the alley's debris. This I used to keep the door from clicking snug into its frame.

4.

I wrestled with whether or not to remain in the little village. My concern for Vera ran deep, regardless of how estranged we were. Sometimes women just need rescuing.

Having nothing in way of a plan, I stopped into a tavern to phone Cara and say that I was chasing a story lead and would not be home until the following day. Her suspicion was palpable.

Night fell and I tried to sort my thoughts into some semblance of a plan. I couldn't even begin to judge whether or not my intentions were pure. Cousin Vera had become swallowed up in a life that I can only describe as leprous. If I could not free her, I could at least confirm that she was not in imminent danger. I believe people have the right to diminish themselves if they so desire.

I buttoned my overcoat against the dropping temperature and once again crossed the little bridge. I stood across the street from Vera's hovel and kept watch. Lamplight shone amber through the second-storey window, but not indefinitely. Shortly after eleven I watched as the bearded man's ugly silhouette extinguished the light.

I stood shivering for nearly an hour, affording Vera's keeper time enough (I hoped) to doze off.

Much to my relief, the wedge was still in the door. Scaling those ancient steps noiselessly was arduous and time-consuming, particularly because my most formidable obstacle stood at their summit.

Exactly how I was going to unlock the apartment door was a problem I resolved to simply deal with by whatever means. Ultimately this meant, after attempting to wriggle it loose and to pop the lock using my driver's licence and my lapel pin, kicking the flimsy door open.

The bearded man had been snoring on the sofa where we'd had our dirty tea. The crash of the breached door woke him instantly, but he was too groggy and stunned to prevent me from tearing across the living room and flinging open the door to NEITHERNOR.

As I'd dreaded, Vera was sealed up within the tiny closet. Her slight frame rested on the metal stool and for a beat I thought she was sleeping, until I noticed that her eyes were open...open yet rolled up in her skull like one in an epileptic throe. Her mouth gaped. In her hands she held the spool of copper wire. The glinting strand was taut before her, like a fishing line in the deep. It fed backward above her head and into the tiny hatch. This time the tiny door in the wall was unlocked and ajar. A fat band of shadow concealed whatever was rutting inside that cubby. Whatever it was, it possessed strength enough to tear at Vera's hair, which caused her somnambulistic body to heave up and then drop down again onto the stool. Her scalp was missing much more than the knitted cap.

The bearded man was growling as he grabbed me. Terror and adrenaline made breaking free easy.

Less easy to escape is the memory of those neatly stacked white boxes beginning to rattle and shake and leap from their perch.

Vera was careless or helpless to the whole nightmare. Not even my shrieking flight could lure her from her in-between.

5.

I drove aimlessly for the remainder of the night and

when I came home the following morning it was to an empty apartment.

Upon Cara's dressing table, which was stripped clean of the little bottles and brushes and mirrors that littered it, a single leaf of notepaper had been taped:

Forrest—
I will write the things that neither of us has the courage to say aloud.
Where to begin? By suggesting that we have grown apart?
No. You cannot separate that which was never together to begin with.
Your phone call yesterday afternoon was the tipping point.
There was no story to chase; I called the paper and spoke to your
editor. I hope this other woman, whoever she is, is able to give you
whatever it is that I couldn't, whatever it is you're lacking. I doubt
even you know what that is.
Locking up the townhouse last night I found a parcel on our doorstep.
I'm embarrassed to admit that I thought you had left it to surprise
me with. But as soon as I opened it and saw the little fetish inside
it became very clear to me that you're walking down a road I would
never even set foot upon. Just being in the same house with it last
night gave me nightmare after nightmare, when I did manage to sleep
that is.
I have nothing more to say. I've gone to stay at Mother's and will
arrange to have my things collected. I don't expect this note to shock
or pain you in any way, no matter how much I may wish otherwise.
— Cara
p.s. — I left your little bauble for you. You'll find it inside your
closet.

I locked the townhouse door behind me and immediately relocated to the only hotel I could afford.

I did not return to the house until the movers I'd hired met me there and carried out the furniture I singled out as being mine. Cara's belongings appeared to have already been collected.

The bedroom closet was never reopened, at least not by my hand. After settling into a small apartment on the far side of the city my first quest was to rebuild my wardrobe, to replace the dress shirts, trousers and various other pieces I abandoned for fear of parting the gate to my own little Neithernor.

It seems my life waxes then wanes. For a time, my cup runneth over, then is drained, after which I strive and scramble to replenish that which has been lost.

6.

I had noted that Cara had once told me something about Scelsi that I have never forgotten. It is this: the eccentric composer refused to allow his photograph to appear in conjunction with any of his musical releases, for he maintained a conviction that his music was much more than a simple outgrowth of his personal imagination. The sounds were a transmission from the greater Soul that transcends all matter and masks. Scelsi was, in his own words, merely a conduit for the music that existed well beyond his own private abilities.

In place of his own visage, distinguished though I later discovered it to be, Scelsi used the symbol (a circle hovering over a straight line) that appeared on the jacket of the recording Cara had presented me with. I have studied that symbol often and with vigour. Cara had always said that for her the image was a cleanly abstract vision of a sinking sun, but to my eye it appears as something else entirely.

Deep Eden

A sh Lake occasionally embodies its name. On November days such as this, when the sunbeams can scarcely press through the leaden clouds, the lake roils grey and ghostly, taking on the appearance of shifting dunes of ash, like incinerated remains of one who somehow survived the crematorium.

How I loved days like this when I was a girl. In those distant autumns I would venture down to the lakefront, Dad and Rita by my side. Together we would toss stones and spy for any boats daring enough to brave the gales. Those days were buoyed by a feeling, very rare and very delicious, that my sister, father and I were the only three people left in Evendale.

Of late this same feeling has become a constant, but it has lost its sweetness.

Perhaps these pleasant memories sparked my desire to make the detour to the beach today. Was I clinging to the thin hope that somehow the sight of Ash Lake in late autumn might uplift me, give me the clarity to make sense of the senselessness that is now the norm in Evendale?

Standing on the beach, I scoop up a handful of fog-moistened stones, then let them drop un-hurled. As I make my way back to the jeep, I listen to the surf whose waves sound much like mocking asthmatic laughter.

The fuel gauge begins to flash 'E' as soon as I turn the ignition, so I begin to woo the vehicle, coaxing it to carry me far enough to reach the Main Street filling station that still, as of last week, had fuel.

Veering into the narrow station, I leave the engine running and run out to test the pumps. The first two are bone-dry, but the third valve spits out unleaded. As I fill the jeep, I wonder how much fuel is left in this town…how much of anything? The residents of Evendale had, up until recently, kept a routine, a choreographed pantomime of a sleepy but still functioning town. There seemed to be a rotation of sorts. A certain segment of the locals remained aboveground to man the fueling station, to switch on houselights on a rotating basis, to plow the main roads when the snow accumulated. But the concern over keeping up appearances to the outside world has waned now that everyone has gone Below.

My memories of this town, pale as they are, paint Evendale as little more than a tangle of poorly paved roads lined with dreary structures. But neither the years nor the miles that I set between myself and my home can account for its present condition. The houses and shops all have the air of heaped wreckage, of withered husks that no longer shelter living things. Most of the spaces advertise themselves as being for lease. A few of them are boarded up with slabs of cheap wood, like coffins bound for pauper's row.

The street entrance to Venus Women's Wear is sheathed in brown butcher paper. A sign in the display window advises potential customers that the boutique is closed for renovations. I make my way to the alley beside the shop and find the side door unlocked.

There is no light inside the shop, but I do not require any. My time Below has sharpened my ability to see in the dark.

It takes me several minutes to find the dress that Rita had described to me: purple silk with a dragonfly embroidered in glittering black thread over the left breast. This was the first time she had ever requested anything since going Below. How I had hoped that her desire could have lured her up and out, into the light. But Rita never comes above anymore.

I zipper the dress inside a plastic garment bag with the Venus logo and the store's address printed on the back, then I carry it back to the jeep and drive on.

Loath as I am to admit it, I now find being above rather unsettling. The airiness, the brightness, after those first few heaves of revivifying oxygen, sours quickly. More and more I want to be Below. But I do not *want* to want that.

I turn onto Apple Road to complete my errand. In addition to the purple dress from Venus, Rita has also requested that our late mother's silver-handled mirror and hairbrush set be collected from our home.

Hypocrisy abounds; after robbing Venus I fish out the keys for my childhood home. We keep it locked up snugly. Perhaps we are afraid to lose our past, meagre as it is.

I take the hairbrush and mirror from Rita's dresser. Noting their condition, I rummage around father's workroom until I find a can of silver polish and a soft rag. A canvas grocery sack hangs from the foyer coat rack. I pluck it from its perch and fill it with a few canned goods, a jar of instant coffee, and some packets of oatmeal. I find five bottles of water left in back of the pantry.

I begin my journey back to the mine.

The Dunford Incorporated coal mine first began operating shortly after World War II and had been Evendale's main employer for the next four decades. But then a tragic tunnel collapse took the lives of a dozen miners. Eventually, through resulting lawsuits and legal fees, this accident also took the life of Dunford Inc. The company declared bankruptcy and shut down the mine in 1983. It has stood in the arid field on Evendale's outskirts ever since.

I escaped Evendale in 1991, moving to the city in search of myself. At that time there were rumblings of a new company purchasing and re-opening the dormant mine, but it was not to be. When Dunford Inc. laid my father off (mercifully, a year before the collapse) he used to tell my sister and me that there was hardly any coal left in those shafts anyway. I'd always thought these words were merely a way for my father to balm his wounded pride, but given that no one has seen fit to resume clawing at those tunnels, perhaps he was speaking the truth.

Either way, the site was left to rot; its towering iron scaffolds bowing like aging men, its subterranean maze resting hushed and hollowed like some vacated netherworld.

As to the origins of the mine's more recent and more rarefied role in the lives of the townspeople, accounts differ depending on whom you ask. That a posse had formed to rescue a child who had scrabbled down into the shafts on a dare and gotten lost seems to be the most common account. But the age and gender of the strayed child varies from teller to teller. A point that *does* run uniform through this folklore is the discovery of the greenish light.

The search party had apparently bored through one of the walls of the farthest tunnel. Their claim was that the lost child could be heard sobbing and pleading on the far side of that rugged culm barrier. When their picks and shovels and clawing hands finally pierced through, they found neither boy nor girl, but instead a luminescence. Were they the beams of some strange fallen sun long interred in the Earth's bowels? The gleam of a green jewel lodged within a great crown? I can only theorize based on the testimonials that have been whispered to me below, for I have never seen the light myself. Nor has Rita. But unlike me, she is convinced of its existence.

My sister loves to brand me as the eternal skeptic, one

unwilling to accept that there are things that lurk beyond the reach of our five meagre senses. Honestly, I cannot say that I'm even that, for a true skeptic would be eager to disprove the myth of the emerald light, to expose the folly of those Below. While I will concede that yes, there may well be a greenish glow in the depths of the mines, I suspect that its presence is some natural anomaly, some phosphorescent property in the carbon, or an optical trick that arises when the human eye struggles against absolute darkness.

Still, I am not so convinced of these empirical theories that I am willing to creep down into those far depths to prove or disprove anything.

✖

I am only a few hundred yards from the gate to the mine site when I witness the impossible.

At first my brain doesn't properly register that what comes trundling out of the roadside bracken is a dog. (The sight of something moving in Evendale is now so rare it truly startles me.) I press down hard on the brake pedal and the pouch spits out the tinned foods into the jeep's foot-well. The creature plods onto the road, pauses to turn its dismal face toward me. I put the jeep in Park and step out, taming my enthusiasm so as not to startle the poor animal.

It is a yellow Lab. I crouch down and coo to her. She comes to me with neither reservation nor love.

That it has been foraging and roaming for some time is obvious. But I am unaware just how badly the poor beast had been faring until I run my hand along its matted coat and feel the fence slats of its ribs pressing against the fur. I race back to the jeep and retrieve the tin of Spam I'd taken from our pantry, along with one of the bottles of water.

The dog is now lying as though the littered asphalt road is her bed. I uncap the bottle, pour some of the water into my cupped hand, hold it out to her. She laps at it with a pale tongue.

I peel the label off the Spam, open the tin and shake the meat out onto the label. This I slide before the dog. She sniffs it, perhaps in distrust or disbelief, then begins to lick and gnaw the pinkish cube.

As I sit beside the dog, her tail now faintly wagging, I hear the sound of a helicopter. Shielding my eyes, I look past the rim of the escarpment to see the small chopper coasting on the ashen sky. A TV reporter perhaps, or an airlift ambulance; someone merely passing over Evendale. That is what Evendale is now, perhaps what it has always been; a place one passes by or through or over on their way to somewhere else. Is this why the exodus Below has been allowed to occur without any outside notice at all? Or is there something other at work here?

"Do you want to come home with me?" I ask my new companion. Every inch of me goes cold once I realize that I have referred to those dank and cultish tombs as home. The dog looks at me with her teary, tired eyes. I pick her up and gently pile her onto the passenger seat. Then I drive to the far end of the road.

※

Dad had been part of that first group that tore the barricades from the mouth of the entrance pipe and breached the mine for the first time in years in search of a supposedly lost child. I only learned this a few months ago from Rita. She told me that the men were glad to have my father among them, for he was the only one left in Evendale to have worked the tunnels when Dunford Inc. was still in operation. I suspect it was more than his knowledge of the shafts that made Dad a welcome member of that search party. He had always been a calming presence in our home, so I can only imagine what a balm it must have been to have his wise and careful suggestions offered in his sonorous voice, especially once they were down in that stinking darkness.

Just what it was Dad saw in that green radiance Below I never came to know. I only know it changed him. The fallout of this encounter was drastic enough for Rita to plead with me to fly home and help her find some means of bringing him back around.

When I returned to Evendale I discovered a catatonic shell in the shape of my father. He never spoke, scarcely ate, slept nearly eighteen hours a day. I insisted to Rita that a hospital was the only place for him; there he could receive not only medical attention but (perhaps even more importantly) psychiatric care. Rita, despite asking for my help, stubbornly refused to admit Dad, stating that this was a family problem and therefore could be fixed by the family. I suppose I should have protested more passionately, but I didn't. It seems I also inherited the same caginess that Rita possessed. Perhaps it's a symptom of growing up in a small town, but propriety and fear of scandal, however slight, always seems to automatically trump common sense.

Three weeks ago, Rita and I finally agreed that hospitalization could not be put off any longer. Dad had always been a strapping man, so his rapid mental dissolution was a sobering and painful wake-up call to my sister and me.

The night before we planned to drag Dad off to receive help, he snapped out of his depression. Late that night my sleep was broken by the clanging of pans and the thudding of cupboard doors. Rita's bedroom door was shut when I walked past it to investigate.

I switched on the kitchen light and found my father preparing a goulash so redolent with spice I teared up the moment I entered the kitchen.

"Dad?" I'd said to him.

"Hungry?" was his reply.

I told him no, then watched as he left the ingredients to simmer on the range. He sat down at the kitchen table and asked me to switch off the light. I did, and together we sat in the lunar glow from the window, listening to the food hissing in its pot.

"Can't sleep," he admitted, answering a question I never posed.

"You've probably been sleeping too much."

"Well, I'm awake now."

Something in his choice of words unsettled me.

"Your sister told me that Sadie-Anne next door boarded up her house a couple of days ago."

"Yes, I saw that. Any idea why?"

"Probably to become a pit-canary like the others."

I swallowed what little moisture there was in my mouth. "Why are people running down there, Dad? What are they running to?"

His silhouette shrugged.

"I know about the glow down there, Dad. Rita told me. Is that what the pit-canaries are moving to the mine for? Are they looking for the light?"

If my father was fazed by my questions, he contained his emotions, just as he had always done with all things. Dad: even-keeled, stoic, strong, like a lake of still black water.

"I think maybe they're after what's on the other side of that light," he answered at last.

"What's beyond the light, Dad?" Worry and tears mangled my voice into something thin and reedy. "What did you see down there?"

It seemed like a long span passed. We sat in stubborn silence like two monks lost in contemplation. The goulash bubbled over the pot rim and splashed onto the burner, hissing as though maimed.

"Been dreaming a lot lately," he said at last. "Funny thing, that. In my whole life I think I can remember one, maybe two dreams. And those were from when I was a boy. But lately…" His voice trailed off.

"There was this one dream," he said after a long pause. "I must've had it three, four nights in a row. I'm in this meadow, real peaceful, real pretty. I'm standing beside an old-fashioned watermill and I'm holding a large bucket with a rope handle. The mill's wheel is turning slowly, but the weird thing is, the only noise I can hear is the creaking of those wooden gears. I can see the brook moving along, I can see it being lathed up by the paddles and I can see the runoff gushing back down into the brook, but the water moves completely silently. You know how sometimes in dreams you just know things about things? Well, in this dream I knew I had come to this brook to gather water to bring back to my village, which was on the other side of this great stone building that this watermill was attached to. Maybe they were grinding grain in there or something, I don't know. But I was there for the water because the villagers were all dying of thirst.

"I reached down to scoop up some of that quiet water, when this awful, awful feeling came over me. I stared down into the brook and noticed in the reflection that a figure was now standing above me on the bank. I tried to cover my eyes because I didn't want to see who or what that figure was, but the next thing I knew I was standing face to face with it. It was a woman, a very strange, very thin woman. She was trying to tell me something, but she was as mute as that water, so she traced some symbols in the air with one of her stick-like fingers. She spelled out that the water was poison. I nodded to show her that I understood. Then you know what I did? I filled that rope-handled pail and carried it back to my village and when I got there, I took a wooden ladle and I doled out that poisoned water to all my wretched-looking neighbours. When that awful deed was done, I poured the last sip into my own palm and drank it myself. Then I woke up."

I wasn't sure how to react to my father's account, but I was desperate to keep him talking, so I asked him what he thought the dream meant. Again, he shrugged. Then he rose to tend to his food.

"The light's coming," he announced. At the time I believed he was referring to the sun that had begun climbing above the hedges beyond our kitchen window. Now I am not so certain.

That was the last time I spoke to my father. The next night, while I slept, he moved Below.

※

The day's organic gloom makes it seem much later than it is as I edge the jeep off the lane and along the entrance driveway of the mine. At one time this passage was truncated by a heavy iron gate bearing a sign that warned of the legal repercussions and physical dangers that trespassers could endure. Today that gate hangs permanently open and the sign is covered over with spray-paint.

The floodlights on their tower perches shine on me, weakly, like a pair of potted moons. I gather up the groceries and the dog that I carry and comfort as though she is my own flesh and blood. As I cross the gravel lot toward the mine entrance, I tighten my grip on the Lab, for she's begun to whimper and squirm.

"You're okay, girl," I assure her, "you're okay. What should I name you, hmm? What do I call you?"

But the nearer we draw to that rugged tunnel with its downward pitch, the more the dog begins to panic. I know that my clutching her against her will is purely selfish. How I need her companionship, her vitality, her love.

As I struggle with her up the wooden rungs and into the tunnel, the dog begins to growl and bark in a sad, effete protest. No doubt she can sense the offensiveness of whatever lurks Below. She wriggles free and charges for the tunnel's mouth. I cry out and lunge for her, but she leaps heedless of any risk. I hear her claws scrabbling against the ladder. A moment later I see the dog tearing across the gravel plain. She nears the road and is soon gone.

I slump against the cold black wall of the shaft and I sob. It is the kind of outburst usually reserved for children; the frame-shaking, convulsive weeping that threatens to tear the soul up by its roots.

The sound of approaching footsteps causes me to fight for composure. How sad is it that even now, under such conditions, we pit-canaries still feel the need for personas?

"Everything alright, miss?" one of the sentinels asks me, the light on his hardhat beaming in the blackness like a lustrous pearl.

I nod, pick up the sack of food and brush past him, negotiating the wooden slats with care as I make the long descent toward the platform where the carts are nested.

A family of four sits at one of the platform's picnic tables, eating peanut butter and saltines.

The people come to the upper level in shifts. For most of them this is as near to the surface as they're willing to go, despite the dangers to their health. Strategically installed fans spin constantly, both here and deeper Below. They do their best to draw the methane out of the tunnels and to coax fresh air down from the surface. But they have been rotting down here since Dunford Inc. shut down production, and I remember Dad saying that even when those fans were new it was always a risk spending too much time "under the crust."

"One of the drivers will be up shortly," the mother calls once she sees me climbing into a cart. I turn back and look stonily at them, at their wan faces smeared with soot, the clothing that hangs loose and grubby upon their malnourished frames. They are like a faded photo of some anonymous Dust Bowl family in a history book.

"Never mind," I say, releasing the brake. The ancient

wheels squeak, and the cart begins to roll toward the greater descent.

Down I go, down, staring numbly at the roughly textured tunnel. I begin to imagine the juts and pockets as being some strange and tedious grammar in Braille, some record of a world that had existed below ours for unknowable years, their entire secret history spelled out here in angled carbon.

These walls are veined with thick cables that feed power to the vent fans and to the garlands of uncovered light bulbs. To my eye these strung lights have all the impact of a few fireflies straining to illuminate a canyon.

The cart reaches the final swoop of the track and I ease up the handbrake to soften the final thud that always comes when the track ends. The carts are inexorably fed into a pent-in platform constructed out of lumber grown soft from too many years in the methane-reeking chambers.

There has yet to be any theft or pillaging down here, but I do my best to conceal the sack of groceries all the same. The converts here have commented about how this profound fellowship and egalitarianism is somehow a sign of renewal, of change. I think it is only because things haven't yet gotten desperate enough. They'll start scavenging and rending sooner or later. It's simply a question of time.

The only proper shelter at this level is the rescue chamber that the miners once relied upon in case of a collapse or other accident. It is a pod where one could hole up until help arrived. Now, with its oxygen tanks long drained, its food devoured, and its water guzzled, the chamber serves as a curious spirit house, a shrine that the people have embellished with mementos of those whose spirits they claim have been glimpsed beyond the emerald light, or with fetishes meant to represent things unfamiliar but still experienced.

I sit down at one of the picnic tables where Rita is knitting a scarf. I watch her for a spell, watch the way her eyes habitually move from her needles to the tunnel a few yards away.

"You get my dress?" she asks without looking at me.

"Yes, and the other things you asked for. I also got some food. Not much though. There's water, too."

A young girl, perhaps fifteen, moves past our table and makes her way to the decorated tunnel mouth. Rita and I both watch as she crouches, and slides her hand into the gap. She seems to be feeling something in that chute, something that appears to greet her touch in a pleasing way. For a moment it looks as though the girl is about to enter the void, but she ultimately lacks the required conviction. She shuffles back to her mattress at the far end of the tract and lies down.

"Have there been any changes?" I ask Rita.

"Define 'changes.'"

"Anyone else gone in...or maybe come back out...there?"

"Don't be stupid." She puts her needles back in her canvas bag along with her yarn. I study her as she carries the silver hairbrush and the handheld mirror into the pod and adds them to the shrine. As she exits the shrine, she refuses to look at me.

"I'm going to try on my dress," she says, as if daring me to object.

She is on her way to change in one of the old miners' shower stalls—there is no running water here, but the mouldy plastic curtains that partition the stalls at least offer privacy—when the ground begins to quake.

This tremor is longer than all previous ones, more forceful. Immediately people begin to murmur, in prayer or in vexation or simply in fear. The rocking ultimately subsides. A wave of relief passes over the people of the tract.

A moment later, there is another tremor.

※

Few become true pit-canaries. While the townsfolk dwell Below, there is another level, another extreme that only the most devout have courage or madness enough to explore.

Beyond the tract, where the mattresses and bags are strewn, stretches another tunnel. It is stiflingly tight and perilously ragged. It must have been bored by something cruder than even the crudest manmade tool. Only those who have dared to squeeze through that aperture earn the stigma of pit-canary because, like their namesake, those birds go beyond, into certain peril, into a kind of underground Event Horizon.

As to what forged that tunnel, I could add my theory to the dozens that have been posited, but what would such a thing prove? The tunnel is somehow connected to the emerald light. This I believe. I also believe that both this cryptic tunnel and the emerald light are the products of something even greater and stranger than both those two things combined.

Somehow, we, the people of Evendale, awoke something down there. Now that something is in turn beginning to awaken all of us.

The change is undeniable. Everyone Below feels it, but because it is so indefinable, we do not speak of it. We simply accept its presence within us, like a growing contagion, an elusive virus.

This is a cold, unwanted revelation, like happening upon a lump in one's breast or testicle; the kind of discovery that makes one yearn for normalcy, tedium, for all those ditchwater-dull afternoons and daily routines that we so foolishly felt needed to be stripped away by novelty and change. Yes, it is that kind of wordless knowledge that there is no going back. Even racing up to the sunlit yards of Evendale would be a small and flimsy defense. And so, we wait for what I hope will be, if not an answer, then, at the very least, an ending.

I'm told that early on some of the men wanted to place bright orange sawhorses before the mouth of that unmapped tunnel as a warning to keep away, but before they could return with their barricade, the mine had produced its own.

The vine sprouted from one carbon wall, drooped across

the down-sloping chute and then poked through the black rock of the opposite wall. Blooming out of this twisting verdant cable were five bellflowers, vibrantly red, as though coloured by arterial blood that raced through transparent petals. Deeply fragrant; even the methane fumes were made sweet, so strong was their perfume. The flowers hung inversely. Set against that gaping hole in the mine wall they were positively incandescent, the beginnings of some fresh new garden of paradise. I studied those flowers often, perched upon my plastic lawn chair, coughing into my sooty hands.

I still watch the flowers and I wait. Wait for my father.

Two weeks ago, much to my shrieking protests, he left the camp here on the tract and he became a pit-canary. He said he'd dreamed my mother had come to him through the emerald light and that she'd encouraged him to experience what dwelt on the outer rim of that light. Dad once said he believed the light was actually the breath of some living thing, large and ancient and wise. An entity that had been here long before we crawled out of the swamp, something nested, something waiting...

He'd also said he thinks this creature, whatever it is, is calling us to descend farther and farther down so it can give us some new kind of fire, the kind that lights up the depths of space.

I'd asked him how he came to know this, but he said nothing.

Only two pit-canaries have come back to the tract in the whole time I've been here, but it seems to be enough to keep people believing, waiting, wondering. The first was an elderly woman who'd owned a cake shop on Main Street. She said she'd heard trumpets and bells in that tunnel, and that the green light had welled up to touch her and for one brief but glorious moment she was able to hold her own heart in her hands. She'd said she'd weighed her heart for hefty sins. She had determined that it wasn't yet light enough, so she'd come back up to fast and pray. She stayed above. I never found out what happened to her.

The other pit-canary who returned only lived for a few seconds. He came crawling out of the tunnel screaming in agony. He screamed and he screamed. He even tore out the vine of bellflowers. When two of the men dragged him out, they discovered that he'd been torn open, but the innards that spilled from his jagged and gaping wounds were fossilized; white and smooth and solid, like hand-carved entrails on a marble statue.

Only after the commotion ended did someone comment about how the red bellflowers had already grown back across the tunnel mouth.

✖

Another tremor.

And another.

It won't be long now…whatever 'it' is.

The bellflowers begin to ring. Their chiming is open and almost without a source. They swing like their namesakes in a belfry. And like those chapel bells, these glassy-sounding flowers seem to rouse the faithful to service.

One by one the people begin to crawl through the tunnel. Where they had once given a wide berth to avoid, they now scramble and fight to penetrate. The emerald glimmer is now visible within the tunnel, cresting upward like a tide of foul sewer water. Rita and I watch as the last resident wriggles toward that ill light.

Rita begs me to let her go, but I hold her back. Impulsively, senselessly, she wrestles that damned dress over her head, tugging it over her filthy T-shirt and jeans.

I feel the collapse occurring in the tunnel beneath us. It shakes the ground. The chorus of screams from those who'd raced into the forbidden chute are muffled by the falling black rock, but they are no less terrible.

Is this what you lured all of them down there for? I wonder.

"Dad!" Rita cries, over and over.

I shriek for her to follow me into the rescue pod. Eventually she does. I shut the door, praying that the cave-in won't reach this upper level and that it ends swiftly. There is no oxygen in the tank, but we need shelter from the mushrooms of black smoke that begins to fill the tract. Chunks of coal smack against the pod like the shower of stones in Revelations. The light leaks up through fresh fissures in the ground.

Eventually the thunder wanes. I look through the pod window, expecting to see only blackness. But there is a distinctive glimmer, greenish and persistent, even against the thick filter of coal dust.

I close my hand over my mouth.

She pushes past me.

I follow her, choking on the fumes and dust.

The emerald light presses through the collapsed tunnel, shining like a lamp covered with perforated black felt. For a long time, we simply stand. Then something squeezes through the piled rocks. It rolls nearer to us with patient velocity.

I turn to Rita, who looks bolted in place. Terror blanches her face and makes her jaw hang slack.

I step forward.

"No!" I hear my sister scream, seemingly from the far end of the world. "No, goddamn it!"

I reach down, pick up the luminous object, and turn back to Rita.

I roll this newfound gift in my palm before halving it with a forceful twist.

"It's from our Father," I inform her with a knowledge that seems to originate outside of myself.

Rita reaches for her half but quickly drops her hand. She watches in mute but visible agony as I bite into the apple.

The Patter of Tiny Feet

Against his better judgment Sam stopped the car and allowed his Smartphone to connect with Andrea's. The earpiece purled enough times to allow him to envision Andrea sitting with arms crossed, eyeing her vibrating phone, ignoring his extension of the olive branch. Choking back the indignation he truly believed was righteous, Sam obeyed the recorded instructions and waited for the tone.

"Hi, it's me," he began, trying not to be distracted by the escarpment's belittling sprawl of glacial rock and ancient forests. "Look, I'm sorry I stormed out like that. It was childish of me, I admit. I'm happy about your promotion, I truly am, it's just…well…I suppose I was a little shocked by how much your new position alters our plans." He was lecturing again. Andrea had accused him of it often enough. Was he also being high-handed, as she liked to claim? "Anyhow, I really do have some scouting to do, that wasn't a lie. But I wanted to call you before I got too far out and lost the signal. I've got my equipment in the car with me. I'm going to snap a few locations just to get Dennis off my back. I should be back in a few hours, so hopefully we can talk more then. Don't worry, I'm not going to try and get you to change your mind about anything. I…I guess I just need to know that a family's not completely off the table for us. It doesn't have to be tomorrow, but at some point in the not too distant future I'd..."

He could feel himself babbling. Already his first few statements had grown hazy; he winced at their possible fawning stupidity.

"I'll see you when I get home. Love you lots."

The jeep that was scaling the road behind him gave Sam an unpleasant start when he spotted its swelling reflection in his rear-view mirror. The deafening beat of its stereo, no doubt worth more than the vehicle itself, caused the poorly folded maps on Sam's dashboard to hum and vibrate as though they were maimed birds attempting to flap their crumpled wings. The jeep rumbled past and the girl in its passenger seat was whooping and laughing a shrill musical laugh that Sam half-believed was directed at him. He started his engine and cautiously veered back onto Appleby Line to resume his half-hearted search for a paragon of terror.

He'd been truthful about the mounting pressure from Dennis, a director who possessed the eccentricities and ego of many legendary filmmakers, but completely lacked their genius. After helming two disastrous made-for-television teen comedies Dennis broke off to form his own miniscule film production company, Startling Image. Freak luck had furnished his operation with a grant from the Ontario Film Board, which Dennis said he planned to stretch as far as it could go. His scheme was to produce shoestring-budget horror films that would be released directly to DVD. Dennis believed this plot was not only foolproof but in fact an expressway to wealth and industry prestige.

Although Sam's experience in moviemaking allowed him to see the idiocy of Dennis's delusions, being a freelancer required Sam to accept any jobs that came his way during leaner times. Location Manager was an impressive title on paper, but with anorexic productions such as *Gnawers*, Startling Image's inaugural zombie infestation film, Sam found himself working twice as hard for a third of his usual compensation. He was contracted for a major Hollywood studio film that was going into production in Toronto next spring. He had only accepted Dennis's offer in order to bring in some extra money. The draconian hours, the director's tantrums, and the risible script for *Gnawers* would have all been worth it had Andrea kept her word.

But now it seemed there would be no need to furnish their guest bedroom with a crib and rocking chair and a chiming mobile on the ceiling. Instead there would only be Andrea's customary seven-day workweeks, her quarterly bonuses spent on ever-sleeker gadgets and more luxurious clothing. Sam's wants were simple: to know the pleasures of progeny, fatherhood, to watch someone born of love and blessed with love growing up and sequentially awakening to all the wonders of life. His grandfather had advised Sam years ago that there comes a time in every man's life when all he wants is to hear the patter of tiny feet.

Now thirty-eight, Sam had come to appreciate the wisdom of the cliché as well as the cold sorrow of realizing that this natural desire might shrivel up unfulfilled. What then? Sunday afternoon cocktails with Andrea's fellow brokers, with him chasing an endless string of movie gigs until, perhaps, he could found a company of his own?

Only when the car began to chug and lurch in an attempt to scale the road's sudden incline did Sam realize he'd allowed his foot to ease off the gas pedal. He stomped down on it, and the asthmatic sounds the engine released made him wince. This far up the escarpment, well past the Rattlesnake Point Conservation Area, the road hosted surprise hairpin turns that required a driver's full alertness. Sam shook the cobwebs from his head and willed his focus on the narrow road before him.

Had he not been so determined to exceed Dennis's expectations, Sam might have let the peripheral image pass by unexplored. But his determination to prove his worth, now not only to Dennis but also to Andrea (maybe even to himself as well), inspired Sam to edge his car onto the nearest thing the narrow lane had to a shoulder. He gathered his hip-bag and exited the vehicle. With eyes fixated on the alluring quirk in the landscape, he began to climb the rocky wall that fed off the laneway.

The stiff pitch of a shingled roof was what had commanded his attention after a rather long and uneventful drive around the escarpment. It jutted up, all tar shingles and snugly carpentered beams, amidst the leafless, knotty treeline. As he climbed upward and then began to wriggle across the inhospitable terrain, Sam questioned the housetop's reality. Had his anxious state conspired with his imagination to impress a structure where one could not be?

A few more cautious footsteps were all that was required to confirm the substance of his glimpse.

It was a wooden frame-house whose two storeys might have sprouted stiffly from the overgrown rockery that ringed its base. Blatantly abandoned, Sam couldn't help but note how the house's battered walls, punctured roof, and boarded windows did not convey the usual faint melancholy or eeriness that most neglected homes do. Instead, there was an air of what might be called power. Sam wondered if the house had drawn strength from its solitude, become self-perpetuating, self-sustaining, like the mythical serpent that nourishes itself by devouring its own tail.

The site was so tailored to his wishes that for a moment Sam almost believed in providence. Lugging the film crew's equipment up and along this incline would be arduous, but he was confident that it would be worth the extra effort. Given the minuscule budget for *Gnawers*, even Dennis could not balk at the richness of this location.

The place was almost fiendishly apt. They would have to bring generators here to power the equipment, and a survey of the house would be required to gauge its safety hazards, but it could work. More than work; it could shine.

As he entered the clearing where the farmhouse stood, Sam lifted his hands to frame his view in a crude approximation of a camera lens. This simple gesture was enough to transform his roaming of the derelict grounds into a long and elaborate establishing shot. One by one he took in the set-pieces that may well have been left there just for him: the crumbling stone steps that led up to the empty doorframe, the rust-mangled shell of a tractor that slumped uselessly at the head of the gravel clearing, the wind-plucked barn whose arches resembled the fossilized wings of a prehistoric bird of prey. It was glorious, perfect.

Sam wished he had someone there to share it with. But surely Andrea would not draw as much pleasure from this as he did. Her interest in movies extended only as far as attending the local premieres of any productions Sam had worked on. Beyond that, Andrea's world revolved around crunching numbers for her clients.

For a cold moment Sam imagined one day teaching his daughter or son the thrill of seeking out the special nooks of the world. For Sam, movies were secondary. Their presentation invariably paled against the sparkling wonder of discovering the richly atmospheric settings that often hide out from the rambling parade of progress: art deco bars, grand old theatres, rural churches, and countless other places like this very farm.

He fought back the wring of depression by freeing the camera from his hip-bag and beginning to snap photos of the potential set. Moving around to the rear of the house chilled Sam, even though the April sun was still pouring modest warmth on the terrain. Perhaps the sight of the high shuttered room was what had unnerved him. Regardless, it would make an excellent shot in *Gnawers*. With this many possibilities, Sam's mind began to thrum with startling revisions that could be made to the script.

A round wooden well sat at the edge of the property, mere inches from the untamed forest. Sam approached it, struck by just how crude it was. The surface had not even been sanded. It still bore the mossy flaking bark of the tree from which it had been hewn. Sam might have mistaken it for the stump of a great evergreen had the mouth of the stout barrel not been secured with a large granite slab that was held in place by ancient-looking ropes. Or were they vines?

Regardless, the well or cistern could have been part of the topography, for it did not look fashioned in any way, merely capped. It was as if a massive log had been shoved down into the mud. Its base was overgrown with weeds so sun-bleached they'd come to resemble nerves.

Sam frowned at the thought of how its water might taste.

The house had no back door, so Sam hastened his way to the open doorframe that faced the incline, excited by the prospect of the house's interior.

The forest had shared its debris with the main hall. The oiled floorboards were warped enough to appear as a heaving sea of wood. The floor was carpeted with broken boughs and leaves and dirt. Sam clicked several shots of the living room with its lone furnishing of a broken armchair; of the pantry that was lined with dusty preserves; of the kitchen with its dented woodstove.

To his mind he'd already collected more than ample proof that this location would suit the film, but just to cross every T he opted for a few quick shots of the second storey. After that he would go back home. He had a strange and sudden need to snuggle up to Andrea, in a well-lit room, with the world held at bay beyond locked doors.

Something in the way the main stairs creaked underfoot gave Sam pause. He came to question whether the house was truly abandoned after all. It must have been the echo of the groaning wood, but the sound managed to plant the idea that the upper floor was occupied.

"Hello?" he called, only scarcely aware of the fact that his hand had begun fishing one of the contracts for location use out of his hip-bag. Drawing some absurd sense of security from the legal papers in his fist, Sam scaled the steps, praying they would not cave beneath him. He listened for noises that never managed to overpower the ones caused by his own motions.

An investigation of the first two rooms revealed precious little beyond more dust, greater decay. Sam's discovery of a dismantled crib in the front bedroom caused a lump to form in his throat. Why should he be so moved by so banal an image—slatted wood stacked in a corner? No doubt because he and Andrea would likely never have to do the same in their home.

His emotions were running unbridled, a delayed response to his argument with Andrea. One last room and then home to see if his own desire for a family could be rescued or simply left to erode until his heart became as rotted and as hollow as this house.

The final room sat behind a door that was either locked or merely stuck in a warped jamb. Amidst the gouges on its surface was a carving of a humanoid figure dancing upon what Sam assumed was intended to be a tomb. In place of a head the figure bore an insect with thin legs represented by jagged slashes in the door wood. Beneath this glyph the word SEPA had been scratched.

Sam wriggled the iron doorknob until frustration and mounting curiosity impelled him to wrench it, slamming his weight against the door itself.

If the owner had secured the door with a lock, it had snapped under Sam's moderate force. Still, Sam allowed a quick pang of guilt to pass through and punish him for the damage he'd wrought on the house. But really, who would ever discover it?

The window in the room was half-covered by planks, but poor workmanship did not allow the wood to block out the light or protect the grimy glass. A cursory glance led Sam to believe that this room has been used for storage, for there were more items here than in all the other rooms combined: a long table, a wall-mounted shelf upon which books and what looked to be little wooden toys or figurines had been set. There was even a thin cot mattress carpeting the far corner. Bulging black trash bags were heaped along one wall. Sam daringly peeked into one of the open hems, discovering a bundle of old clothing, men's and women's both, wadded up in a gender-melding tangle.

All the items in the room suddenly quilted themselves together in Sam's mind, forming a larger picture that suggested the house was someone's home. He felt his bones go as cold and stiff as pipes in midwinter. Fear had bolted him to the spot. He listened, cursing himself for lumbering through the house so brazenly, so noisily.

Ribbons of sunlight slipped in between the askew planks. Sam's gaze followed them as they seemed to spotlight the coating of dust that covered the mattress, the rodent droppings that littered the brownish pillow. The table reposed under streamers of cobweb and the titles on the book spines were occulted by dirt. A bedroom or squatter's den it might have been, but no longer. Sam exhaled loudly with relief.

After three or four shots of the room he indulged himself by stealing a few pictures of the neglected items: first the grubby bed, then the desk, and finally the items that lined the bowing shelf.

He regretted blowing on the row of books once the dust mushroomed up, flinging grit into his eyes and choking him. When the cloud settled Sam squinted his runny eyes at the spines: *The Egyptian Book of the Dead, De Vermis Mysteriis, The Trail of the Many-Footed One.* Leaning against these clothbound books was what looked to be a photo album or scrapbook. Sam carefully shifted this volume to face him and pulled back its plain brown leather cover.

Photographs that looked to have been torn from entomology textbooks were sloppily pasted next to Egyptian papyri that, if the ugly handwritten footnotes were to be trusted, all dealt with an Egyptian funerary god named Sepa. There were also sepia-toned photographs of tiny churchyards. Some of the graves appeared upset. Misspelled margin notes repeatedly praised the Guardian of the Larvae of the Dead. Upon one of the pages was a poem in faded pencil scrawling:

Arise O Lord of the Larvae of the Dead!
Burrow! Squirm! Appear!
Your tendrils drip with dew from the caverns of Hades,
the jewelled filth from Catacombs of Ptolemais,
& the great silent dark that holds fast between the worlds.
Glut on the meat of the temporal realm so that I
may gain yet one more day of life above the tombs!

Sam closed the cover and wiped his fingers on his jacket. His attempt to return the scrapbook to its perch was made sloppy by his unsteady hand. Something fell from the shelf and landed on the table with a clunk. Not wanting to touch anything else in the room, Sam tugged his jacket sleeve down to protect his hand while he lifted the Mason jar from the tabletop. Whatever the brownish substance was inside, it certainly had heft. Sam rotated the jar slowly, trying to discern its contents despite not truly wanting the answer. He took a step toward the window. Through the boards he could see the capped well, looking much like an ugly coin lying within the weedy lawn.

Holding the jar up to the light, Sam saw enough to suggest that what it held was indeed a wad of centipedes preserved in some sludgy liquid. His stomach heaved, and he quickly returned the jar to the shelf. Next to it Sam noticed what looked to be a wooden phallus. But this sexual aid was spiked with a number of toothpick legs. He did not bother to count them.

Shock was the only force that retarded Sam. Had his brain

not registered the sight of the closet door opening, had his eyes not caught the suggestion of the shape in the darkened alcove, he would have run wildly, been out of this house, been racing through the sunlit woods, his car keys in his fist.

But the image of the seated cadaver was strange enough, *stunning* enough, to momentarily stifle Sam's instinct to flee. Its flesh was the colour of fresh concrete, causing it to glow like grey, smouldering embers within the lightless closet. The legs were spindle-thin, and the chest was sunken. Its head was obscured by a cowl of some kind.

What an awful way to be interred, Sam thought. He marveled at how the mind almost short-circuits when its limitations are exposed.

When the figure suddenly rose and bounded into the room it was clear it had not been left to rot in some locked farmhouse room. It had been waiting in the closet, like an ascetic in a confessional. Its face was shaded by what looked to be a flowing habit of fringed brown leather that crackled as the figure advanced, sounding like something dry, something moulted.

Sam wondered if he had stumbled into one of the improved scenes he'd been imagining.

But in the movies the dead do not move this quickly.

In a swift and seamless motion, the monkish figure reached into one of the piled trash bags, causing it to tip. The bones it held clattered out onto the dusty floor like queerly shaped dice. The skulls stared with grinning indifference as the figure clutched Sam with one hand, while the other raised the chunky femur and brought it down like a primitive club. Sam never even had time to scream.

✖

The pain in the back of his skull woke Sam. It also played havoc with his perceptions. What else could explain the presence of the moon or the fact that everything else around him had been swallowed by darkness?

He pressed his hands down on the cushiony surface beneath him and slowly, achingly, pushed himself upright before slumping right back down again. The air was frigid and damp. He could see his breath forming ghosts on the blackness. Confusion over where he was quickly gave way to a sharp panic as memories of the farmhouse shuffled their way back into Sam's consciousness like cards being dealt: the tomes and the symbols and the terrible grey attacker.

With an unsteady hand Sam prodded his trouser pockets, pleading silently that his Smartphone was still there. It was, though its screen was cracked. He mashed at it with bloodless fingers, trying to connect with the world by any means possible. But the device's only use was as a source of weak glowing light. Its graphics were but a smear of colour.

Sam waved the phone about like a torch. What it illuminated was an upright tunnel of textured wood. Grubs and clumped soil dangled here and there. The atmosphere was uncomfortably moist.

The well...

Craning his aching head, Sam watched as clouds scuttled across the moon's face and he wondered how long he had been down here. The light on his phone began to flicker like a guttering candle.

A shadow suddenly blocked the moon. It was a human silhouette, one that swiftly stretched across the crude mouth of the well.

The figure, now bent over the rim, made a gesture.

Only after Sam had screamed out "Help me! Please!" did he conclude that this shadowy visitor must be the man who'd attacked him.

Words came down the chute, ricocheting off the wooden walls. They were indecipherable, guttural, almost inhuman. Regardless of whether there was meaning to them or whether it was merely the vibration of the alien voice, the ground began to shift in response to the stimuli. And soon Sam felt himself being flung as the cushioned base upon which he'd been lying began to rise and scale the side of its den.

It was immense. Sam foolishly wondered how long it must have taken his attacker to find a log large enough to shelter such a creature. By the moon's pallid glow Sam could just see the man aboveground raising his arms to imitate the flailing mandibles of the great scuttling thing that bucked its head in mirror-perfect mimicry of its keeper's gestures. The barbarous words were now being bellowed in a euphoric tone. Their rhythm matched the clacking of the thick stingers that parted and shut on the insect's rump.

Horror and irony besieged Sam in a great steely wave. He could only listen to the sound he'd so longed to hear: the patter of tiny feet. Only this time they were multiplied a hundredfold. Sam almost laughed, and a second later his light went out.

The Rasping Absence

Trent Fenner was unable to gauge his supervisor's reaction to the re-edited news segment. Upon the mounted television, animated galaxies spun like tops within simulated space.

"Astonishing as it sounds," (Trent never liked the way his voice sounded on television, even after two years of reporting), *"some physicists suspect that the longstanding model of reality, which suggests that our universe is made up of atoms, is in fact wrong. This mysterious substance that they are calling Dark Matter, along with a repulsive force dubbed Dark Energy, make up ninety-six percent of our universe. It seems that the universe is much darker than we suspected.*

"Dark Matter cannot be seen. It neither reflects nor deflects light, and it seems to be part of a reality completely distinct from our own. And yet, billions of Dark Matter particles surround us. As Dr. Douglas Newman of Newfoundland's EXCEL physics laboratory put it, 'Dark Matter represents the distinct possibility that our universe is a vast haunted house, where billions of these mysterious particles pass through the walls, and even our bodies, every day without our knowing or feeling it.'"

Lester shifted in his seat as the image on the screen changed: Trent and Dr. Newman were entering the orange-painted cage of a mine elevator. The conveyor cables emitted a low hum as it lowered the cage into the bowels of the mine.

Trent's face filled the screen. The sight of him dressed in a hardhat made Lester chuckle.

"Some of you might be wondering why physicists like Dr. Newman would go looking for Dark Matter some five hundred metres underground in this abandoned iron-ore mine here on Bell Island, Newfoundland, instead of looking up at the heavens. But in order to obtain a particle of Dark Matter that is untainted by cosmic rays and other contaminants, scientists have to go deep underground. It's eerily appropriate that we're going looking for the Dark within the dark…"

"This is where Newman describes trying to catch Dark Matter particles, yes?" Lester asked, his finger held on the remote control's Advance button.

"Using frozen germanium plates, right," replied Trent.

Lester nodded. He paused the video on a simulacrum of Dark Matter, which the show's animators designed as swarms of bluish-purple specks that swaddled our galaxy.

"I like it," Lester confessed. Perspiration caused his bare, pinkish scalp to glisten like a glazed ham.

"The script I gave you for my new epilogue, was it okay? I tried to sound more reassuring in this version."

Lester dismissed Trent's concerns with a sweep of his hand. "The closing speech works. I wouldn't worry about viewers getting upset. This Dark Matter stuff might rattle their nerves until the next commercial break, but in the end Canadians are more concerned about brass tacks; government spending, gas prices, teachers' strikes."

"You're probably right," said Trent. The tension that had been mounting within him ever since he first began his investigation on Dark Matter then reached a breaking point. He sighed roughly, releasing a bit of the mounting pressure. "I have to admit, this story kind of got to me."

Lester offered a wry smile. "Kid, what have I always said about you? That you've got a reporter's nose but not his skin. Yours is too thin. This field will chew you up if you take every story inside of you. Reporters have to be objective for more than just ethical reasons. If you make every assignment personal, you'll crack."

Trent attempted a smile.

Perhaps sensing his tensions, Lester slapped his hand on his desk as a purging gesture (Bleakness be gone!). "You know what I think you need right about now? A vacation."

"Well, as luck would have it..."

"This break will be good for you and the family. But isn't it going to be kind of a whirlwind for you, just getting back from Newfoundland yesterday and heading up north tomorrow?"

"We're actually leaving tonight. Melissa's packing as we speak."

"I bet the little one's excited."

The very mention of Jasmine sent a calming wave through Trent's mind.

"You have no idea. Melissa told me Jasmine's been talking nonstop about the holiday since I left for the east coast."

"You'll all love Pine Bluffs," Lester assured him.

"I'm sure we will, Les. Thanks again for the use of your cottage."

"See you back here in two weeks?"

Trent shook Lester's offered hand. "In two weeks."

⁂

Evening air gusting through the open car windows rejuvenated Trent as he followed the bias in the two-lane roadway. Toronto long behind him now, he strained to untangle the stress knots in his psyche.

"Hello? Earth to Trent?"

He glanced over. Melissa dangled a bottle of water between her fingers. Trent uttered an apology. Melissa uncapped the bottle and handed it to him.

"You've been a million miles away all evening. Did something happen at the meeting today?"

"No, Lester liked the recut footage. Well, as much as Lester likes anything."

"So what is it then? Your episode's been approved and now you're on a country holiday with your charming wife and beautiful daughter."

He glanced at her. Melissa winked.

"Oh, I know," Trent began, "believe me, I know. This is just what I need. Stupid as it sounds, this story got under my skin."

"That's not stupid at all," Melissa returned. "It's a freaky subject. But it's just a theory, isn't it?"

"Well, they do have evidence that Dark Matter is all over the universe, but it's so alien they can't figure out its purpose. It just blows me away that there is scientific evidence, proof, that everything we know about reality makes up only four percent of the universe. Four percent! For all our talk of colonizing Mars or beating cancer, we're like one tiny candle guttering inside a massive cave. And the cave wasn't designed by us. Or even for us. "

"You know what I think? Even if everything we know is only a little candle that's going to be snuffed out a billion years from now, so be it. We're here now, and that's good enough for me. "

Trent brought her hand to his lips. "Me too," he said through a kiss. How he wished that it was the truth.

The last mottles of daylight appeared as burnished coins as the hatchback approached the tiny hamlet.

※

They were gobsmacked to discover that their holiday accommodations were nearer to a beachfront bungalow than a humble cottage. The cold supper they ate on the back deck seemed to nourish not only Trent's body but also his spirit. At bedtime the three of them were lulled by the susurrus of the distant surf. All was right.

Still the shadows managed to puncture this airtight calm.

Dream spirited Trent back into the bowels of Bell Island. But now the laboratory was submerged in brackish water.

Trent tried to swim but couldn't. He felt shoed in weighted boots, which made all movement taxing. The liquid was thicker than mere H2O and seemed unwilling to part for him. Instead, it resisted with a pressure that threatened to fracture his bones. The fluid crowded his nostrils, sprang between his clenched teeth to seal his throat like caulking. He knew his only hope was to surface.

He pushed off with a titanic effort. Bits of sediment rushed past him as he swam, yet he saw only black.

As he wriggled upward, the texture of the liquid began to thicken. And this brought an epiphany: Trent was not swimming at all, nor was he about to break the surface of a quarry-like pool.

He was being dragged up through the earth, punching through soil, sediment, and concrete, until at last the bed of all ages sought fit to birth him into a realm of unbearable light and warmth.

Twitching, helpless, Trent could do little more than stare up at the men and women encircling him. Their hands gripped the lemon-yellow guard rails, their lab coats glowed like chalk lanterns. Strangers to a one, their expressions varied from utter disbelief to primal horror.

Trent tried to speak, but the sound that emerged was a coarse rasping, like a hacksaw dragging into wire. It echoed through the emptiness above him.

He shot up in bed with a strangled cry. His terror had not disrupted the shallow tide of Melissa's breathing.

The ashen glow through the windows and the ache behind his eyelids established that it was too early to be awake. Not wishing to risk being dropped back into that nightmare lab, Trent slipped out from beneath the sheet and prepared for a run.

Only the geriatric residents of Pine Bluffs seemed to be up and about at this hour. Their congenial waves or bids of good morning as Trent jogged past their storybook cottages brought a pleasant feeling.

It was chillier along the shore, but Trent used this as motivation to run harder. The lake was the colour of caramel. Gulls alternated between circling the overcast sky and swooping down to peck at the vivid carrion of yesterday's French fry cups and hamburger wrappers from The Snack Hut.

He turned his attention to the impressive bluffs after which the village had been named. They formed an ambit at the shore, arcing into the water like a great bookend of sun-baked clay.

Birches and pines spiked the incline's face, lent teeth to its summit. It was evocative of a moon crater's rim—a resemblance that made Trent uneasy.

Movement in his periphery evidenced that Trent was not alone.

He turned his head enough to see the beach's only other sunrise visitor: a whip-thin man whose over-tanned skin was the cast of shoe leather. He was dressed only in a gaudy pair of swimming trunks (Trent didn't enjoy the way the Tiki mask pattern seemed to study his approach) and a dull metal medallion, which looked to be the Star of David, hanging from his spindly neck.

The man was too absorbed in his task to give Trent even a nod. He appeared to gathering sand from the hem where the bluffs melded with the shore. The man's own slender hands were his only tools. He clawed up handful after handful of the wet granules, stockpiling them into a variety of plastic shopping bags.

"Floodwall?" Trent asked with a smile. When the man did not react, Trent repeated himself, assuming that his own lack of breath had made the question inaudible.

A great mantis in both posture and movement, the old man collected his bagged sand. Several of the bags had already begun to split under their own cargo; clumps and granules hemorrhaging back onto the ground as the man tied them to an almost comical-looking bicycle half-digested by rust. Trent was now near enough to observe that the medallion, which seemed to weigh the man like a ship anchor, was not a Star of David, but a symbol far more cryptic. The bauble was obviously handmade, and crudely at that. Trident spokes and leaf-like curlicues jutted out every which way. And at their point of convergence, was that a rudimentary face?

The stranger straddled his bicycle and began to pedal. He nearly toppled, the sight of which caused Trent to gasp and reach feebly. Velocity righted the cycle, and soon the pack mule of a man reached the dirt road and was gone.

A sneaker wave crashed down, its reach broad enough to wash Trent's feet. He looked over as the foamy wake ebbed, revealing the pit dug by the old man. The hole was now filled with frothy swirling water, which gave it the appearance of an inhumed cauldron.

...toil and trouble...

He reversed his course and began back to the cottage, walking at first, then, inexplicably, breaking into a wild run.

Seeing Melissa carrying a breakfast tray out onto the back deck brought not relief, but greater panic, for Trent now saw what he stood to lose if he didn't reach safety in time.

His imaginary pursuit ended with his rambling up the wooden steps and all but collapsing into one of the Adirondack chairs.

"Hi, Daddy!"

Trent hadn't even noticed Jasmine seated in one of the great seats until he heard her birdsong voice. Her tiny hand was patting the sanded plank of the chair arm. She leaned forward, her heart-shaped plastic sunglasses darkening her eyes, a smile brightening her already cherubic face.

"Good morning, sweet-pea," Trent huffed. "Did you sleep well?"

"Yep!"

"Me too."

Melissa gave him a peck and a mug of coffee-with-cream. "How was your run?"

Trent nodded. "This is a nice place."

"Beautiful," Melissa corrected.

"When can we go swimming?" Jasmine asked.

"We'll see," Trent replied. His gaze snagged on a brooding cloud in the east. "We may be in for a storm."

※

The storm didn't come that day. By noon the sun had burnt through the steely padding of clouds.

Trent returned to the beach, this time with his family, and this time it was now a hive of activity: voices, splashing, a cacophony of radio music; the air fragrant with birch wood and grilling meat.

Trent, Melissa, and Jasmine staked their claim by laying out beach towels on a little patch of sand.

"C'mon, you guys!" Jasmine cried, her chubby feet stomping divots into the sand. Trent took her hand and she tugged him toward the water. The bluffs darkened the edge of his field of vision, but Trent refused to acknowledge them.

The sight of Jasmine so enraptured by the rustic pleasures of sun and surf soothed him. After a while Melissa took over watching Jasmine to allow Trent some swimming time.

He submerged himself beneath the waves. The cool dimness, the isolation, the air held tight in his lungs: he felt he had somehow slipped back into his dream.

His surfacing was dramatic, or so he believed. For one awful instant he wondered whether he had indeed become the shrieking thing. But none of the other bathers seemed aware of his existence.

The undertow must have been stronger than Trent realized, for it had whisked him several metres nearer to the bluffs. He was facing them full-on now.

They were the antithesis of the beach, with its all its life and noise and ceaseless motion. The bluffs were austere and silent and staid. Even their trees appeared unwavering. Such stillness made it very easy for Trent to spot the tiny figure traipsing along the top of the bluffs.

Trent cupped his hands and splashed some water on his face in the thin hope this would cleanse the apparition. When it didn't, he made his way back to shore.

Melissa and Jasmine were huddled under the meagre shade of a staked umbrella.

"Jasmine's shoulders were getting a little pink," Melissa explained.

"Why don't we head back now? I'll drive into town for more groceries."

"Aw, I don't wanna go!" Jasmine cried.

"We'll come back tomorrow, sweet-pea. Besides, I need you to pick out the ice cream for dessert."

It was all the incentive Jasmine required. They returned to the cottage just long enough for Trent to fetch his car keys, and then they piled into the hatchback and drove to the barn-like grocery outlet they'd spotted on their way in.

Cornucopia was its name; a co-op that looked to be run by survivors of the Age of Aquarius. The cashier was congenial, chatting up Trent while she tallied their bill. Melissa and Jasmine took the bags to the car while Trent finished the transaction.

"Oh," the cashier blurted, her eyes locked on something beyond their large show window, "here comes old Isaac. Have you seen him pedalling around the village yet?"

Trent heard the copper pipe chimes above the entrance begin to clang. He shook his head but could not bring himself to turn around.

The cashier spoke softly: "Comes in here every afternoon without fail. And he always buys the same stuff. Canned goods mostly; soup, lentils, that sort of thing. I kid him about stockpiling for Doomsday, but I don't think Isaac gets the joke."

Trent heard the methodical scuffling of feet passing across the oiled wood floor. He grabbed his receipt and hastened for the door.

⁂

Trent spent more energy trying to keep his anxieties in check than he did cooking dinner. The food was delicious, but Melissa wasn't swallowing his forced joviality. Over dessert Jasmine began to show signs of too much sun and surf, so Melissa tucked her in early. When she returned to the deck she was armed with two glasses of white wine.

"So?" she asked.

Trent shrugged.

"You've not been yourself since you got back from that damned assignment. What's troubling you? Still this Dark Matter business?"

He sighed with authentic resignation. "I honestly don't know. I just have this heavy feeling. I've had it since I went down into that damned lab. I don't seem able to shake it."

"But you've covered stories far more disturbing than this, hon. Teen shootings, sweatshops, terrorist cells..."

"I know, but I was able to wrap my head around those. I'd almost always uncover at least some of the causes behind the problem: poverty, loopholes in corporate law, whatever. Those cases would always offer at least some promise of a solution. But this..."

His words trailed off. Melissa reached over and entangled her fingers with his. They sat and looked skyward; Melissa at the gleaming stars, Trent at the cold hollow between them.

✳

Trent did not dream of Dark Matter that night. He did not dream at all. Dreams require sleep, and Trent knew none. Even his reliable trick of monitoring his breathing failed to lull him.

He shut his eyes and fought to shut off his brain.

But Night was lodged within his head. Constellations shimmered and blinked. They were smeared across the seemingly endless curve of his calvaria, like his very own planetarium.

Between and beyond the nuggets of silver light stretched the vacuum of dead space; still and lightless and seemingly silent.

Seemingly, for there was a grating, grinding sound; underlying and ever-present, like the gears of some unfathomable machine turning, slowly turning...

He was being drawn into the black gaps. Trent felt himself being pulled like a hooked fish into that abyss where even the flesh is forbidden. He struggled to pull back, but was lost in a magnetic field. Black grit whisked about him like granules in a sandstorm. It stung and froze his flesh. In a mere heartbeat Trent felt himself encased in scales of this light-eating armor.

There was purpose in their assault.

The specks of nothingness dug into Trent's flesh until every pore became a socket embedded with a minute onyx eye. At once, these billion eyes sprung open. Trent Fenner became Sight itself; omniscience, the chariot that bore all the Dark Matter whose reality was not ours. In this new unlighted form, Trent tasted the colours of sounds, he seized the great cold knowledge that secrets itself within the rasping of the stars.

He understood, knew. No, more: Trent was Radiant.

He opened his eyes to find himself in a mortal's bed, his sight instantly, mercifully dwindled down to a pair of mortal's eyes that witnessed the bedroom in pre-dawn gloom.

Although he was not an emotional man, even in times of duress, Trent began to cry. The fount of his sorrow was so deep it was incomprehensible to him. He pulled his aching body out of bed and crossed the cottage to the room where Jasmine slept soundly. He meditated on how dear she was to him.

How incredible it is to be able to love, he thought.

Almost mindlessly, Trent donned his sweats and his runners.

He took to the dirt road, allowing blind instinct to guide him.

✳

The footpath that fed off the shore and up onto the bluffs was thoroughly unremarkable; an almost unnoticeable strip of dirt that was only nominally less stony and weed-entangled than the untamed areas on either side of it.

Trent found the incline almost insurmountable. The sheerness of it caused his thighs to tighten and, seemingly, to ignite. His breathing was ludicrously laboured, as though he had reached some impossible altitude, when in fact he was scarcely above the tree-line. His fatigue baffled him. He had run much harder, over much more arduous terrain, and for much longer spans of time.

By now the sun was layering the lake with a netting of glints. Magpie-like, Trent fell under the spell of the distant shimmer until an obstacle on the path tripped him up. The object entangled around Trent's ankles, acting as a tripwire. He smashed down on the path, the breath instantly banished from his lungs. Pain speared through his ankle. His hands, bearing the bloody stigmata of tiny stones, reached down to remove whatever had ensnared him.

It was a plastic shopping bag. Dregs of wet sand lined its inner creases.

He was tearing it from his feet when he noticed the shadow staining the path.

Trent twisted his head to a painful degree, but all he could discern was a figure made coal-smudge-anonymous by the rising sun behind it.

Righting himself put on more weight than his ankle could bear. Trent stumbled to one side and came to rest upon the bluffs.

Isaac (Trent could clearly see him now) had turned away from his intruder and resumed working. The same swimming trunk Tiki masks watched Trent even when the old man couldn't be bothered.

Trent found himself oddly entranced by Isaac's labours. The crouching old man reached blindly for handful after handful of wet sand, culling it from the pile of bulging shopping bags beside him.

Isaac made a sudden sense to Trent: his eccentric attire, his aloofness, his peculiar reputation among the locals. He was an artist. Trent had interviewed enough of them last year for a story on homeless people who elaborately decorated alley walls and sidewalks with chalk drawings, many of which were astonishingly beautiful.

His journalistic instincts stoked, Trent pulled himself up and hobbled over to peek at Isaac's work-in-progress.

What he found was a hole bored deep into the bluff. Isaac was crouched at the lip of it, pouring handful after handful of clumpy sand into the aperture. Unless this was some Zen practice, Isaac was engaged in a fool's chore. Trent eyed the pit, then that morning's stockpile of beach sand. It was like a reverse version of the old fable about bailing out the ocean with a teaspoon.

Reposing next to Isaac was a chunk of dark matter.

Of course this black rock (likely volcanic glass) wasn't true Dark Matter, but its similarity to the computer-generated models used in his news story was strong enough to frighten Trent.

"I let it out." The creaking voice reminded Trent of an old gate swinging on rusty hinges. "Don't tell nobody. I let it out, but it wasn't nothing but an accident. Righting wrongs takes time, but I'm trying. See? I'm trying."

Another fistful of sand was ground between Isaac's palms like baker's flour. Into the hole it fell. Another reach, more sand. Trent could actually see Isaac's joints bucking and twitching within his scrawny frame like pistons of bone.

"Is there anything I can do? Why don't I get you some breakfast? You look like you could use it."

Isaac shook his longish head. "Too late for that now. All the eggs are broken anyway. You think you're smart enough to put them back together? I'd like to see you try!" There was a flare of indignation in his voice. He clasped the wiry medallion and brought it to his lips.

"Can you tell me what happened here, Isaac?" He had slipped into reporter-mode; a state of mind that brought Trent both comfort and confidence, if for no other reason than that it afforded him a sense of detachment from his surroundings.

"I'm trying to fix this!"

"Fix what?"

Isaac fed a few more grains to the shadow.

Trent tried to swallow but found his throat a sandy tunnel. "What's down there, Isaac?"

"Hardly anything now," Isaac replied. "I told you, I let it out. Every night I'd hear it scraping and scratching inside the earth here. Every morning I'd pray that the noises would stop. Finally I came up here and did what I thought it wanted; I dug it out.

"I know it was a mistake. I know that now. So all I can do is try to right the wrong and try to fill the whole thing up so it'll stop leaking out."

"So what will stop leaking out?"

"It's spoiling everything, everything it touches. And that

big empty is getting into everything. I found this black rock here to plug the hole. I thought it would be fooled by the black colour, that it'd think this was still an open hole. It didn't work." Isaac held up his crude pendant. "I'm pretty safe though. I built myself a seal for protection. I'm airtight. But you? I don't see a seal. You're a fool coming up here without one. You're a damned fool."

An eel of nausea began to wriggle in Trent's stomach, swimming up with such velocity it seemed to set the whole Earth spinning. He shut his eyes and saw dark amoebas splattering and splashing against his eyelids; tassels of midnight lustre that shrivelled as quickly as they thrived.

He was absorbing them now, eating this Dark Matter, his eyelids chewing the particles, his brain digesting them. Whether they were invading him from the open bluffs or whether he'd been contaminated in the old iron-ore mine was irrelevant. These seeds were beginning to hatch. They sprouted teeth and they were eating him, gutting him. Trent could feel them chewing up his muscles and bones, rendering him hollow. They passed through him like a rapid, ravenous cancer. And once he'd been voided of organ and bone, sinew and breath, Trent experienced the awful rasping sound as the Dark Matter grated and spun and revelled in the great absence within him.

He touched his chest. The lack of a protective talisman drained all the strength from his body.

Now intoxicated, Trent staggered helplessly back along the path.

Despite this drama and din, Isaac remained riveted by his task.

✵

Trent hid among the pines until he felt he had his contagion under control.

He eventually returned to the cottage, telling Melissa that he'd gone for an especially long run this morning. She informed him that they were going to the beach after lunch. Trent layered himself in clothing to keep anything from radiating outward.

"You're going to roast!" she declared as Trent exited the patio door.

He stood dumb, dazed.

"Beach, mommy!" Jasmine cried.

They walked.

The beach was even busier than yesterday. Youth was everywhere. The only people Trent spotted who appeared older than him were the shore-bound fishermen stationed in their lawn chairs in the shallows.

They staked out their spot. At Jasmine's bouncing insistence, Melissa helped her wriggle into her water wings. Trent, overdressed in long trousers and a jacket, refused to lower himself down onto the granules. Nor would he heed the voiceless beckon of the bluffs. He looked out across the water and wondered how many more days of sunlight were left.

"Trent!"

He turned to see Melissa hunched before Jasmine. "For the fourth time, where is her lifejacket?"

Trent looked about foolishly. "I...I must have left it at the cottage."

"I wanna swim, mommy!"

Melissa sighed. "Can you go back and get it?"

"Hmm?"

"Never mind," she huffed, pushing herself to her feet. "I'll go. Watch her, please. She's got her water wings, so she can go in, just not too far."

"Right."

"Trent?"

He looked at her.

"Watch her."

He pushed his mouth into what he hoped was a reassuring grin. Judging by Melissa's reaction, it was not.

Trent took Jasmine's hand. Her palm was like a tiny silk pillow. Together they parted the water.

Jasmine slid her fingers free and began to stomp the shallows. Her steps caused water to bounce up like miniature fountains in the air. The tide flowed and ebbed. Overhead, gulls spun out precise spiral patterns.

A slow and silent tide also touched Trent from within. In no time it subsumed him. Trent saw the sky as a great murky ocean, pouring its Dark Matter down like sand through a sieve.

The scope of it, the indifference it exuded as it went through its bewildering machinations—these stifled Trent.

All was silent and dim; human activity was fading, like candles guttering out one by one.

But then the candles began to brighten, raging against this meta-darkness. There was a flaring.

There was a crescendo of ugly sounds.

Trent snapped his head, and the Dark Universe was once more hidden behind a bright and busy mask. A stark image filled his eyes: a tiny figure in a shell of many colours, twitching just below the water's surface.

"Mister!" yelled a male voice.

The fishermen had sprung from their lawn chairs as quickly as their aged bones would allow. Their poles were jerking about as though they had live wires in their spinners.

The men were waist-deep in the water now. One had scooped a bulky shape from the waves while the other ever-so-gently manoeuvred the fishing line.

The sight of Jasmine's head hanging limp and heavy from the crook of the fisherman's arm summoned in Trent a feeling that was far worse than being emptied. It mangled his heart. The alpha and omega of all life blazed from the crushed and dripping form that was drooped over the old man's arms like a boned fish.

With trembling hands the second fisherman removed the last loop of the nylon line that had wound itself around Jasmine's neck. They laid on her on the sand. Trent scuttled over to her, howling, his movements as alien-looking as a crab's crawl. He positioned Jasmine's head and attempted the Kiss of Life.

Even in the cold, thick mire of his dread, Trent was somehow still aware of his contagion. The grinding voice in his head assured him that he would not be saving Jasmine, he would be poisoning her; breathing into her the tainted black particles of the mine shaft and of the gutted bluffs.

He sat up to draw in a fresh breath. Jasmine was still.

An eagle-like scream pierced through the murmurs that were swirling above Trent. All heads turned to see Melissa standing near The Snack Hut, the lifejacket hanging needlessly from her fist. She dropped it and ran forward.

Trent arched down to exhale again. He was abruptly shoved aside.

He remained slumped in the shallows, his clothing growing cold and heavy with the tide, and watched as Melissa did what his toxic self could not.

Jasmine convulsed. Melissa began to weep as she turned her child onto her side and saw water and saliva trickle out of the tiny mouth. Jasmine began to cough, and then to cry. She sounded like a mewling cat. Melissa kissed her sand-encrusted hair and sobbingly urged her to breathe, breathe...

"Thank God," one of the fishermen said. "Thank God. I'm terribly sorry, ma'am. Your little one, she was starting to stray over to where our lines were cast. We tried to warn your husband. We didn't see her go under. We didn't know she'd gotten tangled up right away. I'm just... Thank God, ma'am." He patted Jasmine's head delicately, as though she might shatter at his touch.

✳

Melissa carried her back to the cottage, cooing to her, telling her how brave she was and how none of this was her fault. By the time they reached the back deck Jasmine was no longer crying.

Trent lagged behind, a pack mule burdened with all the cargo that was infinitely less precious than Jasmine.

He was not yet at their yard when Melissa flung open the sliding glass door to announce that she was driving Jasmine to the hospital to be examined. She did not ask Trent to join them.

Their vehicle roared out of the driveway and down the country lane. Trent dropped the beach items on the lawn and shuffled to the cottage's living room, where he fell into one of the wicker bucket chairs.

It was dusk before Melissa returned. She entered the cottage with a bag from a fast-food chain. She uttered only two words to Trent: "She's fine."

She and Jasmine dined in the kitchen. Trent did not join them, but instead went to lie down.

The night deepened. Melissa had obviously opted to sleep next to Jasmine in her bedroom.

When Trent had at long last managed to shake the pieces into a pattern, he understood what had to be done. Still dressed in yesterday's clothing, he crept to the doorway where he lingered to watch the two most beloved things in the world to him sleeping peacefully.

Melissa had intervened in time. Jasmine hadn't been poisoned by him. But Trent could not run the risk of such a thing happening again. The indifference of the universe, which had somehow come to house itself in his heart, had to remain his alone. He could not let it leak out to spoil his loved ones.

He slipped outside and began to walk. He tried to jog but found that his black lungs were strained even by the mildest activity. It was coming to a head much quicker than Trent had suspected.

It was still dark when he reached the empty bluffs. Isaac was likely enjoying a well-earned rest somewhere.

He found the chunk of blood-black glass that doubled as both marker and plug. He rolled it free, allowing fresh Darkness to geyser up and out, but only momentarily.

Trent climbed down into the pit and began to rake the cold earth down onto himself. The grains wedged themselves beneath his fingernails and they gloved his palms. He pulled down enough sand to keep him snug. Then he reclined his head and waited.

Pent with folded limbs and arched neck, Trent shut his eyes and tempered his breathing. The sand seemed to be grinding in his ears, chirping in the mad language of birds, or in the secret tongue of the Conqueror Worm.

The longer Trent lingered, the more acute his aerial sense became. In time he was able to see clearly, despite the narrow womb that would not birth him, despite his tightly shut eyes. He had been right. Melissa would never know it, nor, thankfully, would Jasmine, but he was right. Science had delivered Trent into this heart of darkness, but Nature had provided him with the means to save his family from this fate.

Trent's eyelashes were dewy. He could feel the Dark Matter gathering on his skin like some type of cosmic pollen. It was vacuum-cold, but Trent had already reached the point of acceptance.

Above, Isaac arrived and resumed his labours. A fresh quantity of beach sand was flung. As was his custom, Isaac did not look down into the pit as he worked. He knew well enough what was down there; something primordially impure, something that needed to be sealed in for good and all. He had lugged up fewer bags than usual, sensing perhaps that his chore was not as endless as he'd long believed. Intermittently he fingered the sigil around his neck.

Though neither man was aware of the other's presence, somehow, at that horizon where all thought dovetails, both men intuited that today, at long last, it would be accomplished. Today would be the end.

Scold's Bridle:
A Cruelty

"**D**o we have an understanding then, Mr. Biskup?"

Ivan Biskup disliked the way the smile was growing across the face of Peters; his neighbour, the unbidden guest to his garage workshop.

"No," Ivan returned. "No, we don't. Not yet at least." He plucked a rag from the pocket of his trousers to wipe away the perspiration that jeweled his weathered face. The iron workshop was a stifling cell. The open garage door afforded no breeze but only the rays of the Dog Day sun to pour in like molten slag. "I don't even understand why you, why *anybody*, would want a book like this, let alone have something made from it."

The chunky volume sat upon one of Biskup's worn workbenches. The book's gold-leaf edging sparkled under the fluorescent lights. *Cruel & Unusual: An Illustrated History of Torture Devices* was the book's title. The cover seemed to shout these words, with its thick, ominous typeface. Beneath the title was an arrangement of four photographs, each showcasing a different invention born of humanity's boundless creativity and cruelty. Ivan recognized one of the items as an iron maiden. The other, he assumed, was a gallows, or some hideous rack-and-rope contraption designed to dislocate living limbs like corks popping from bottled champagne. The other two were line drawings of devices too esoteric for Ivan. He scratched the back of his neck.

"I teach history," answered Peters, though Ivan had forgotten his question, "I want a device for a visual aid. It will help me teach a lesson. The neighbours tell me you work wonders with wrought iron."

There was a fluttering noise as Peters flicked open the book to an earmarked leaf. He tapped his finger on the page, coaxing Ivan to look.

The image might have been of a helmet. Ivan squinted his eyes and studied closer, concluding at last that the contraption was a mask of some description. Its frame was of curved iron bands and jutting screws and a few ornamental curlicues. Poking up from the top of the mask was a pair of donkey's ears, fashioned in crudely hammered metal.

"You're either joking or crazy," Ivan said. His indignation had been made plain. "Folks around here aren't going to let their kids see something like this in school. I don't care if it is from some fancy history book. What's this thing supposed to be anyway?"

"It's called a scold's bridle. It's also sometimes referred to as a brank. In medieval times, authorities would employ it to remind certain people of their station in life."

At that instant, a young mother pushed a pram along the sidewalk in front of Ivan's exposed workshop. The woman gently rocked the carriage with one hand while with the other she waved a blue teddy bear before the open hood. Neither action consoled the infant, whose cries were piercing and persistent.

"Good morning, Allison!" Peters cried. He waved and grinned at her. Allison waved back tiredly. Peters then turned back to Ivan and mumbled, "That kid sounds like a boiled cat. Imagine hearing that at three in the morning?" He shuddered with disgust.

Ivan reached over and closed the book.

"I'll pay you," announced Peters. "I know you need the money."

When he saw the expression on Ivan's face, saw the way the older man puffed up his sizeable frame, Peters raised his hands in a gesture of peacekeeping.

"Please," he began, "don't take offence. It's just...well, I watch. I see things. I'm good at taking little pieces of detail and seeing how they fit into a larger mosaic. This workshop, for instance. When my wife and I first moved onto this street, we'd see throngs of people on your driveway every Saturday and Sunday."

Ivan nodded mournfully. "My sales. My Edwina used to help me every weekend..."

"I remember. I think almost every house on the block had at least one piece of your ironwork; fireplace tools, patio furniture, garden gates."

"Every house except yours," Ivan replied. He, too, was good at noting details.

"That's why I'm here; to correct that. Besides, it's been a long time since you've had one of your sales. I'd imagine your bills are piling up. And before you ask, I deduced this after your wife passed last year. My condolences, by the way. You haven't hosted a sale since. I remember that day in January when your car wouldn't start. You had it towed and I haven't seen it since. The repairs must have been outside your budget. You've been practically housebound."

Ivan emitted an unintentional sigh of lament. "*If* I make that mask," he began, "what were you thinking of paying?"

Peters named a sum that stole Ivan's breath.

"I don't believe you," Ivan said thinly.

Peters produced an envelope plump with bills.

At Peters' insistence, Ivan counted them, fumblingly.

"How does a schoolteacher come up with that kind of money?"

"Family," Peters said plainly. "Now, let me go over a few

of the key details." He once again opened the torture book to the chosen page.

"The scold's bridle shown here is modelled on a donkey's head. I gather this was a pretty common design; make the guilty party resemble a jackass, that sort of idea. But I came up with this rough sketch on this paper." He produced a sheet from his shirt pocket. "The bridle I want is made to look more like a rabbit. See the ears?"

Ivan moved his head vaguely.

"As for the mouth clamp, the book suggests an iron band lined with adjustable screws, points facing inward. These can be tightened to various lengths, depending on how deeply the punisher wants to push the screws into the wearer's gums..." Peters continued to explain gleefully, before finally asking, "Do we have a deal then, Mr. Biskup?"

Ivan's gaze was tethered to the bulging envelope on his workbench. "Yes...yes, I suppose we do."

✷

He did not begin to work on the project until the sun had begun to sink, dragging with it some of the swelter. After a pauper's supper of canned soup and an apple, Ivan wended his way to the garage.

The iron muzzle was the most labour-intensive of the bridle's components. Mr. Peters had requested that the bit be lined with a gravel-like coating of barbs. A pair of chains linked the mouthpiece to the muzzle, and the whole contraption was framed by a network of flat iron bars bent to fit the exact measurements Mr. Peters had left on his sketch.

The following evening Ivan went about ornamenting the scold's bridle with the jackrabbit ears of thin metal. He even added six pieces of jutting copper wire to the muzzle; whiskers for the bunny's polished metal nose. The gum clamp was lined with double rows of screws and the mask's interior was enhanced with thick spiky bolts. He scored the interior of the eyeholes and peeled back the pointed metal jags so that the wearer's eyelids would, theoretically speaking of course, be nicked with each blink.

The third night was just a matter of tightening and buffering.

On the appointed morning, Peters came to collect. The metal monstrosity was secreted inside a white cardboard box that bore the insignia of a wine Ivan had never drunk. Peters peeked into the top, then gave what might have been a very faint nod. He neatly folded over the carton's flaps, picked up his spoil and strolled down Ivan's driveway without so much as a word.

✳

From that day onward, guilt—inexplicable, burning, ever-present—became Ivan's erstwhile companion. It weighted his frame like a millstone. When he did manage to steal a few hours of sleep it chewed on his psyche, causing dreams of tortures too gorgeous to ever be recalled by a civilized mind. Indeed, Ivan felt as if he was trapped in one of the devices from Peters' book. He thought of the schoolchildren seeing what he'd wrought. He found that thought unbearable.

However, he had paid his bills and still had cash left over, enough to keep himself in drink for several weeks.

Finally, his guilt crested over into burning curiosity.

Ivan lay on the bed, listening to the windup alarm clock ticking at him from the nightstand like a clucking tongue. It punished him until daylight finally broke.

He sat up too quickly and for a moment the room lilted, yet it did not rob him of his clarity. He needed to know, needed to be reassured that he had done nothing wrong. Of course, his mask had been fashioned in good faith, as a teaching tool, but nevertheless, this rationale could not keep the ugly guilt at bay.

He rose and dressed. This morning he would have closure.

Not until he was out in the street did it occur to Ivan that he hadn't bothered to check the time. It was early but clearly not too early; women and men on the street were jogging or were beginning their morning commute in their smart-looking business attire.

He thought he'd made it all the way to Peters' house without being seen when the front door was startlingly flung open. Peters stared hard at him. His white Oxford shirt was buttoned to the collar, but the tie was hanging from his right hand like a limp scourge.

"Ivan!" he said with audible shock.

"I..." he began, clearing his throat as he struggled to find the words, "I just came to..."

Peters raised his hand and chortled softly. "I know why you're here." He pushed the door open wide. "You want to see your creation in its new home, yes?"

"Something like that, yes."

Inside, the house was warm and stale. Heavy drapes kept out the light, kept the rooms obscured.

"Nice place you've got here," lied Ivan.

"Come with me," Peters said. "You'll appreciate this. The scold's bridle is not only beautiful, it works. Come. Wifey's in the kitchen making breakfast." The wave of his hand was childlike, playful.

Dread retarded Ivan's rounding of the corner. When he finally willed himself to advance, his fear became manifest in the shape of the woman at the stove. Ivan could no longer move. His breath leaked out in a low moan. It felt like his organs had been replaced with ice.

She sheepishly sat down at the kitchen table whose single place-setting was for her husband, who casually sat, took up his fork.

The scold's bridle crowned the woman like some gruesome headdress. The metal ears jutted up as though she was a startled hare listening intently for some encroaching predator. Aside from the cage on her head, the woman's attire was quite normal, almost banal. She wore a robe of lavender satin. She was looking at Ivan, looking into him. Ivan could see her brilliant blue eyes, shimmering with tears of agony, shining out from the shadows of the Lepus mask.

"Dear, we have a guest," said Peters. "Set another place at the table." His tone was noticeably firmer now, more like a military commander than a spouse. "Have a seat, Ivan."

Ivan nodded. Thoughtlessly he pulled one of the high-backed chairs out from under the kitchen table and sat down. He was happy for the support, for his legs seemed to have lost all their strength.

Peters' wife retrieved a plate, coffee mug and juice glass from the cupboard.

"Here, let me..." Ivan said as he attempted to stand.

"No," Peters said coldly. Ivan looked at him and Peters shook his head. "No," he repeated.

She was facing them now. The metal bands that Ivan himself had manipulated so cunningly were now revealed in all their hideousness. The morning sun shone through the window with ironic brightness, causing the torture tool to gleam.

Ivan could only suppose that the woman was pretty, so smothered were her features. Through the slats Ivan could see her eyes, wide and wet with tears. They were the only human feature he could discern inside that orgy of cold metal.

"She likes rabbits," Peters explained. "A jackass mask would have been too harsh."

She stepped closer in order to set his place. As she leaned in Ivan was able to hear faint gagging sounds and the awful chink of teeth-on-metal. Her breathing was sharp but uneven, drawn and exhaled solely through her nostrils. A dark wet thread suddenly sprouted from the muzzle. It left a small red stain on the linen tablecloth.

"My god," Ivan gasped before pushing himself erect. He turned and began toward the front door.

"I told you it was for teaching," Peters called, but Ivan was already out the door. The rest of Peters' spiel fell on deaf ears, for Ivan was too absorbed in shock and self-loathing to hear. The only words that managed to rise above the murmur were "You're culpable, you know!"

Ivan rushed out into the day and squinted from the accusatory sunlight. He staggered back to his home. Once inside he went straight to the garage where the cordless phone was perched near his workbench. He had it in his fist and was about to dial when Peters' words bored into him. He had been desperate, yes, but even this and playing up the grieving widower routine would only get him so far with the authorities.

Panic set in. The garage became stifling. Ivan flung the track door open. He breathed in greedily, his mind racing.

Ivan was so lost in his panic he did not hear the approaching footsteps.

"Are you Mr. Biskup?" a strange voice called. Ivan jumped at the sound of it. "Sorry, I didn't mean to startle you."

The woman in his driveway was not wholly unfamiliar to him. He'd seen her before: the young mother from the basement apartment down the road.

"Mr. Peters said I should talk to you," she said.

"Talk to me?" Ivan sputtered.

Allison. Was that the name Peters had called her?

"He said you'd understand," she continued. She moved to him, revealing her fatigue-ravaged face, her teary, reddened eyes. "It's my baby," she said. "He won't stop crying. Day and night. I've tried everything; singing to him, midnight feedings, taking him for long drives. Nothing works."

Ivan's hand autonomously found his mouth and gripped it.

The woman held out a tattered envelope. "It's all I can afford. I don't need anything as elaborate as what Mr. Peters ordered. Here, I drew a sketch."

She unfolded a colourful paper from inside the envelope. It was an ad from a magazine or catalogue. The infant in the photograph had been distorted, its wide and innocent grin gagged by a hectic thumbnail drawing of a chin strap and blinders and a spiked ball-gag forced between the tiny lips.

"I love my son, you understand? I love him. I'm not doing this to punish him. I just need some peace and quiet. I'll only need this for a while...just a little while...just until he learns."

Crawlspace Oracle

Afew moments under the strange red lamps of the restaurant was all that was required to cause Rhiannon to wonder if she was dreaming. The long bus ride through the rainy afternoon certainly hadn't helped matters, nor did the reason behind her trip: a reunion with a woman she'd considered, at best, an acquaintance in the office where she'd worked before Iain and marriage and the birth of the twins. It had been a long time since she'd ventured out on her own. She now regretted that her first outing was to this anaemic town that was notorious for being a haven for dismal weather and washed up entertainers.

For reasons Rhiannon could never unearth, these entertainers seemed to migrate to this colourless burg to collect their meagre pensions while waiting to die.

Today, Rhiannon had seen plenty of bleak weather, but only one example of the latter feature; when she'd deboarded at the bus depot she'd witnessed a scarecrow-like man on crutches attempting to juggle a trio of shining spheres. He'd watched Rhiannon hopefully as fluid (rain, perspiration, or tears, she could not tell) streamed down his cheeks. He'd made a pitiful sound as she'd walked by, clinging firmly to her purse. His whimper had been like a baleful note blown on an old wooden flute.

Rhiannon had no intention of ever coming to this town, or of seeking out Hyacinth again. The very thought of Hyacinth provided Rhiannon with pangs of guilt, pangs that worsened when her memory trawled up specific details, such as the lavish gift Hyacinth had given her for the baby shower. But seven years had passed since that time and there'd not been so much as a single call or Christmas card between them.

But once Rhiannon had arrived at the curious eatery and was able to see Hyacinth in the flesh, she wondered if they'd both been living on different calendars. If she were to use Hyacinth's face as a gauge, it looked as though decades had passed since their last encounter, for Hyacinth appeared old and drawn and brittle.

Rhiannon wondered if this was partly due to the strange macrobiotic diet that Hyacinth had spent the first part of their evening explaining in detail. She'd ordered queer, tiny delicacies from the menu and had requested a small pot of boiling water and an empty mug, in which she steeped some pungent herbs that she'd bundled in a small piece of cheesecloth.

"I can't thank you enough for inviting me to dinner!" Hyacinth said. "But I can't allow you to pay the tab."

"Please," answered Rhiannon with a casual wave of her hand, "it's my pleasure. I only wish we'd done this sooner."

"Time is a startled bird flitting away from us, as my father used to say. Well, since you insist on buying dinner, if there is ever anything I can do to repay you, you may consider it done."

Rhiannon grew cagey once she recognized this opportunity to state her true motivation for this reunion. The opportunity was too perfect, both in timing and tone. It thrilled and unnerved her at once.

"Funny you should say that…" she began, anxiously. The words were swirling about her head, just out of reach.

Hyacinth flared her sallow eyes with interest. "Oh?" she said.

"Yes. I was hoping to pick your brain about money." Rhiannon flinched at her poor choice of words. Hyacinth's expression darkened.

"No, no, not like that! I'm not asking for a loan or anything of that sort!" sputtered Rhiannon. "I'm just looking for some advice."

"Oh."

The cord of tension that Rhiannon had felt tightening between the two of them began to slacken, to her immense relief.

"You see, Iain's had quite a good year at the agency: four quarterly bonuses on top of his annual salary increase. We're looking to invest this extra money, put it toward something sound. It's not a huge amount, but Iain's pretty convinced we can make a respectable profit if we play our cards right."

Hyacinth shaped her sapped expression into something vaguely happy. "First off, I am truly thrilled for you; all snug with a husband and those little darlings you made. I'm tickled to hear that you have money besides. But when it comes to investing, I'm afraid I wouldn't know one market from another."

"But those stories in the *Gazette*..."

"Those..." Hyacinth said dismissively, "...those articles were inflated."

"They referred to you as Queen Midas," Rhiannon said. She felt a peculiar pride when her comment caused her guest to visibly blush. "But you never gave those reporters the secret of your success, did you?"

"I'm only as good as my guide," Hyacinth confessed.

"Your guide? So, you do have some sort of an advisor?"

"Some sort, yes."

A fine balance was required for Rhiannon to probe her guest further without seeming rude.

"Do you have a card for this person?" she asked. "Some way I can reach them?"

Hyacinth stared past her dinner companion, toward the restaurant's front window and through it. Rhiannon wondered what, if anything, the gaunt woman might have been looking for on those miserable streets.

Whatever she was scanning the soggy night for, Hyacinth suddenly appeared to have found. Her eyes brightened with fresh inspiration.

"I like you, Rhiannon. I always have. More than that, I trust you. And so, yes, I will show you. I will let you in."

With that, Hyacinth rose and tugged her long coat from the pole by their booth.

"You mean now?" Rhiannon asked, flustered by her own lack of preparation. The world suddenly seemed to be spinning too quickly.

"Of course!" Hyacinth gushed. "Come along. My car is just around the corner."

"I…it's just that…I mean, surely their business will be closed by now."

Hyacinth was already halfway to the door.

The car Rhiannon was led to was far humbler than what she'd envisioned a woman of Hyacinth's standing would drive. She squeezed into the littered cab and endured the deafening rumble of an unmuffled engine. Her head was aching by the time Hyacinth chauffeured them off the main roads and down a maze of bleak-looking side streets.

When she noted the house before which Hyacinth stopped her car, Rhiannon was bewildered. Could the woman be playing some type of joke? She'd never known Hyacinth to have a sense of humour.

This confusion cooled into apprehension once Rhiannon closed the car door and watched her guide scaling the cement steps that connected the ugly lawn to a residence that was not much larger than a storage locker, and every bit as tasteless. It was a frame house, stunted and misshapen. It was as if an unskilled carver had whittled this stingy dwelling from a greater house, then tucked their shameful creation on a poorly lit backstreet in hopes of concealing it. The roof bowed where it should not, and the walls stood in a manner they could not, and the patina was the grey of curdled mushroom soup.

Hyacinth unlocked the narrow front door and held it open for her guest.

With that, as if on cue, Rhiannon's surroundings conspired against her. A pair of men rounded the corner and began shambling in her direction (their voices deep, their laughter at some imperceptible joke scary), the lone streetlamp on the block began to flicker, the rain resumed falling.

She crossed the lawn and scaled the steep concrete steps as quickly as she could.

The realization that this entire adventure had been a grave mistake, which had been nagging faintly at the corners of Rhiannon's attention from the moment she boarded the bus to come here, fully erupted the instant she crossed the threshold of Hyacinth's house. What she was feeling was not the threat of immediate danger, but something vague, something dizzying in its menace. The nearest Rhiannon had ever felt to this sensation was déjà vu. She wondered if she had perhaps dreamed this reunion with Hyacinth years ago and was just now discovering that her dream had been an omen, a warning to avoid this detour on her life path. But it was too late now to heed.

"Just throw your coat anywhere," Hyacinth said as she shut and bolted the door. "Would you like something? Water or tea?"

"No, thank you." She kept her coat on.

Hyacinth moved down the little hallway and snapped on the kitchen light, revealing a countertop piled with unwashed dishes and rows of hanging cupboards with their doors open, flaunting their vacancy. Queen Midas was evidently nearer to Old Mother Hubbard.

Glancing discreetly through the archway to her right,

Rhiannon saw a living room that was empty except for a folding lawn chair whose seat held a stack of rumpled magazines. The kitchen was as lacking in furniture and appliances as it was in foodstuffs. Rhiannon noted a small hotplate and a barstool stationed before the warped countertop. And that was all.

"I apologize for the state of the house. Don't think I'm not aware of the fact that it has seen better days."

"Oh...I..." stammered Rhiannon. "Are you in the process of flipping it?" she asked, her voice soaked in hope.

"No," Hyacinth replied. "I've been living here for some time now."

"What about your money?" Rhiannon immediately regretted her choice of words and scrambled to reframe her panicked interrogation. "What I mean is, surely you can afford to live a bit more comfortably than this."

"I have before. I hope to again. But the money's gone."

Rhiannon wished that the woman's tone wasn't so cheerful.

"I'm confused. I thought you had this excellent advisor, that the advice he'd been giving you was sound."

"Oh, it is. It's very sound indeed. The fault lies with me, not my advisor."

"How so? Did you not take their advice?"

"For a long time, I did. As my father did before me and his father before him. But it's all about correctly interpreting the message. That's the key. I've not been interpreting the messages properly, obviously. Or maybe it's that the nature of the messages has changed."

"I don't follow."

Hyacinth stood leaning against the cluttered counter, studying her guest, scrutinizing her.

Rhiannon looked away and loudly cleared her throat. "Um...did you happen to have that advisor's phone number?"

Hyacinth shook her head. "No need."

She crossed the tiny kitchen and pulled down the gingham towels that hung from a mounted rack. The removal of the towels revealed a door of whitewashed wood.

Hyacinth pulled this back from its jamb, unto a black void, or so it seemed to Rhiannon, whose legs were losing their strength. Fear had rendered her helpless. She stood mutely, watching as her host clawed at the debris on top of the stained refrigerator until she found a large black flashlight.

Though she appeared to merely be testing the batteries, Hyacinth had the light upturned so that its beam shone against her chin, a sight that stirred in Rhiannon frightening memories of ghost stories around bonfires during those awful weeks when she'd been left to fend for herself at summer camp. She recalled how immersive those tales had been for her, the horrible impact they'd had, tainting the strange world around her as something seething with hidden peril.

Standing here now, in this dingy kitchen, Rhiannon came to appreciate how true those impressions had been.

Without a word, Hyacinth turned the flashlight to the open door and began her noisy descent of the basement steps.

Recognizing this opportunity, Rhiannon turned to charge for the front door, but a chanced view through the living room window crushed her plan of escape.

The straggling figures she'd seen moving down the unfamiliar street when she'd arrived were now loitering by Hyacinth's rusted car. Or were these the same figures? No, for where there had been but a pair, there was now a group. Forlorn-looking women now stood alongside the imposing men. They looked to be huddling under the sputtering streetlamp like moths.

Rhiannon reached into her purse for her phone to call a cab, or perhaps call Iain. She stole another look. The figures were ordering themselves. They were lining up single-file along the sidewalk.

"Everything is ready," announced Hyacinth.

The sound of her voice made Rhiannon squeal. She spun and looked into a flash-lit grin.

"You look frightened."

"I am!"

"But there's no reason to be. I'm coming with you, it's fine."

Hyacinth began down the basement stairs first, which made Rhiannon feel just secure enough to move to the doorway and look down at those ruddy steps; anything to keep her focus off the strange congregation outside.

The basement was no longer a wall of blackness. In addition to the gleaming finger from Hyacinth's torch, it now hosted an intriguing sheet of prismatic light; something festive, carnivalesque.

It was to this cloistered aurora that Rhiannon moved, one hesitant stair at a time, until eventually she found herself standing amidst the cluttered cellar.

The room was reminiscent of an army bunker, with its stifling confines and its drab cinderblock walls. It also looked as though it hadn't been properly cleaned since the analogue age.

Hyacinth was standing in wait between two towers of stacked plastic bins, an unnerving smile staining her face. She turned and wriggled herself down the tiny row, then crouched down, her shadow now stretching amongst those flickering trails of multicoloured light.

Rhiannon manoeuvred through the maze of detritus to find her hostess squatting before a tiny hatch door that was set into the wall just above floor-level.

"Come see," cooed Hyacinth. Politeness (and, if she was being honest, the curiosity of the unknown) moved Rhiannon toward the open doorway, but as soon as she was able to see the room and what it contained, this curiosity instantly twisted into fear.

The illumination guttered from a lanky strand of Christmas lights, which had been wound about the beams that served as the thick bones of the house itself. Insulation bulged between the wooden beams; pink as lung tissue, fluffy as candy floss. The floor of the crawlspace was but a single board that stretched from the doorway to the far end of the hatch like a ship's fatal plank.

And it was there, upon that long runner of un-sanded pine, that Rhiannon saw the body. It was as large as life and its presence among the festive bulbs was confusing, uncanny, terrible, and yet, irrefutably, shockingly, just...there.

The figure was slumped at the back of the room. Its head was swollen, and its eyes were shimmering, bulbous things. The mouth was gaping but expressionless. It was dressed in a dingy leotard that lent its body the lumpy, colourless appearance of bagged flour.

Hyacinth pulled herself through the crawlspace opening and proceeded to slither across the long plank, toward the crumpled form.

"My grandfather built him," she explained. "He helped my family flourish during the Great Depression. We've looked to him ever since." Hyacinth fussed with the figure while she talked, adjusting its posture like a fretting mother would with her child, pushing the cobwebs from its head using the heel of her longish hand. "I'd be lying if I told you that we've always benefited from his words, but really, it's a matter of interpretation. That's the art of it. Are you familiar with *Sortes Sanctorum?* It's divining one's fortune through a seemingly random flip of the Bible page. Great-grandfather was a believer and he taught my grandfather. But grandfather took it beyond the gospels. He felt that the great pattern was everywhere, in all things at all times. So he devised this."

Rhiannon watched as Hyacinth reached around to the back of the figure's plaster head. Its mouth began to glow with faint amber light, which revealed the too-wide grin of the dummy to be a fabric-covered speaker, the kind that might bring one feelings of nostalgia if one had memories of wartime gatherings around a cathedral radio to listen to melodramatic plays. Rhiannon had no such memories and therefore the mouth was horrible.

Static gushed from the dummy's speaker/mouth. Underneath this incessant whir Rhiannon could hear faint strains of music and distant voices all struggling to be heard, to emerge from the static like fish breaking the surface of deep water.

The great lidless eyes began to spin. They were twin plastic discs, each bearing a spiral pattern. They glowed as they spun around and around and again. Was Hyacinth attempting to hypnotize her?

No, this effigy was a radio receiver, its dial-eyes prowled the bandwidths in search of transmissions.

Hyacinth nestled close to the thing and whispered something into where its ear should be.

Rhiannon had already begun backing away from the colourful crawlspace, but when she heard the doll speak as if in response to Hyacinth's question, Rhiannon turned and ran.

On hands and knees she scaled the wooden steps, dragging herself toward the landing.

Her hands had managed to slap down on the linoleum of the kitchen floor when Rhiannon felt something grip her ankles. She screamed and tried to kick, but Hyacinth was unnaturally strong for so slight a person. She scrabbled upon Rhiannon's prostrate form, looped her wiry arms around Rhiannon's waist and heaved her clean off the stairs.

"Shhh," she cooed, "shhh...shhh. It's fate, darling. It's not about you or me."

Swiftly and inexorably, Rhiannon was being pulled back toward the hatch in the wall.

"All we ask is that you listen, just listen."

Rhiannon was thrust through the square aperture. The wooden lane was filthy and rough. The blinking lights made her nauseous. And the sight of the horrible mannequin reduced her backbone to putty.

Closer to it now, closer than she would have ever wanted to be to such a thing, Rhiannon could see that the effigy's body was nothing more than a hollow frame of chicken wire wrapped in a cheap white leotard. The pattern of the wire mesh was pushed firmly into the fabric, creating the illusion of reticulated flesh. And yet the gardener's gloves that capped the hands betrayed the thing's true nature: it was nothing but a pathetic scarecrow, without so much as a post to perch upon.

But scarecrows with their heads of straw and sackcloth cannot speak as this thing spoke. Its voice was as ugly as its shell. The spiral eyes spun around and again, pulling in random fragments from countless broadcasts. Hyacinth's advisor was a child of Babel.

Time seemed to halt for Rhiannon as she faced the thing and planned her escape. The angled beams forced her to crawl like a slug. She tried to push herself back toward the hatch.

She felt the draft and heard the slam of the hatch door as Hyacinth sealed her in. There was the recognizable clunk of a lock being fastened, followed by the roar of heavy things being dragged, both of which rendered the crawlspace door immovable.

She kicked at it, hammered at it until the heels of her hands began to swell. All the while the cheery lights continued to flash, and the endless babble of Hyacinth's advisor mounted.

Rhiannon's joyous moment of inspiration that came when she thought of using her cellphone to call 911 turned black and came crashing down around her when she realized that her purse had slipped off her shoulder during her struggle on the stairs.

Her screams shredded her throat but roused not so much as a sound from beyond the door.

Some time later, the Christmas lights went out and the only the illumination that remained was the mannequin's endlessly spinning eyes and the amber glow of its fabric mouth.

※

Three days and three nights passed before Hyacinth finally deemed to unlatch the crawlspace door. But by then Rhiannon had shed all conceptions of time and lost every ounce of will, strength, resistance. Like Lazarus, she slinked, broken but alive, out of the open hatch door, a living creature from a stifling crypt. Some Logos, some obscure alchemy of sound and isolation, had altered her world. It was powerful enough to transform Rhiannon's tomb to womb, potent enough to spore her back among the living, her head brimming with messages. She felt as though her skull was on the verge of cracking, erupting like a volcano, so gigantic was this fresh knowledge.

Hyacinth had been keeping vigil. Her tiny form was propped upon a scuffed wooden stool and she held a burning white taper in her hands. The melted wax ran down in rivulets, splattering upon the already waxy skin of Hyacinth's unsteady hands. Rhiannon looked at her face, so ghastly in the candlelight.

She looked past Rhiannon. The sight of the effigy lying broken and silent inside the crawlspace did not faze her. She returned her gaze to Rhiannon.

"*Yes?*" she whispered. "*Yes, please...speak.*"

Speaking just might relieve some of the unbearable pressure in her head. Rhiannon opened her mouth, but for what purpose? Was she going to scream? To beg for pity?

She heard a voice resounding in her skull, could feel words shaking over her palate, but the statements she was making bore no resemblance to the ones she was trying to make. Many of the words were from languages of which Rhiannon had no knowledge. Some of the sounds were not even words but were instead almost musical: the blurt of a trumpet, the pluck of a cello string.

Hyacinth's face became a mask of delight. She puffed out the candle and sat it smoking upon a stack of old books. She advanced to Rhiannon, wrapped a switch-thin arm around her back and guided her toward the basement steps.

The climb was almost impossible for Rhiannon, whose ankles buckled with each footfall. By the time they reached the kitchen she had lost all feeling in her legs.

She was frightened to discover that the main floor of the house was not appreciably brighter than the crawlspace, for the windows had been sheathed in tarpaper and every lamp she passed had its lightbulb purposely smashed.

With care, Hyacinth guided her form, which grew weaker with each tick of the clock, into the living room and sat her in the folding chair Rhiannon had spotted on the way in.

"This is only temporary," Hyacinth purred, her tone maternal and assuring. "We'll get you a chair befitting a woman of your stature as soon as we're able to understand your message. Can you hear what I've been saying to you? No, no, don't try to speak. Just blink your eyes once for yes and twice for no. That's it. Good. And can you understand what I've been saying to you? Very good. Do you know what it is that has happened to you? No. Well, that's to be expected, my dear. Don't let it alarm you. It will take time."

Hyacinth moved around to the front of the chair, hunched slightly to level her eyes with Rhiannon's.

"There are some people outside, some really lovely people. They've been waiting a long time to see you. May I send them in?"

Rhiannon's arms felt like concrete. Unable to lift them, she closed her eyes to press away the tears that were welling up and blurring her vision. Hyacinth took this to be an affirmative answer and squealed with delight before rushing to the front door.

The first pair to make the hesitant entry into the living room were the men Rhiannon had seen laughing on the street the night of her arrival, the men who'd loitered in the pooled light of the streetlamp, the men who'd scared her. They held hands as they approached her. They asked about the nature of their father's illness.

Rhiannon's cry for help translated into a staccato message, something in Spanish or perhaps Portuguese.

The men sighed and shed tears and blessed her for this message. Before they exited, they handed a small and crumpled envelope to Hyacinth, who was already greeting the next visitant.

Iain was the sixth or seventh to approach. The sight of him brought Rhiannon a relief that bordered on bliss. She tried in vain to rise. Crying out his name yielded only static. She felt trapped in a nightmare, the kind where she would try to scream but found she had no voice, and all the while the danger—calmly and with notable relish—would close in upon her, mangling her body with a weapon or forcing something thick and fibrous deep inside her mouth, her cleft.

But dear Iain did no such thing. His assault was something far more insidious.

He wrapped his arms around her momentarily, kissed her oily brow.

In her ear he whispered, "Will we be successful?"

Rhiannon's reply was instant, confusing, and delivered wholly without her consent.

Never had her mate appeared so pleased.

This would be the only memory of his face that Rhiannon would have to cling to over the next three years, the first of which was spent solely in that horrid folding chair, meeting with an endless procession of guests.

Hyacinth kept the tarpaper on her windows and succoured her new doll with her choicest teas and macrobiotic delicacies. She cleaned her bucket twice daily without complaint and washed her with a loofah sponge soaked in tepid rosewater.

Iain made good on his promise to Hyacinth. He procured for them a handsome and firm stone cottage in the city's historic district. Gardeners and contractors were hired to see that the house and its humble grounds were kept in good repair. The windows were two-way smoked glass, which assured privacy while not depriving the occupants a view of the elegant street.

Rhiannon was given a chair befitting her at last; a throne-like apparatus of sand-coloured plush and a white lacquered Hepplewhite frame. She was stationed in the bedroom at the top of the stairs (the master bedroom went to Hyacinth). A second chair, comfortable looking but not as regal, was placed before Rhiannon so that her visitants would feel more at ease during consultations.

A year or so later, Iain finally made his return. Though he still managed the books for this little soothsaying enterprise, this was the first time he'd made a pilgrimage to its source.

Rhiannon's recollection of him was faint, dulled by exhaustion and trauma and time. The young woman who clung to him was wholly unfamiliar to her. The twins who cowered behind Iain had grown immensely during her absence.

"Hello, Rhiannon," Iain said weakly. Then he turned to the young girl at his side. "Sit," he bade her. "Ask." He then instructed the twins to go outside and play.

The young woman was reluctant to obey, and once she found herself facing the glassy-eyed hag with her tea-stained teeth, her marionette-like body, her frumpy floral gown, her black-soled feet with their thick yellow toenails, her voice refused to come. Rhiannon knew the feeling well. Seeing the girl in this familiar helpless state, that of nightmare, that of her very existence since the night in the crawlspace, made Rhiannon pity the girl. She did her best to show empathy through her unfailingly vacant gaze.

"Can you tell us," the girl began pausing to clear her

throat, "will our baby be a healthy one?"

The power inside Rhiannon, over which she had no agency, shared its prophecy.

Iain smiled. His young lover began to cry. He helped her to her feet, and they escaped the room together, like some awkward three-legged hybrid joined at the hip.

Twenty-three weeks after their consultation in the stone cottage, the last of which were filled with punishing nausea, the word was made flesh.

Wriggling, its tiny limbs twitching as though being prodded with an electrical charge, the child's first mewling cry was distorted from the mucous that sealed its mouth like fine stretched fabric. Iain swaddled its body, still greasy with the fluids of the womb, and carefully lifted it from the bed. The cord was still connecting the baby to its host. Iain could feel the lump growing in his throat, could feel himself tearing up, yet he still managed a smile. For and from this child, great things had been predicted.

After the Final

Are you out there, Professor Nobody?

I'm hopeful that these words will somehow reach you, wherever you might be, whatever you might be.

In my starker moments I find myself questioning whether you were ever really here at all, whether those sermons that spilled from your dusty throat were not simply the vestiges of one of my lavish nightmares.

But if you did truly grace a classroom with your singular presence, if the trances you evoked were indeed real, then I cannot help but cling to the hope that you might return to your most dedicated pupil, one who you left behind on this shadow-encrusted planet.

Do your thoughts ever stray to me, Professor? Rarely, I would wager; rarely, if at all.

I have roamed many roads, exhausted so many different methods, all in the hope of finding you. Every one of my efforts has come to nothing. But how could it be otherwise? After all, how does one even begin questing after a man known only as Nobody, a man whose vocation is that of a secret shepherd to what he calls "the true macabrists"?

Macabrist. It was your phrase, yet it rang so true to me that I cannot help but regard it as a grand truth, every bit as immutable as love or fear or pain.

I shall never forget that first after-hours lecture when you defined a macabrist as "a person whose dreams are as a great charnel ground, one that is dimmed by personal eclipses and slaked by a private Styx." I remember how you stated that the macabrist is free of faith, strictly speaking, but that if they were to invent a religion it would be based not on the supernatural, but rather on the "grubby *sub*natural; the Underworld. Indeed, we trawl up our philosophies from our unconscious, and they emerge dripping with abjection."

I remain determined to gain full admittance to the great subnature, Professor, if only to prove to you that I am worthy of seeing the darkness, that I am truly *of* the darkness.

Do you see how assimilated your teachings have become with me? Your "little lectures on supernatural horror," as you somewhat dismissively called them, made me feel as though I had been granted admittance to a buried sphere from which I'd been wrongly banished before being condemned to being born into this world.

I'd always thought I was the only one who longed for some grue-dimmed subnature, a grimy cosmic cellar. But in you I had, at long last, found one who understood. You voiced things which had always felt like shameful intuitions to me, impulses that I had to keep pent at the back of my mind, perennially praying that they would not leak out to condemn me among the Normals. But you uttered your bent observations plainly, with a boldness that could only have stemmed from experiential knowledge. You exuded a confidence I could never possess.

You taught us that the Horror toward existence is not only real but is in fact more real than we are, that it is the boundless gory foam upon which all things, known and unknown, merely bob like so much flotsam.

I was the best pupil you could ever hope for, Professor. If only you would return to experience the fruits of your teachings. I can still see you creeping toward the classroom door on that last night; can still hear your parting words echoing through the halls of my brain: "Good luck on the final."

I waited for that final examination, waited an unmentionable span of time. After more anguished nights than I care to recall, I came to suspect that the final was not to be held in the cozy confines of your classroom, but in the world at large.

And then it all became so obvious. For what were your lectures if not impressions of life beyond the theoretical, echoes of the palpable nightmare that succors us all?

So I began to prepare for the final.

My preparations were unique and rigorous. I used the Earth as my reference material. I tested myself in a variety of ways.

I now have so much to show you, Professor.

This place, for example: the dank storage locker where I, Maximilian and the others have taken temporary refuge. Instinct instructed me that this city was a good place to stop and try once more to make contact.

※

You'll likely recognize this regulation notebook I'm writing in. It is one of the dozens that I rescued from the ashes of your old schoolhouse. I have stained their leaves with the details of my lavish nightmares, and of the awful waking deeds I've committed. (A curious development: I can no longer discern which entries are recollections of my dreams, which the record of my worldly actions.)

Do you know that I carry with me a charred fragment of the lectern behind which you once preached, Professor? This blackened splinter is reticulated and warped, and perhaps this is apt. Each night I swaddle it inside my jacket, which doubles as my pillow. I do not sleep well upon it.

Sometimes my fitful slumber is banished by the sound of a school bell. Although I am aware that it is only a passing siren or a car horn or a distant scream, I still instinctively bolt up, thrilled by the possibility that your class is once again in session, that you have returned with fresh teachings from the perimeter.

Perhaps—may I be forgiven for any hubris—I can teach *you* some fresh lessons as well. For example, how you would have relished the trip Maximilian, his entourage, and I made to a neglected estuary in that degenerate little town north of the border. There, under a shawl of polluted cumuli, I hearkened to your tales of the great plague ships that had once damned these shores, how that fleet had emerged from a noxious mist; gliding gracefully into port, their rudders manipulated by a fell spirit far beyond mankind's grasp. You'd said their hulls had been brittle wormwood, their sails the pelts of gods long crucified and flayed, these galleons that crept into port and let their cargo of vermin come vomiting out. Rat backs seething with infected tics, their innards black with disease, these creatures that scuttled into every nook of the city, plopping toxic droppings into the grains, tenderly nibbling on slumbering flesh.

I did what I could to recreate and reify this myth, Professor, using a special white powder I'd concocted. I watched the Normals wither inside their pathetic little houses, crumpling like puppets with clipped strings. I of course was unaffected, having donned my proper vestments.

If only you'd been there with me to bask in these delights.

※

Maximilian has set up his Observatory in another locker a few doors down from mine. Though he was never part of your class, I always believed he was sympathetic to our cause. The wedding of his technical prowess with my instincts resulted in what might be the best tool a cruddy human has to follow your spectral trail, Professor: the Observatory.

In the early days, just after your departure, Maximilian seemed to be suitably intrigued by my vigorous hunt for you. My passionate descriptions of your lectures, along with my more persuasive tactics, eventually caused Maximilian to agree to help me find you. He was, I believe, sincerely hoping to meet you, to learn what you had to teach. But as the months crawled past without any sign of your return, Maximilian began to lose patience. Our sessions became briefer and more hopeless in tone. I knew it was only a matter of time before I lost Maximilian.

When I broke the news to him that we would have to travel further, he was most resistant. It required me to use an even greater incentive, but eventually he acquiesced.

Earlier today, however, he informed me that he's had his fill. He begged me to give up the vigil. This (needless to say) will never happen. But I managed to deceive Maximilian into believing that tonight would be our very last attempt to call you back from the rim of the darkness. Based on this lie of finality, Maximilian reluctantly complied.

As the grey daylight bled out in gloaming, I donned my vestments and set out to meet with Maximilian at his Observatory.

I feel I should pause here in order to describe my vestments to you, as I'm sure you would approve of their design, which is every bit as pragmatic as it is aesthetic. With my vestments I become the plague doctor of old; guising my face beneath a gasmask with a long beak of black leather. My ratty wide-brim hat adds a ceremonial touch, and my ragged duster coat is suggestive of a shroud. With a walking stick of lashed femurs in hand, I love to stroll the poisoned wastelands.

Earlier this evening, as I made my way to Maximilian's

locker, the clamped doors became an indistinct swath of corrosion and rust in my peripheral vision. Boulders of grey clouds had smothered the last of the daylight and made the sky appear heavy and low. There was a distant purl of thunder. (The rain never comes.)

Maximilian was pacing about the Observatory's open doorway when I arrived. The smoke of one of his trademark black cigars swirled about his head like a personal fog. He was wearing his October Coat; a threadbare dressing gown of silk emblazoned with a tapestry of autumn-coloured leaves. It billowed about him in a dervish sweep. I gave him this coat some months ago, when we began our quest. I made Maximilian promise me to only wear his vestment on auspicious occasions; namely the sessions when we try to Observe you, Professor.

I waved to him but he did not reciprocate. His first words to me were, "Tonight is the last, J.P." His tone was one of resignation, even melancholia. "The others and I had a meeting this afternoon and we just can't do it anymore. If tonight's probing fails, if we don't get a response, we'd like your permission to move on."

"Move on to *where*, exactly?" I asked him, hoping he would see that one city is just as doomed as the next. I then enforced the point that my work was not yet done. Maximilian, visibly deflated, flicked his still-fuming cigar onto the littered asphalt. He looked soundlessly skyward. Perhaps for him the clouded constellations offered instruction; I know little of the mechanics of his Observations.

"Let's go," he said coldly before striding back into the Observatory.

The others were seated around the musty cube of a room. The woman quietly sobbed while mindlessly spinning the gold band on her finger.

I moved to one of the grubby plastic lawn chairs that were splayed crescent-wise before the hanging bed sheet that doubled as a curtain.

Maximilian disappeared behind this crude drapery. His and the other shadows beyond it began to move.

I heard muttering, then the sound of someone screaming.

The sheet was peeled back, revealing a man; gaunt and naked and quaking. He was seated in a chair made of metal. There were wires taped onto his brow. His limbs were tethered with leather belts.

Maximilian gave no word of explanation, but our familiarity with the ritual meant none was required.

He roughly pried the man's jaws apart in order to administer the tangerine-coloured liquid he regularly prepares in small batches. In no time the lashed man's screaming ebbed, allowing Maximilian time to check the wires. In a few moments the man's eyes became like saucers as the lysergic medication took hold.

Maximilian switched on the antiquated television set that he'd wired up to the man's head.

The images on the screen were hazy with snow, but were unquestionably those of some subnatural state, a place replete with monsters; squirming things, things akin to plucked birds or stillborn infants, things that were withered or bloated or mere hissing fog. They swam upon the screen, all these abominations, churning upon & within the fabulous unshaped Dark.

The lines began to form; a topography of sorts. Waves of ugly dull light, like a phosphorescent sludge, passed across the monitor.

I rose from my chair in order to better study the screen, to better scry the horrors.

We were searching for you, Professor, peering like seafaring folk looking into a fog, squinting for the signal fires on the shore. After all, where else might you have gone but beneath the surface?

But you were not there. We found no sign of you inside that foamy Hell.

"This specimen should be freed," Maximilian pleaded. He slapped the television's power switch. Of his own accord, Maximilian ordered the woman to "remove him." Too shocked by this display of insolence, I soundlessly watched as the spindly specimen in the chair was carted off, to where I neither know nor care. Maximilian, head down, stepped out of the room and into the chilly lot beyond it.

I sat in the Observatory trying to ignore the overwhelming sense of nihilistic hopelessness that was tiding up within me. I looked about the Observatory and saw only blackness; truly the only thing ever witnessed here by Maximilian or me.

I rose and shuffled outside.

Maximilian was standing stoically. Bluish smoke streamed from his freshly-lit cigar. His October Coat was wadded on the ground, as though it had been flung there in a rage.

"No more," he said beseechingly. "Please, J.P., no more."

"We can't just resign from it," I said. "It's a part of us."

"It's a part of *you*," he corrected me. "But after all these failures, can you not see that I was right all those months ago?" He sighed, placed his hand on my shoulder. It was the first time he'd touched me in ages. "Things have gotten way out of hand, haven't they? You'll admit that, won't you? This isn't working and you know it, but you probably don't know how to make it stop. But I'm telling you, J.P., it's very easy: just let us go. I want to take my family and leave here, this place. We won't try to stop you, J.P. We won't even tell the authorities. I give you my word on that. We don't want any trouble. We just want your permission to leave."

"And go where exactly?" I returned. "The plague's widespread. It affected more than just Crampton." (I know it was a lie, Professor, but at the time I was desperate to maintain your vigil.)

"We're willing to risk it, J.P. Let us go."

I started to laugh. It was a reaction that shocked me just as much as it did Maximilian, who glared at me with disdain.

"You really don't get Nobody's message at all, do you?" he spat.

"Why don't you enlighten me?" I said, angered by the insolent suggestion that he could comprehend your little lectures on horror better than I do.

Maximilian ground the cigar under the toe of his shoe. "It's horribly simple. Think for a moment and you'll get it. The message is; there is nothing to do, there is nowhere to go, there is nothing to be, and most importantly, there is nobody to find. *There is no Professor Nobody! There never has been! It's you, J.P. It's you.*"

"...preposterous..." I muttered. "...absurd ..."

Maximilian held up his hands. "Think back. I was your therapist, remember? Your parents sent you to me because you were suffering delusions. There was no Professor Nobody, no plague. You *killed* them with homemade anthrax. I was there. I saw it. Then you took us; my wife, my son..."

"We're not your 'companions,' J.P., we're hostages, prisoners. And we want you to let us go. It's over, J.P. I've been trying to help you see that for weeks now, trying to get you to turn yourself in. But I'm giving up on that. You can keep searching for Professor Nobody if you want to. I won't stop you. But I'm asking you to let us go. Maybe you'll do better trying to find him on your own..."

※

I don't remember restoring my companions or leaving the Observatory. The next thing I recall is slumping down upon the curb and staring down at the trash heaped there; old wadded newspaper that scuttled from the slightest breeze, and mashed beer cans. Someone had twisted some plastic drinking straws into a rudimentary effigy of a human figure. I stared at its knotted limbs for a little while, wondering if this was the final you had mentioned.

Was this your litmus test to distinguish the true macabrists from the dabblers?

Even if I was wrong in my theory, it was still the only logical next step in the process of the search for you, Professor.

I gathered my ritual implements and returned to the Observatory in the wee hours. Just as I had done with the schoolhouse after you'd abandoned it, or with the white powder I unleashed around the town: I blasphemed in order to send you a Calling.

Maximilian and the others were chained to the wall, slumbering on the Observatory floor, looking like well-fed slugs in their sleeping bags. The chains that bound them looked like spun silver under my lantern light.

As the signal pyre blazed, I stood and watched it through the jaundiced lenses of my plague doctor mask. I saw one of the figures inside trying ineptly to escape, to break their bonds while the flames scurried up their limbs in waves. They resembled fire-tarantulas, scuttling up and down the walls, leaving vastation in their wake.

I had hoped this arachnid light would have guided you, like a plague-ship being navigated safely to shore.

A little while ago, I indulged in a tour of the leavings, and inside I found a marvellous treat: one of the skulls had its jaws welded into a perpetual shriek, and the gold in its teeth shone like beetles' backs.

But as exquisite as this horror was, I am still left wanting.

✖

How like the thunderheads you are, Professor. You prowl the sky, near enough for me to sense you but far enough away for me to doubt your presence. And like those prowling clouds that never unleash their rains, you never fulfill your promise.

Who shall swallow these horrors with me? Who out there

can comprehend the poetry of this half-toppled abattoir land?

Who else might draw equal delight from this endless nightmare of being?

And the storm in my head rumbles its retort:

Who understands this horror?

Nobody.

Nobody...

The Sullied Pane

"If you're really worried about your parents suspecting us, you might want to wipe that ridiculous grin off your face before we go down to dinner," Maxine said, giving him a coquettish wink. She looped the straps of her bra back onto her shoulders, then turned her back to Xavier in a wordless request for his fingers to re-clasp what they'd so nimbly unfastened a few moments earlier.

Gently, he pressed his face into the soft nest of her hair, which smelled of sea air and spices. "Give me a moment to come down," Xavier joked in whisper. "I'll have my poker face on before the salad's served, trust me."

"Oh? Is this the sort of thing you've done often?"

While still technically a newlywed, Xavier knew his bride well enough to spy that telltale hitch of the corner of her perfect mouth; the seed of a smile that she was struggling to hide from him. It was a reassuring sign that her question was not an earnest one.

"Hardly," he replied. "I just know my family. The law of survival is simple: show no emotion, expect none in return. Do that and we're fine."

Maxine's brow furrowed in consternation. "We're in the home of the grand Whitlocks; it's a *palace*. Stop making it sound like we're entering a war room."

"There may be war if we don't get this bed remade exactly as Mother had it when we arrived!"

Together they moved about the mattress, which was still warm and tousled from the frantic, hushed coupling they'd snuck in just after their arrival at the grand house.

Once the bed had been reasonably restored, Maxine dabbed the sheen of sweat from her brow. "How does your mother keep this place so pristine without a housekeeper? Honestly!" she huffed.

"My brothers and I have been asking that question all our lives. My father has hired a dozen cleaners over the years to try and ease the burden, but Mother always lets them go." Xavier shrugged. "Maybe it's her way of contributing, who knows?"

"What do you mean?"

"My family's money all came from my father's side. He took over the business interests from my grandfather before my parents were even married, and he's handled everything ever since. Once my brothers and I were all grown, I think my mother got lost...maybe even a bit resentful."

"Resentful of what, the conniving harlots of the outside who bewitched and stole her boys from her?"

Xavier lifted his hands. "Easy," he said. "This isn't some Freudian family drama. There's no Oedipal anything here. My mother didn't get jealous or angry after we moved out. She just kind of...drifted. She kept house, walked the grounds, sort of disappeared inside herself for a long time."

"And that's why her invitation to spend New Years' here surprised you so much?"

"Yes," he said, coiling his arms around her. "I wasn't shut out because you and I eloped. All my brothers and I had nothing but radio silence from the home front."

"Until now?"

"Until now."

※

Their walk to the dining room was, to Maxine's mind, more akin to a museum tour than the surveying of a homestead. Every inch of the abundant walnut wood gleamed as though it was encased in glass. The carpet that lined the grand staircase bore the swirl patterns of vigorous vacuuming. The walls all looked to be freshly painted, and the air was fragrant with lemon oil. But these details quickly paled in Maxine's awareness, which was growing evermore focused on her internal anxieties. She could feel the familiar invisible vise clamping over her lungs, and was relieved when Xavier, perhaps able to sense her inner workings, slipped his hand into hers and lovingly whispered an instruction for her to breathe. He stopped her at the bottom of the stairs and kissed her lips before escorting her into the dining hall.

The room was like a film set, so grand was its elegance, so meticulous its maintenance and design. At first Maxine was so taken with the scope of the French windows that composed three walls of the hall, that she scarcely registered the carved table that seemed to stretch from one horizon to the other, or the highbacked plush dining chairs, or the fire that roared inside a maw-like hearth of green marble. Opera music strained from speakers that must have been hidden amidst the bookcases. The panelled wall bore family portraits in oil. There was a large standing globe and an antique bronze telescope by the spacious windows.

Maxine's arm found its way around her husband's waist. She pressed her hip firmly against his; a silent plea for him to not stray from her, not here, not tonight.

The party appeared, much to Maxine's horror, to have divided itself according to fusty traditional roles. In one corner, Xavier's two elder brothers nursed scotches with their father, who looked every inch the elder statesman with his slender face and tamed white hair and eyes like those of a Siberian Husky. Across the room, meanwhile, the wives were helping Mother set out the last of the serving dishes.

Maxine had every intention of following Xavier and inserting herself in the men's corner, but Xavier's mother just at that instant announced that dinner was served.

Noting that the place-cards stationed the spouses next to one another brought Maxine a small measure of relief. Xavier pulled out her chair, as did his brothers for their respective wives. Mrs. Whitlock, however, had to seat herself. Maxine found it strange that the father's outdated views on gender she'd suspected upon entering the room apparently stopped short of chivalry. Both parents assumed the throne-like seats at either end of the table.

Maxine's movements as she passed the serving china around were as stiff and unnatural as her smile, but as the evening wore on, she found, to her immense relief, that Xavier's family was cheerier and looser than she'd assumed. His father asked interestedly about her job in human resources, about her background in drama. Several times the entire group erupted with laughter. Later, the discussion grew sombre and empathetic as the topic shifted to the violent unrest that was intensifying south of the border.

"Well," Xavier's father said, "let us hope the new year we're ringing in tomorrow night brings better things to all."

The party raised their wine glasses to this wish, and then Xavier's mother began to automatically clear the dishes from the table and onto the wooden serving cart.

"Let me help," implored Maxine. There came polite refusals, then polite insistences. Finally, Xavier's mother half-suggested, half-commanded that Xavier take Maxine for a walk of the grounds.

✖

Without, the night was cold and clear, which Maxine found refreshing after the house's warmth and the bounty of food that had been served. Their journey had involved a turbulent flight, an overly complicated car rental at the airport, followed by a white-knuckle drive across the unploughed country roads that wound toward their terminus at the family estate. These factors, along with their unexpected early evening tryst, meant that Maxine hadn't yet had an opportunity to fully drink in her surroundings.

The snowfall, which had caused great stress to her and Xavier earlier in the day, was now a source of magic; it padded the grounds like a pristine quilt, it muted what few night sounds there were out here, it even cast off the occasional glitter when the moon shone upon it at just the right angle.

As she walked arm-in-arm with her husband, Maxine came to appreciate that the care and attention that Xavier's mother lavished upon the inside of the house extended to the property as well. The perennial hedges were trimmed to symmetrical perfection. The seasonal plants were tidily mummified in burlap, guarding them for the spring to come. The grid of stone walkways that ran through the gardens had already been salted and thus stood out like a maze of black marble laid within the snow.

This obvious meticulousness caused Maxine to doubt herself once her eyes fell upon the ugly little structure that slumped at the far end of the grounds. It was the size and design of a large wooden shed. Its roof was noticeably stooped, and its lone uncovered window was so clouded with accumulated grime it was as if pollen had been baked into the pane. The abode sat nestled among ugly brambles. Its wooden frame was colourless. It was almost as if it was a great toadstool that had sprouted up from the earth; the kind of magic hovel Maxine had read about in fairy tales when she was a child.

"Where are you going?"

Xavier's voice came from behind, rather than beside her. This alerted Maxine to the fact that she had somehow unconsciously slipped free of her man's arm and had begun to stray on her own down the sloping lawn toward the strange little dwelling.

"I wanted to get a better look," she explained awkwardly, covertly straining her eyes to spy whatever she could through the murky glass. (She saw nothing.) "I'm sorry."

He stepped off the walkway and added a second set of footprints alongside hers.

"No need to apologize," he said.

"What is it, a storage shed?"

"I think it was a gatehouse once upon a time. Not sure why my parents haven't torn it down, to be honest with you."

A wind pushed over the grounds, rattling the settled snow from the tree boughs and the shrubberies. It also rattled Maxine's bones.

"Come on," Xavier said, wrapping his arm across her shoulders. "Let's get you in front of the fireplace and get a warm brandy in your hand."

The offer was music to Maxine's ears, but her snifter was still half-full when she felt the weight of the day's travels pressing down upon her limbs and eyelids. She tried to politely hide her persistent yawns with her hand, but Xavier noticed right away and announced that they were turning in for the night.

Upstairs, the spacious bed felt gloriously supple beneath her tired limbs. She fell asleep before Xavier had switched off his bedside reading lamp.

Perhaps it was the unfamiliarity of her surroundings, but sleep refused to hold her for anything more than a few short bursts. She reposed, her limbs aching and eyes burning. She listened to the furnace pressing warm air through the floor vents, watched the black kaleidoscope of tree limb shadows as they splayed across the high white ceiling.

Suddenly there was sunlight.

Maxine was confused by the impossibility of the golden light that had begun to glimmer upon the ceiling and the far wall. Dawn was still many hours away; a fact that flirted with

Maxine's curious nature. She rose from the bed and moved to the window, shivering at the arctic draft that oozed through the window's edges.

The vantage from the mansion's third storey only deepened Maxine's already great appreciation of the property, both its scope and its pristineness. Up here, she was able to see the source of the golden light quite plainly: it was pouring from the misshapen shack in the greenery. Seeing now the sheer symmetry of the gardens emphasized how ugly and incongruous the little structure was. It did not belong here.

'Maybe it's you who doesn't belong,' Maxine said to herself, then immediately hushed her doubting mind.

The golden light suddenly became a backdrop for flickering movements. Black shapes began to flitter in the micro-cabin's tiny window; shapes that became elongated into a mass of lean, ropy things that pulsed and flexed like characters in a shadow-play, with the pearly snow acting as a screen. Maxine stared hard at the guttering light from the window, wanting deeply, though inexplicably, to see, to know what was occurring beyond it.

A few moments later she received her answer, or a portion of at it least.

The amber light shrank and was extinguished, and shortly thereafter a figure emerged from the micro-cabin. It turned and secured the stout wooden door, then made haste along one of the stone paths that led from the gardens to the great house.

Identification was impossible at first, given Maxine's distance, as well as the flowing, shapeless garment that the figure wore. But once the figure reached the pooled light from the house's security lamps Maxine could see beyond any doubt that it was Mrs. Whitlock. The colourless overcoat she wore flapped like a cloak in the frigid night wind.

✖

"Good morning, my dear," Mrs. Whitlock said as Maxine entered the sitting room. The warmth in her voice was a quality Maxine had not detected on the afternoon of her and Xavier's arrival.

"Good morning," she returned with reticence.

"Slept well, I hope."

"Very," Maxine lied. "How did you sleep?"

"A few hours, but enough. At my age one doesn't need much sleep."

Maxine's next attempt to further probe Mrs. Whitlock for answers slipped away when the entire entourage began spilling into the room in procession. Morning greetings were exchanged, and, by the hand of the matriarch, breakfast was served by the fire.

Only after the meal was done and the other guests were sitting lazily did Maxine manage to attain a fresh clue to the mystery that, for reasons she could not comprehend, was becoming an obsession with her. Her discovery came when she pushed through the swinging door of the kitchen to ask Mrs. Whitlock if she could help in any way.

At that instant, Mrs. Whitlock was exiting the door that led from the large kitchen to the back gardens. She hadn't noticed Maxine entering the kitchen, but Maxine had noticed Mrs. Whitlock reaching behind the large china hutch, where she retrieved a key.

Exhilarated by the extent of what she might learn this morning, Maxine scuttled across the kitchen's marble floor and crouched at the base of one of the sparkling windows.

Mrs. Whitlock marched briskly along the stone walkway. When she crossed onto the snow, she revealed that she was carting the kitchen's dustbin with her, lugging the cumbersome thing by its rim. Maxine watched this elegant woman plunk the dustbin down onto the snowbank. The matriarch began to struggle with the cabin's door. Perhaps the old lock had shrunken from the cold and thus was refusing Mrs.

Whitlock's secret key, but eventually it gave. The old woman took up the dustbin and disappeared inside the shack.

Maxine sped to the sitting room, shoehorned her slight frame onto the sofa next to Xavier, and then shoehorned her way into the conversation. When Mrs. Whitlock re-entered the room some time later, she did not appear to suspect that anything was amiss. But the old woman's face was flushed. Now and again she reached one of her tapered hands to adjust the bun in her hair, which was visibly looser than it had been at breakfast. Mr. Whitlock took no notice of his wife's rather haggard state, nor did any of his sons, or their spouses. This fact pained Maxine. It saddened her to think of the endless, exhausting chores Mrs. Whitlock must have faced daily in order to keep the great house in such gleaming condition.

Greater than her empathy, however, was Maxine's thirst to uncover why the old woman went to such lengths to keep the tiny cabin a secret.

Her opportunity to discover this secret did not come until much later in the day. The guests and Mr. Whitlock had frittered away the afternoon on board games ('*Bored games*,' Maxine had joked to herself) while Mrs. Whitlock laboured over a pork loin dinner in the kitchen. It was a little after four when she came bursting into the sitting room. She was nearly frantic over the fact that she had forgotten to buy both the heavy cream and the chicken stock required to make the loin's herb sauce.

"Well, we'd run out and get them for you," Mr. Whitlock began, "but I'm afraid we've all had a few." He held up his whiskey glass as evidence.

"Never you mind, I'll go," replied Mrs. Whitlock. "But I'd better leave now. The stores are all closing early for New Year's."

"I'll keep an eye on the loin if you like, Mrs. Whitlock," volunteered Maxine. She stood and stepped away from the gaming table.

Mrs. Whitlock puckered her face. Was this tiny gesture (which Maxine had given for wholly selfish reasons) truly enough to drive the woman to tears? She reached out and clutched Maxine's left wrist and thanked her profusely.

Maxine entered the kitchen and pretended to hear Mrs. Whitlock's whirl of instructions, when Maxine was simply waiting for her opportunity.

It came the instant she saw Mrs. Whitlock's sleek car verging off the winding driveway and onto the road toward town. Maxine abandoned her charade of stirring and fussing in favor of searching behind the china hutch. She caught sight of the dustbin, which now stood empty by the corn whisk broom in the corner.

Turning her attention back to the task at hand, Maxine found the key dangling from a small brass hook that had been screwed into the back of the hutch. She snatched it, then paused to listen to the boisterous laughter from the players in the sitting room. Assured that they were too engrossed in their game to check on her, Maxine slipped out the back door.

The sunbeams must have been melting the snow for some time, for the gardens had lost their smooth carpet of white. They were now a shoddy, patchwork place. Lumpy mounds of mud and matted grass jutted up in between pockets of dirty slush. The stone walkways hosted puddles where twigs and old leaves floated, resembling pools of loose-leaf tea.

Before she crossed the muddy slope to reach the cabin, Maxine checked over both shoulders. She was petrified of discovery.

The planks of the narrow porch were twisted and caused Maxine's ankles to wobble as she strained to find her footing. The little square window was at her shoulder now, inviting her to partake of its view at last. She cupped her hands on either side of her face and squinted to gain a preview of the space she planned to invade.

Through the foggy glass Maxine was able to discern a

single stout room. A small pallet mattress lay on the floor, framed by brittle leaves. A canvas tarp had been draped over whatever else was stored inside. Maxine could just make out a tall sheeted form, like a ghost in a children's storybook. The sight of it unnerved her, and she wondered if this was why the image of the shrouded figure endured throughout the ages. Perhaps there is some profound quality in the shape seen-and-yet-unseen, a quality that touches us at our core.

The milder day allowed the key to fit into the lock much easier for Maxine than it had for Mrs. Whitlock that morning. Maxine knew that her time was limited. For all she knew, Xavier was calling for her from the games table, or perhaps he was standing in the empty kitchen at that very instant, worried or furious over her absence. But she would not allow her fears to dissuade her. Instead Maxine stepped into the cramped cabin and shut its door.

The first thing Maxine experienced inside the cabin was heat. It was the kind of arid, leeching warmth given off by cheap electric heaters. She could feel the static electricity building on her clothing, feel the sweat developing under her arms and at the back of her neck. Being in here put Maxine in mind of a hothouse, but instead of offering her the fragrance of orchids, this space assaulted her olfactory sense with an appalling stench.

The air within was not simply stale, it was thick with the stink of accumulated filth. Dust had not merely gathered here, it seemed to have been cultivated. Great grey mounds of it stood in the corners and along the baseboards. Spiders had been left to weave their silk freely; their creations hung in sweeping cascades from the low ceiling like fishnets. Particles of dust rode in on Maxine's breath. She felt them lining her nostrils. She sneezed loudly several times.

Was this Mrs. Whitlock's grand secret, the fact that she used this cabin as a receptacle? Maxine felt disappointed, but also faintly empowered. It was strangely reassuring to realize that all the matriarch's obsessive cleaning meant that she simply shooed every speck of her family's filth from the great house to here. This shack was the proverbial rug under which Mrs. Whitlock swept everything she did not want others to see. But if dirt was the worst thing the old woman was hiding, Maxine felt ashamed for suspecting something worse. What was dirt anyway but tiny specks of the past? The hair and skin and other substances of the living, ones that time flenses from us with metaphysical patience, pecking away at us until we ultimately become…nothing.

The morbidity of this line of thought weighed heavily on Maxine until she heard someone sigh inside the cabin. At that instant, her melancholia slipped into icy fear.

It was a low, protracted sound; less an expression of despair, more a moan of great release.

'I am alone in here. I am.'

The tall shrouded object now haunted Maxine's peripheral vision. She felt herself shudder. She had to will her head to turn and face the thing head-on.

It was a lumpy, shapeless mass whose height equalled her own. She looked to the filthy floor and discovered a pair of wooden claw-foot carvings poking out from beneath the tarp's hem.

Entranced, titillated, she reached out and peeled back the tarp, revealing a pair of slender wooden posts. Lifting the covering further still, Maxine found herself facing a blurry reflection of herself.

What was hidden beneath the tarp was a floor-length standing mirror. The glass was tapered too sharply at one end and was too swollen at its base to be a true oval. Its shape was nearer to a teardrop. The frame and legs were of cherrywood and had been carved in a highly baroque style, with undulating C-scrolls and voluted forms. The frame seemed to seethe with energy, to pulse and throb. This illusion was aided by the wavy looking-glass, which appeared like a heaving sea that was frozen mid-wave.

But the illusion quickly became palpable. Maxine could see movement. Something was shifting in the room behind her. In the mirror she saw a great shape rising from the dust. It distended and stretched. Its bulk quickly darkened the sullied pane of the cabin's only window. Again, there came a deep moan of release.

Enflamed with panic, Maxine flung the tarp back across the standing mirror and flung the cabin door open. She'd accidently left the key in the lock; a mistake for which she was now grateful, for it meant less time fumbling to fill the slit. Snapping the lock, she held the key in her fist and ran wildly for the great house.

Once back inside the kitchen, Maxine's terror was slightly abated when she found the dinner just as she'd left it and heard the gamers laughing in the sitting room. She returned the key to its hook and joined her husband. A few moments later she spotted Mrs. Whitlock's car creeping up the driveway.

※

The New Year's Eve dinner Mrs. Whitlock had prepared was sumptuous, but Maxine's troubled mind forbade her from enjoying it. She had to choke down her serving just to save face. When Xavier muttered to her, asking what was troubling her, Maxine drew upon her dramatic training. She mimicked the authentic revelry of her fellow diners, even joined them in a raucous countdown to midnight. Mr. Whitlock uncorked the magnum of champagne and poured the foaming liquid into the waiting flutes.

The festivities extended into the wee hours of the morning. Everyone, including Mrs. Whitlock, consumed a shocking quantity of spirits. By three a.m. some of the couples had slipped off to their rooms. Mr. Whitlock was dozing in his overstuffed chair. Others danced mellowly to the strains of waltz music.

Maxine was unfazed by these sights. Her attentions were focused on two tasks; the first was struggling to fight off the effects of too much drink (she wanted very much to keep her wits about her), and the second was to find out where Mrs. Whitlock had disappeared to.

It had been well over an hour since she had eased her husband into his favourite chair and collected the champagne flutes. She'd escaped into the kitchen but had yet to return. Maxine almost managed to trick herself into believing the foolish theory that the old woman must have retired for the night. She recalled the shape in the cabin, the dirt, the heat, the misshapen mirror...

"Why don't we turn in," Xavier whispered to her, pulling her attention from the kitchen door that she'd been waiting to see swing open for the entirety of their waltz. "Let's go have our own party upstairs."

Maxine looked at her husband, nodded, kissed his mouth. "I'll be right up," she growled.

Xavier gave her his usual telltale grin. He began loosening his tie before he'd even exited the sitting room. He bade none of his family goodnight.

When she was reasonably confident that everyone remaining was either too tired, too distracted or too drunk to notice her, she pushed against the swinging door and moved through the darkened kitchen.

Again, there was light guttering from the little cabin in the hedge; again, there was a manic fluttering of shadows, like a murder of crows in flight.

Maxine exited the great house and snuck up on the cabin.

Peering in through the dirty window exposed her to a sight so startling, so raw, that Maxine's brain could only process it in fragments. The flame of the lone candle jittered from the motions occurring in the room it illuminated. Mrs. Whitlock stood bent at the hips, naked as she'd been at birth, gripping the sides of the floor length mirror, which had also lost its covering. The old woman appeared to be watching herself in the glass. Her silver mane now hung loose and flowing. Sweat glistened on the soft padding of her back. Her pendulous breasts swung in rhythm with her rutting.

As to the other, impossible aspects of the scene—the numberless bodies of shadow that positioned and repositioned themselves around Mrs. Whitlock to hungrily knead and caress her body, the tongues of cobweb that licked her or pressed against her own jutting pink tongue, the dissolving faces of grit that leered at the action like a gaggle of phantom voyeurs—all of these details Maxine would later tell herself were simply born of her own imagination. Her brain, so shocked by the matriarch's act of indulgence (or was it one of release?), created a tableau of Id-soaked images to punish her...and perhaps to protect from the even harsher truth about this scene.

Sheepishly, Maxine backed away from the cabin, plugging her ears against the curses and the cries that filled the otherwise silent night in the virgin new year.

✖

New Year's Day slipped past like a dream. It was plain to Maxine that her mother-in-law was either unaware of her spying or was unfazed by it, for the old woman was every bit as congenial, conscientious and clean as she'd been all weekend. As she had no doubt been all her adult life.

Maxine was unspeakably grateful that Xavier had booked them an afternoon flight back home. Their departure in the great marble foyer was filled with hugs and wishes for safe travels. Maxine hugged Mrs. Whitlock especially close. She thanked her for such a wonderful time.

"I hope this year brings you every happiness," Maxine told her. Her sincerity was absolute. She looked her mother-in-law directly in the eye when she spoke these words, and then she hugged her again.

Their car hadn't yet reached the four-lane highway when Maxine frantically urged Xavier to pull over.

"Do you feel sick?" he said.

"Just pull the car over, please."

Xavier carefully edged the vehicle onto the side of the road, fearful that he might sink them in a ditch. He shifted the gear into Park.

He was half-confused, half-elated when he saw Maxine wriggling her underwear down her legs and over her shoes. She undid his seatbelt, his trousers. She mounted him.

Their coupling was surreal, exotic, intoxicating. For Xavier, terror of discovery mingled with the ecstasy of taboo. He looked at his wife, radiant in the bright winter afternoon. He caught glimpses of the vast open fields and the nearby houses, the birds that perched in the leafless trees.

"Promise me something," Maxine said once the deed was done.

"After that? Anything!" Xavier breathlessly replied.

"Promise me you'll never keep anything from me. Anything. Promise me you'll always tell me everything, no matter what it is."

Xavier was visibly confused but he nonetheless nodded his head. "Okay," he said. "But only if you promise to do the same."

"I will."

※

In March of that year, a hurricane that had begun stirring in the Caribbean made its way up the Eastern Seaboard and reached Ontario. The storm felled many structures, including the tiny cabin on the Whitlock grounds. The great house escaped unscathed.

Shortly thereafter, Mrs. Whitlock began to lose weight at a rate that alarmed her husband. Eventually, she was hospitalized, but by this time the cancer in her uterus had metastasized. She succumbed on the 21st of June.

As per her Last Will & Testament, Mrs. Whitlock was cremated, and her ashes were divided into separate urns and sent to each of her sons. For the better part of a year Xavier kept his portion of his mother on a table in the living room. But the sight of it, the very *idea* of it, disturbed Maxine. Eventually Xavier acquiesced and allowed Maxine to move the ashes to a spare room closet, where they sat for a long time in neglect.

Until one wintry day when Maxine was left alone while her husband was away on business. An ice storm had been ravaging the area for nearly thirty-six hours. Many houses had lost power; Maxine's included. It was while she sat shivering in the unlit, vacant house, that she decided to liberate Mrs. Whitlock from her perch.

A single candle lighted Maxine's way as she ventured into the neglected room and freed the urn from its cobweb-laden nook.

The dust it held seemed ever-so-faintly to sigh as Maxine turned it gently in her hands. She sat within the candle-lit chamber long into the night, holding the urn, listening. She allowed her mind to drift into buried fantasies, ones that heated her insides with shame, with delight. Maxine waited until these sensations became almost unbearable, then she extinguished the candle.

Cast Lots

"I'm the clerk, I'm the scribe, at the hearings of what cause I know not."

— Samuel Beckett, "Texts for Nothing"

She finds herself inside a lilting cottage. Gales test the twisted nails that hold the planks of this most humble abode consecutive, firm. The wooden walls creak, as does the bowing cot she rests upon.

The winds are cold and smell of yeast. They insinuate themselves between the slats, snuffing out the low-burning kerosene lamp. There is no moon.

Shifting in a strange bed, with its prodding springs and coarse blankets, the woman is suddenly alerted to…what, a premonition, a memory?

Knowledge; direct irrefutable knowledge that a great peril is encroaching; growing keener, vaster, nearer.

The certainty of this danger rouses in the woman an all-consuming terror, one that reaches a critical mass once she hears the bleating sound that rides the forceful wind. These noises come rhythmically. They penetrate the cottage as surely as a spear.

Flinging back the bedclothes, the woman charges for the door. She is thoughtless in her panic, but is intent only on fleeing, on racing down the first causeway she encounters.

She freezes mere paces outside her door.

There are no roads to tread, for this tiny cottage, she discovers, stands upon a tiny island. The mainland is clearly visible, its dunes baptized in a strange kind of manufactured light, but a raging channel stretches between it and the woman. She studies the choppy surface with its whitish peaks. It is like a horde of ghosts floating past her, endlessly.

Out here the bleating sound is that much louder, that much closer. Peering out across the roiling divide, she pinpoints the source of the noise. Standing on the far shore, planted in the sand like an incongruous tree, is a payphone. Fixed to a stout wooden pillar, the phone is of a style the woman has not seen in years. The metallic clang of its bell is painful, panicked, like the mechanized scream of a maimed creature...

✖

Joyce Felton lifted her eyelids slowly, then immediately closed them again. Though the dream had dissolved, its significance lingered, spiting the daylight that had only just begun to brighten the blinds. Tears slipped from the corners of her eyes. Breathing had become a chore. Joyce knew she had to muster sufficient courage in order to face whatever changes might have been wrought during her sleep. She also knew that there were questions, difficult and delicate questions that needed to be asked.

She sat up quickly and forced herself to see.

The bedroom was as she had left it, complete with the half-drained water glass and an overfilled ashtray on the nightstand. Though these sights might have on any other morning reassured her, Joyce could not ignore the fact that she had endured a disturbing dream, a nightmare where every detail seemed to sweat menace, to shine with fell purpose.

She rose and began to walk, to scrutinize, to hunt for signs of transition.

In the hallway, pale carpet met smartly with moulding.

Walls ran upright. All the light fixtures were functioning.

The number of steps on the main stairway had neither swelled nor diminished. The mums in the vase on the foyer stand had not withered.

A cursory check of the kitchen proved that the milk remained white in its container and that the water still drained clockwise in the sink.

Joyce had almost managed to convince herself that her lot in life had survived this most recent experience in the nightmare-realm, but her confidence crumbled when she chanced a glimpse through the laundry-room window that looked out into the back yard.

The lawn was strewn with the bodies of birds—crows, thrushes, sparrows.

At first Joyce was struck by the awful scenario of the creatures having suffered some epidemic that had stolen their lives. But this theory was usurped by the worse reality once Joyce noticed that many of the birds were still stirring and twitching. Their feathers were fluffed, bills were tucked under wings, tiny eyes were closed.

The knowledge, such as she had undergone in her nightmare, was flushing through her now, in the heatless light of the waking state.

This was how the change always came: a Hand of Death caressing those it had cursed. In Joyce's case, for reasons she could never ascertain, the change had always staked its claim through slumber. It rode in like a Horseman on a mare, spectral and marauding in its pursuit of her.

Sleep's reach, Joyce had learned, was vast. Though this was the first time she had ever seen evidence of it pulling birds from the sky and stunning them into an almost unshakable rest, she was not shocked by this development. Her past experiences had left her utterly consumed by the mounting unreality of oneiric shifting. It grew around her like a rising tide, dragging in any sentient creature that happened to be anywhere near Joyce's prostrate form. Anything lost in this undertow often floundered. If they did survive, they awoke to find themselves inside a wholly different life, a wholly different world.

Joyce hoped, *prayed*, that these winged creatures were too slight and frail to impact her to any degree.

But she then discovered that the birds were not the only creatures to have been sucked into this dream-mire: a man must have been passing by her yard at some point in the night. Had he been trying to break in, Joyce wondered? No matter, for his punishment was to become a mere pawn in an enterprise that was beyond the ken of anyone.

The man was floating face up in her swimming pool.

All strength drained from Joyce's legs. She slipped down between the laundry tub and the dryer, which, she noticed, needlessly and inopportunely, had a thin scab of rust at its base. It was not fear that buckled her, but an exhaustion that is specific to this psychological torture. It was happening so soon after last time. Had it ever truly ceased? Even its respites seemed somehow to be punishments.

Pulling herself erect, Joyce childishly hoped that the man on the water had evaporated as dreams are supposed to do in daylight.

He was no longer in the pool. He was now at the window.

His features became distorted as he pressed his face to the pane. His movements left a greasy trail on the glass. Joyce looked at his face and was offended by its slackness, by the way the eyes jittered beneath their drooping lids. Through the glass she could hear the wet flutter of the man's snore.

"Go away!" she pleaded, her voice waffling unpleasantly between a whisper and a shrill whine. She checked over her shoulder, fearing that Morgan had been woken, that she would see the shape of all that Joyce had struggled to protect her from ever seeing. "Go!" She enforced her plea by waving her hands in a shooing motion.

Drool spilt from the man's hanging jaw, indicating just how deep in the nightmare he was.

Confident that the rear door was out of the somnambulist's reach, Joyce unlocked it and stepped out onto the patio. "Get out of here—now!" she cried. The man's clothes were ragged. He pawed at the air as one love-starved, one desperate for an embrace. He was, Joyce knew, looking to pull her back into last night's ugly island cottage, with its telephone screeching to be answered.

The man shambled listlessly to his left, his right. His condition allowed Joyce to guide him on his way with relative ease. She steered him toward the open wooden gate. Pool water dripped from his clothing. Joyce hated the fact that she had to touch him.

Once he began shuffling down the driveway Joyce slammed and bolted the gate.

Her re-entry into the house had all the drama of a teen sneaking in after curfew. She broke from tiptoeing long enough to snap the deadbolt on the back door, then she moved to the living room and peered through the sheers of the large bay window.

The man was staggering like a drunkard down the centre of the street.

He'd managed to shuffle out of Joyce's view before the terrible squeal of tires, followed immediately by a thud.

Joyce backed away from the window, chilled by the sound of the panicked voices and cries from down the way.

"What's going on?"

The voice came from behind her. Joyce spun to see Morgan, who was rubbing her eyes with the heel of her left hand. Her tangled hair suggested a restless night.

"An accident," were the only two words Joyce managed to pronounce before she began to cry.

Morgan moved to her, wrapped her arm around her shoulders, and asked repeatedly what was wrong. When Joyce was unable or unwilling to respond, all at once Morgan knew.

Her arm slipped off Joyce's quaking frame. "No," she said.

Joyce looked at her, her eyes desperately assessing what, if anything, Morgan might have pieced together.

The girl's expression and demeanour were frustratingly blank. They prevented Joyce from any insights at all. Morgan made her way to the breakfast nook with melodramatic slowness. The padded bench huffed when she slumped down upon it. The girl sat like one mesmerized. She lazily traced the table-top's grain pattern with one finger.

Resignedly, Joyce joined her, studying her from across the narrow nook.

"I want to ask you a question and I want you to answer me honestly. Morgan? Look at me please. I need to ask you something."

Morgan kept her head against the crook of her elbow but did respond with "What?"

"Have you been doing something you're not supposed to?"

Morgan lifted her head at last. "What do you mean?"

"I mean have you been...curious."

Morgan's eyes slowly closed. Her chin rumpled and began to quiver. "I'm sorry," she squeaked.

"I told you never to go looking for her, didn't I? How many times did I say that if you start looking for a castaway, all you end up doing is calling attention to yourself, making the nightmare notice you?"

A thick wedge of tension was driven between them.

Joyce ultimately rose to collect the rudiments of breakfast.

She peered out at the back yard. The birds must have

awoken and flown.

Morgan was unable even to consider eating the bowl of cold cereal that had been placed before her. Joyce smoked cigarettes over her own, allowing the fallen ashes to darken the milk like polluted snow.

The telephone's ring jolted the pair of them—Morgan from the unexpectedness, Joyce from its kinship to her most recent nightmare. They let the answering machine take the call:

"Hello, Joyce? This is Alex from the store. I'm just checking to see if you were aware that you were scheduled to be our opening cashier this morning. Your shift started forty minutes ago, so if you could give me a call back as soon as you get this that would be great."

The sing-song tone of her supervisor's voice both masked anger and betrayed an utter lack of concern for what might have prevented Joyce from fulfilling her retail duties.

Joyce rose and yanked the phone cord from its jack. She returned to the nook and lit a fresh cigarette.

"Can I have one of those?" Morgan asked. There was no longer a need for pretence.

Joyce flicked the pack across the table. Morgan felt as though she might be graded on her smoking skills. She cleared her throat and then confessed.

"I wanted to know...know who she was."

"I told you, you can't," Joyce barked. "Do I have to engrave it on your forehead? You can't and you won't."

"But *you* knew her."

Joyce sighed. "Yes," she said, "but I knew her *before* she fell into it."

"Well I wasn't around *before*."

"I know you weren't."

Smoking was evidently new to Morgan. Joyce noted the way her face was beginning to blanch.

"Let me ask you," Morgan began, "did you know *your* mother?"

Joyce cleared her throat. "Yes."

"Have lots of good memories of her, do you?" Morgan's voice was taking on a keen edge.

"Some."

"Oh? You weren't taken from her when you were still in diapers? How nice for you."

Joyce folded her hands before her. In her mind she counted the seconds until an appropriate pause was reached.

"Did you know I once had two sons?"

Morgan did not know how to respond.

Joyce nodded. She was unaware of the fact that she'd begun to cry again until she felt a tear splash upon her still-folded hands.

"Isaac and Caleb. Well, to be accurate, Caleb hadn't been born yet, but I was in my ninth month. My husband Barry was a firefighter. Or maybe he still is. How can I know? Anyway, we'd just purchased our first house—a little place, a lot smaller than this house. Barry was working a lot, trying to pick up extra hours to pay for all the things we needed. I was trying to get as much unpacking done as I could, but Isaac was only three at that time, so trying to keep up with him and set up house while I was as big as a house myself, well, it tired me out. Plus, about that time Isaac had been suffering from…bad dreams. That must be how it got me…"

Joyce's voice dissipated like wind-scattered smoke. Several moments were spent on a vacant stare that made Morgan both heartsick and frightened.

"I remember," Joyce resumed, "I'd just put Isaac down for his afternoon nap. I was going to finish unboxing our kitchenware, but I was just so exhausted. I curled up right beside Isaac."

Morgan interjected with a rush of apologies. "You don't have to relive this," she told her.

But Joyce's recollection was immune to protest. "We had an antique clock," she continued, "an heirloom. It was inside one of the open boxes in our bedroom. It was a pretty thing, with Roman numerals on the face and little brass chimes that rang on the hour. Anyway, the house was so quiet that day that all I could hear was the refrigerator buzzing in the kitchen and the ticking of that pretty little clock. As a matter of fact, I pulled that ticking sound into my dream.

"I must have dozed off fairly quickly, and the nightmare came right away. In it, I was walking up a steep country road. The incline was so extreme that I could barely climb it. At one point my legs gave out. I fell down but I still couldn't stop climbing. I began to crawl, to pull myself along the asphalt, looking up to the top of the road.

"The sun was very white. It hurt to look upward, but I could just make out that there was a silhouette at the top of the hill. It took what felt like forever before I was able to make out what it was—a stuffed chair, a wingback, antique...but battered. The chair was turned away from me. When I got a bit closer, I could see that something was sitting in that chair. There were spiky tufts of hair sticking up above the back. The upholstery was blue with a very ugly pattern of gold running through it, a zigzag thing that made me nauseous if I looked at it for too long.

"Standing next to the chair—and I'd forgotten all about it until just this very moment—was a little wooden table. There was a glass on the table, like a champagne flute. It was filled with this shining liquid. It was the colour of amethyst.

"I almost made it to the top when I suddenly froze. I can't remember exactly what it was sitting there, waiting for me, but I was overcome with...awfulness. I tried to turn around, to get back to the bottom of the hill, but there was a magnetic pull that was forcing me closer to that chair.

"I tried to resist. I pressed my fingernails into the asphalt until they broke off. I even tried to bite down into the ground. Somehow it worked. I'd managed to stop moving forward.

"So, the thing in the chair came to me.

"The chair came grinding down the sloping road. The sound was hideous, the shrill scraping sound of wood being dragged along the ground. I remember seeing the chair legs splintering and breaking apart. The closer it got, the worse it became. The upholstery was not patterned but stained with all these foul blotches. And I bet if you try really hard you can guess what the upholstery was made from.

"And then the chair was *right there*." Joyce held her hand before her face to emphasize her point.

"The thing in the chair stood up and lifted me off the ground by my eyelids. I started to scream, and then the nightmare ended."

Morgan felt she should speak. She did not speak. "When I woke up," Joyce added, "my babies were gone, and I was in a little townhouse with a different lot in life. The stranger who insisted he was my husband got tired of my hysteria pretty quickly. It took him less than a day before he had me hospitalized. I was stuck inside there for weeks. But I got out of that situation too, eventually. Anyway, something good came out of it. I kept the name Joyce. I used to love James Joyce's story 'The Dead.' I really think I did…such a long time ago."

"I sent an email," Morgan finally confessed. "I found an online service that claimed they could track down lost relatives. It was that day we argued last week, remember? I was angry at you, and hurt, so I emailed them to ask for information. But I'll write them back and cancel, okay? I'll tell them to forget it."

"Don't bother."

"No, really." She reached for her phone, which sat charging in the kitchen wall socket. "I'll do it right now."

"It won't change a thing."

Morgan withdrew her hand.

"What happens now?"

Joyce said nothing for a time, then: "What happens is that everything shifts."

"How can you be sure?" Morgan retorted. "Nothing's happened to us yet."

"Oh, it has. We just haven't seen it yet. Everything's always changing, in flux." Joyce crossed her arms across her chest, a posture that made Morgan uncomfortable, so great was its kinship to the dead in their eternal rest. "I don't know if there is a message in this whole thing, if there is any kind of lesson to be learned, but if there is, perhaps that's it: that nothing is ever stable, that we're never in control, no matter how much we believe ourselves to be."

Morgan was visibly deflated. Thinly, she asked, "Do you know how all this started?"

"No idea. But I think this...nightmare, vision, whatever you want to call it, has been around forever. I don't think we create the dream, we just experience it, get claimed by it. It takes from us, but weirdly enough, it gives to us too. I've had other children, other possessions. But I don't choose them. I just kind of...observe them."

"Like in a dream?" Morgan asked.

"Like in a dream. One thing I *have* figured out is that you had to have met someone in waking life before they can be pulled into this. Sort of like the way you dream about ordinary people, even the dead, when you dream. Your mother used to do my hair, as you know. That's how she got dragged in."

Joyce's subsequent shudder was so violent that Morgan asked her what she was thinking. "That man, the one in the yard...I think I saw him panhandling in the alley behind the house last week. I even gave him a five..."

Despite her confusion, Morgan felt that further questions were futile.

The room donned silence like a garment, flaunted it for too long. The doorbell's chiming broke the spell. Morgan flinched, gasped, and then rose to answer it. Joyce reached across the table and gripped Morgan's arm. "Don't. It will be the police looking for witnesses to the accident. We're not getting involved."

There was a knock, then a stillness that lasted well into the afternoon. By then Morgan had migrated to the living room, where she stared at the television with its volume deliberately high. Joyce remained in the kitchen, smoking until the package was depleted.

Out of frustration and defiance Morgan rose from the sofa with a huff. She gathered her rolled mat and her petite gym bag.

"Where are you going?" Joyce asked her.

"Yoga. It's Wednesday."

"You can't."

Morgan shrugged. "I say I can."

The jangling of keys, the rattling of Joyce's nerves; she bolted toward the front door. "Wait! Don't go. It's not safe, do you understand? Not safe!"

Morgan pretended that the woman's blubbering, her clinging grip, didn't faze her. "I'm not going to sit here and rot like some prisoner."

"Well then, I'm coming with you."

✳

Joyce stationed herself upon a bench against the yoga studio's far wall. She was like a stoic bird watching emotionlessly as the women reached and twisted their bodies in mimicry of beasts, and then, at a turn, in reverent imitation of the holy ones who prostrate themselves on *sajadas* facing Mecca.

The studio was warm and the score that leaked from hidden speakers was a lullaby of chimes and babbling water. Joyce felt buoyant, cleansed. Her guard seduced, she allowed her heavy eyelids to draw shut.

The nightmare did not grab her until after she was awoken. The yoga instructor who'd nudged her offered a warm smile and said something that Joyce didn't hear. The studio was empty.

Joyce rose and began asking about Morgan. The instructor's nonplussed expression spoke volumes. Numb, Joyce slipped out of the studio.

Dusk was thickening around her. The streets were a pale haze, the people mere moving props. Joyce found her way home by instinct. She fully expected her key to no longer fit the lock, but in the end, she did not have to test it, for upon her arrival she found the house's front door slightly ajar. She pushed it open and stood in the vacant frame.

To the uninitiated the disruption to the house would have been viewed as a robbery, but Joyce was keenly aware of the incongruous details: the thick coating of dust that suggested years of neglect despite the fact that she had left the house only hours earlier; the indentations in the carpet where a furnishing had once sat; the ceiling fan that dangled from its wires, as if something immense had recently stormed through the confining room.

Joyce ducked under the destroyed fixture. Chunks of plaster crunched beneath her soles. She followed the tracks in the carpet, which led her to the stairway.

The chair that was missing from the living room had been dragged to the top of the stairs. It was facing the top of the landing, its back to the steps.

Joyce felt herself moving backward. She pressed her back against the foyer window.

The figure that was seated in the chair was, Joyce reasoned, designed to seem familiar, much the way recognizable forms pass through one's dreams.

"Morgan..." Joyce whispered, knowing how desperate her guess was, how foolish.

The shape in the chair rose, swelled. The chair was cast aside and went tumbling down the steps until it finally became wedged between the wall and the banister. Its upholstery was shimmering wet. It reeked foully.

What had once been seated now stood. The thing was colossal, tangled, yet it moved with a grace that defied its size and its anatomy. Every time it lowered one of its lumps onto the next carpeted step there came a thunderous knock-ing, metallic and deep and echoing endlessly. The creature began to contort itself, to flaunt its non-humanness by halting for a second or two so that Joyce could absorb each repulsive asana.

Joyce shut her eyes.

Weeping, she sputtered, "Now I lay me down to sleep..."

Notes on the Aztec Death Whistle

It was the dream home for which you'd always been yearning, and at last, after many years of patient drudgery in the halls of academe, you found yourself able to purchase it. But your freedom came at a dear cost. You'd only truly managed to garner wealth after winning such a high degree of fame and fortune thanks to your unsanctioned archaeological dig in Tlateloco, Mexico.

Yet even before you connived your way into the historian's limelight, you had already done quite well for yourself, hadn't you? For years you'd drawn a handsome salary as a tenured professor of Cultural Anthropology at McMaster University, Hamilton, Canada.

But this was not enough for you...not nearly enough. You just had to be noticed, be revered, be perceived as the one who had done that which couldn't be done: you 'discovered' the notorious Aztec Death Whistle.

Of course, the newspapers that ran your story around the globe didn't know about the ruthless tactics you'd employed in order to make that discovery, did they? Even the most diligent journalists who covered the story were unable to dig up the ugly facts about it that you buried: your engaging a gang of mercenaries to raid the little village near Tlateloco, the way you'd watched them torture an elder to death just so you could obtain the location of the secret ceremonial pit where long ago the Aztecs buried their human sacrifices.

No, what you showed the world instead was a charade, the mirage of the humble scholar whose painstaking research had led him to that pit of the dead. It all appeared so innocent.

Why, even your research notes exuded studiousness. See? I have set them here upon your marble-top desk. Beside these pages is the worn satchel of pig leather you used to cart your notes around Mexico. It is hand-stitched and is branded with a strange mask in profile; the Nahuatl words "*Huehue Ichta-catlatolli*" (meaning "Ancient Secrets") embossed in careful one-inch characters just above the satchel's clasps. Wreathing this tantalizing message is a mosaic of images—gods in profile, potted fires, skulls whose expression is almost gleeful. Many of the images have been woven into the leather with a variety of colourful threads, making this object as much a tapestry of mythology as a case.

Set beside this satchel is a stack of pristine white pages, each one marked with handwritten script, crisp and focused. I have no doubt that this is the most careful text you've ever penned...

NOTES & OBSERVATIONS COLLECTED DURING MY EXPERIENCES WITH THE AZTEC DEATH WHISTLE

Tlatelolco, the Ruins of the Aztec City State:

The Aztecs developed their notorious Death Whistle before the Mithraic Mysteries, before human-ity looked for the meaning of life in arcane scrolls, before the resurrection of a Saviour.

The process of the whistle's creation would com-mence with the careful selection of sleek, firm bones, ones that had once sat nestled in living meat but had since been flensed by the cruel hands of time. Only

the choicest parts would be culled from the fly-swarmed mound that festered at the bottom of the death pit in Tlatelolco.

These bones would be placed upon large slabs of stone. There, they would be hammered into nuggets. The nuggets would then be plunked into mortars and pummeled into a fine dust.

River water would be collected and carried to the place of seclusion. Earth taken from those places that had been blessed by the gods would also be ferried there. The warlocks, called 'nahualli' in their native tongue of Nahuatl, would then blend these elements to form a slimy clay. Into this mixture the bone dust would be swirled and folded. Finally, this morbid clay would be scooped up and shaped by the skilled fingers of the nahualli. Skulls would be formed, with gaping jaws and eye sockets like the pocks on the face of the moon, or like the conch shell of the lunar god Tēcciztēcatl.

It was through the shriek-wide mouths of the skulls that the precious noise of the whistle would escape.

Once purified and made firm by midnight fires, the whistles were then decorated with suitably grue-some adornments; snakes or squiggly lines of pyre smoke, hexes, all brushed on with a paint made from poisonous berries and from dung.

On ceremonious occasions, the dates for rites whose character is too extreme to hew with the timid mindset of contemporary man, these whistles would be blown.

The sound they would emit was the very voice of the damned in Mictlān, the Aztec Underworld.

Or such is the tale the elders tell. The whistles become a ligament between this realm and theirs, a terrestrial tool the damned can use to lend voice to their otherwise unheard cries. The whistle's scream is the song of torment and torture, unimaginable and unending.

How can one even begin to describe the sound? A piercing sine? The sound of fingernails scraping across old tin? It is a hideous, most unmusical noise, yet its power is all-encompassing and immediate. Once one hears it, one is owned by it to one degree or another.

This is a sound that rouses and wrests. Settled dust is stirred by its piping. Hidden shapes are lured out. Latent wishes spring up like fresh weeds in the mind of the hearer. Mictēcacihuātl Herself is said to smile when the Death Whistle blows, and the priests' blades are drawn and raised.

Until this past century, when a team of archaeologists with which I was involved accidentally disinterred one from its resting place amidst the ruins, the Death Whistles were believed to be mythical. We'd gone to the site in search of villagers' relics, which, based upon years of research, were believed to be in the area. We were shocked and excited by our happening upon one of the Death Whistles. News of our find spread like wildfire.

Human nature being what it is, the lone discovered specimen was quickly molded and replicated. These cheap copies were exported to line the shelves of trinket shops around the planet for no other purpose than vulgar, unvarnished greed. No stock was placed in the whistle's sacred nature or its powers. It became, like all things to modern men, a toy.

Only the original artefact was shown any degree of respect. It was preserved under glass in the British

Museum of Antiquities, where tourists gawked and snapped photos and made light. There it remained...

Indeed, there it remained, Professor. Until last week... when you stole it.

You smuggled it all the way here, to your private bungalow on the shore. You didn't think that anyone or anything would hear when you stood on your deck and blew into the whistle's ancient slit and unleashed the ungodly scream.

The sound ripped across the snow-piled shore of the beach, now abandoned for the winter. It stabbed through your lavish bungalow as well...the bungalow that had been vacant, but now held me.

I want to thank you for leaving behind all these notes about the Death Whistle. They've been a great aid in explaining just what I am, the power that now lives inside me. Since you dug up that whistle, I felt I'd been living in one prolonged nightmare, but now I have entered another.

All dreams are quests. I undertook mine, and as my prize I found my portal out of Mictlān. You did that for me. You gave me a signal to follow, you gave me back my voice. Along with a new body I could use to once more roam the mortal world.

I hope these words I'm now adding to your notes are legible to you, and that they help as you move down there in Mictlān. Your notes have certainly helped me. I hope this confession makes you understand, though judging by your face when you saw me crawling through your living room wall (me being all pungent smoke and clattering, carbonized bones) it did not look as though you were able to understand anything that was happening.

Can you hear me down there as I call to you with this fresh, screeching voice your stolen Death Whistle has given me? I hope you're able to appreciate what the Death Whistle has done for me...and what it made me do to you.

[Police were summoned to Professor Somner's
private beach house on the morning of 31st March,
after the hired groundskeeper discovered the
shorefront door of sliding glass had been shattered and the white sheers were flecked with
dark stains. Detectives entered the homestead
to face a grisly scene; the entire study was
coated in blood, a glass case containing many
rare Aztec artefacts was smashed and the relics
destroyed beyond repair, and numerous papers
were torn and left to fester in the pooled
blood around the study. Police are reluctant to
confirm that the blood was that of Professor
Somner. Though presumed dead, his body has yet
to be found.]

Headsman's Trust:
A Murder Ballad

"Life is flesh on bone convulsing above the ground."
— E. Elias Merhige, *Begotten*

Just how the Headsman trapped divinity within His axe blade is a riddle I am not destined to solve. But I have borne witness to the Cut-Lord's miracles. They evidence the power of both the blade and the hand that wields it. This is sufficient to keep me in servitude to Him.

Once I shared a stout daub house with my Mother and Father. There was stew in my bowl daily and mown hay to bed down on nightly. If such an arrangement constitutes happiness, then for a brief time I was happy. But then Father abandoned us, forcing Mother and I to till the land and re-wattle our drooping roof and lay shivering in our cistern, hiding from the bands of highwaymen that stalked the trails near our land.

Mother seldom showed emotion, but I was not afraid to cry or curse my Father; which I did often at first, more rarely as the seasons passed.

It was on the very night when the Moon first pulled blood out of my body to stain my nightdress and thighs that the Headsman darkened our door.

The moment Mother spotted His monumental frame plodding toward our house she began to plead. Mother's fear of death ran deep. I see now that she could never have let go, could never have properly received the Headsman's lesson.

So instead she struck a bargain with Him: her life would be spared and in exchange I would become His charge, His Trust. With horrifying ease, He wrenched me from Mother's ankles where I clung, screaming. He whisked me off and chained me to His wagon. I have been at His side in the many Moons since that night.

✷

We emerge like the spawn of the forest that encloses this village. As if aware of our destination, the mares draw our carriage to the clearing. Once they reach the execution platform, they halt. I tie the reins to my footrest and leap down from the driver's bench. Our carriage is a slight but ominous thing, canopied in midnight-blue leather and fastened with thick iron bolts. The whole contraption appears to my eye as a grand foreboding book, one that holds fast to its secrets. I move to the back and unlatch the iron grate.

The Headsman climbs out from the wagon. He is looming and lanky. His arms, while thin, are sure.

He is already hooded when He lumbers into view. His hood is dun, and the eyes that stare through its only openings are citrine and intensely focused.

We have been travelling for what feels to be a ceaseless summer, an interminable span of swelter and insects and sweating peasants. Of late it feels that we are wayfaring to the very edge of the world. We have nearly reached the sea.

Our rituals rarely deviate, so the fact that we have not yet collected a coffin for today's victim troubles me. When I inquire about this the Headsman tells me:

...*in due course*...

My duty is to tend to the block and I see to this as soon as the Headsman passes me. The block is stored within the wagon. We employ it for each beheading. Its surface has been smoothed by the blood that voids out of His victims. This human grease softens the woodgrain. The block now has the silken texture of a woman's thigh.

The Headsman stores His implement in an oblong box of stone that is lidded with a nameless tombstone.

Once the Headsman has inspected the scaffold for today's task He returns to the carriage and uncaps the oblong box. The gravestone lid groans as He pushes it from its mount. Trapped air flows upward. It is heady with apple and pine, poppy and sage. On the eve of the first execution where I served as the Headsman's Trust I watched Him prepare entanglements of these and other flora with great care. He'd sowed the dank bottom of the trough with them, making a fragrant bed upon which His unwieldy axe reposes. I do not ask the Headsman about this practice, though I believe that the indwelling spirits of these plants bless the weapon. Never have I witnessed the Headsman burnish it nor lean it to the whetstone, yet the blade has lost none of its lustre or its edge.

A drum begins to beat.

The ceremony is commencing.

I could list the minutiae of these proceedings—the vengeful accusations of thievery or wortcunning, the mock trials, the prayers for the condemned—but a greater picture can be painted without such trivialities.

The drum lures the villagers from their hovels and huts. They congregate before the platform as the guards drag out the latest woman to be convicted. She squints, for the sun undoubtedly pains her after such a long span in a windowless cell. She does not utter a sound, not even as she is guided up the scaffold steps and her head is pressed against the block.

The drummer goes still, and the mob falls silent in anticipation of the Headsman's song.

The Headsman assumes His stance, adjusts His grip on the handle of His weapon. It is customary for the Headsman's

Trust to avert their gaze out of respect for the condemned, but something, some impelling force, inspires me to lock eyes with the woman on the block. I know the blade will fall at any moment, so I wring every detail I can from the sight of the woman's wide, lunatic eyes. Her lips are peeled back over her misshapen teeth. She trembles, though not from fear. Her body quakes with silent, mirthful laughter.

Then comes the Headsman's song: the crisp flit of the axe swinging downwards, the briefest of squawks from the victim before her neck is parted, the muffled thump of the wetted iron edge sinking into the block. The crowd gasps.

Along with its song, decapitation has its scent, one that chokes the air like a swollen cloud. It stinks of copper and mud and yeast.

The head lops forward, like some sluggish creature. It wobbles down into the basket. Wordlessly the Headsman reaches down and grips it by its mane. Like Perseus, He holds this morbid trophy aloft. The drained face has already assumed a ghostly shade of white. Gore dangles from the halved neck like ruby pendants.

Occasionally the heads manage to retain a wisp of their original awareness. The eyes will shift and blink in frantic confusion, the tongue may wriggle as it gropes for speech. However, this does not happen today.

The Headsman drops the spoil back into the basket, pushes it to the edge of the scaffold with His boot.

Like crows, the villagers swoop in to grasp at the carrion. There is arguing and shoving as they slink back into the village in a messy procession. The dripping basket is held above them. Different villages put these ruined heads to different uses. Some give them a burial in alignment with their native faith, others preserve them in brine where they are said to become a divination tool.

What they do with the head is of no concern to me or the Headsman. Our mission is markedly different from this.

A boy named Matthias worms his way to the headless corpse. He holds up a stone bowl to the raining neck.

Not far from this village, at the hem of the forest's shade, there stretches a broad heath. There the heathgrass sprouts as tall as men, and even on the stillest days these blades sway under strange winds from elsewhere. Upon this heath is a cluster of standing stones. How long they have stood no one knows. The winds that bully the heathgrass also erode these stones. Occasionally large pieces are lopped off. These pieces are often fashioned into bowls, as today's villagers have done.

Matthias has followed us dutifully throughout this scorching season, skillfully gathering the precious blood and then feeding it as offerings to the gods of certain hidden places that the Headsman regards as sacred. Matthias wanders off, his bowl brimming. The blood will be meticulously borne to the heath and poured upon the standing stones, food for the power that pulses inside them.

Matthias was born to serve the standing stones. He has shared with me the methods his parents employed to groom him for this role. As to why I was recognized to the role of Headsman's Trust I do not know. Perhaps the Headsman perceived some shift in my soul, a quickening that has transformed me alchemically into something purer than I was before. I do not sense it myself. But just before the season turned the Headsman informed me that I was no longer to collect the blood offerings, I was to tend to the block.

Today I am to be shown yet another step in this sprawling ritual.

The Headsman lifts the carcass from the block and sets it upon the platform. It is like a morbid enactment of the bridegroom laying his love upon the marriage bed.

We disrobe her.

"We should wash her," I say. My request is met with a rigid denial.

Instead the Headsman hands me a crude map that reveals

a path to the hovel of the casket-maker. I am to collect the custom coffin for the recently fallen. He attempts to bolster me for what I will witness at the casket-maker's hovel. He orders me to make haste.

The midday heat swells the veins in my hands, causes my breathing to become laboured. I yearn for the shade of a glen but my path snakes through open country.

The casket-maker dwells and works in a pithouse far from any village, far from any burial ground.

The sight of her homestead steals my breath. I am impelled to lower my tired frame, to cross my legs and sit in contemplation of this mound-like structure. Being a pithouse, the dwelling is a bored-out hole in the earth that is roofed with a rigid entanglement of bones. Fibula and femur, scapula and tarsal; they all nest into one another as if Nature Herself had forged this skeleton, the remains of some fabulous arachnid that had skittered across the plains with the mammoths. The bones are the colour of old wheat. They nestle so tightly together that no view of the pithouse's interior is possible.

After a respectable amount of time has passed, I rise and approach. An odd sound creeps into my ears.

Crickets.

To hear one or two of them chirping in the daylight is not uncommon, but what I hear is not the thin creaking of a few stray bugs, it is an orchestra. Their serrated song gives the afternoon a nocturnal pulse, a rhythm ill-suited for raw light and heat. It is instead the cool, murky rhythm of twilit mires, of waning embers, of the charm hung above the bed before slumbering, of secrecy, of dim potential.

Their song passes over me, through me, and I imagine that my heart is altering its beat to match this pulsation. I move closer to the pithouse, the womb that houses the crickets. My face is practically pressed against the spiky mesh of bones. I can see precious little through the weave, but I can hear the chirping fully now and I can smell the heady stench of mud and milt. It is sickening and arousing at once.

There then comes a sonorous creaking which joins the cricket orchestra like the faint rumble of distant thunder. The creaking pulses low, then high, low, then high. Its pace is measured and patient. I press my eye to one of the few slits in the bone shelter.

Within the pithouse, something shifts. I can almost discern the shapeless form. It reposes in the centre of the shallow hole. Needles of sunlight manage to pierce the darkness through the tiniest of apertures, pressing in like unwanted seawater through a ship's hull. These bright threads form a luminous crosshatch. As my eyes grow accustomed to this, I am better able to spy the figure in the hut.

I can only presume it is a woman, for the figure is dressed in a luxurious gown, one that suggests nobility. The hair is piled hectically upon the pale head. I cannot discern the face. If woman she is, if *human* she is, she is seated in a frame chair, one that rocks slowly back and forth, creating that measured creaking. The chair is composed of pale wood. Or is it bone?

Instinct presses me backwards. I scuttle back from the hut. The crickets continue to chirp.

Leaning against a warped, canker-laden tree is the coffin. It is a wicker casket. The thin branches that form its woven body are the grey of morning fog.

Suddenly remembering my task as if newly woken from a dream, I scramble to my feet and creep over to collect the casket. I am glad to be ignorant of whatever arrangement the Headsman has with the casket-maker. I simply take up the coffin and flee.

My load is mercifully light, but its shape makes carting it a chore. I lug it on my back and can feel the knots of its branches pressing into my flesh. I do not offer the pithouse a backward glance. Soon the only cricket-song I hear is the one that stains my memory.

✳

The light is already fading to a late-afternoon shimmer by the time I return to the scaffold, where I find the Headsman waiting in what appears to be the same standing position as when I departed. I plunk the coffin down and begin to breathlessly explain what I have seen.

Unconcerned, the Headsman simply goes about His task. He removes the wicker lid and from the inside of the coffin He produces a length of fabric. I aid him in unfolding this. The long sheet feels coarse against my palms. It is a shroud, dyed midnight blue.

We begin to wrap the headless body. The shroud is a sullied thing, woven with many kinds of thread and soaked in the waters of the Moon. Or so the Headsman tells me. When this task is complete, I help the Headsman lift the swaddled body and deposit it inside the coffin.

Once we replace the lid, the Headsman orders me to step away and turn my back. This I do, all the while trying simultaneously to both hear and not hear the words He mutters over the casket. I wonder what gestures the Headsman makes, what substances He might use to anoint His victim.

Eventually He announces that it is time.

We take up the casket. I am at the foot of the box, following my leader as He marches steadfast through the forest and across the great heath whose stones seem to study us as we pass and whose billowing grasses urge us to *hush*...

The Headsman does not utter a sound and I dare not break our shared trance by asking any of the thousand questions that swim in my brain, foremost of which is where our destination will be.

We move west, further and further. Even the sparsest of villages are now behind us. Eventually we three are crossing a terrain that no hermit or even beast would occupy. We are nearing the sea. In all my years, it is a sight I have never seen and the prospect of it fills me with exhilaration, with dread. Rocky cliffs jut up all around us, like the grasping fingers of a great hand. They strike me as being the parents of the heathstones, which now seem tiny and frail by comparison. Between the rocky spikes of the cliff I catch my first faint glimpse of the sea.

"May we stop?" I ask.

When the Headsman does not reply, I ask Him again, and yet again. I want so very much to race to the cliffs' edge and take in that boundless green expanse, to hear its roaring surf, feel its cold spray against my skin.

Our path suddenly juts in a sharp incline. I feel the cadaver shift in its box, placing all the weight on my end. My exhausted arms wobble as I struggle to keep our cargo aloft.

When I spot the mouth of the great cave that yawns at the end of our path, I somehow intuit that it is our destination. After a few more paces the Headsman proves my hunch correct.

Once the casket is set down upon the stony ground, I am only able to take a few steps nearer to the sea before my body betrays its exhaustion. I collapse against a boulder. My arms and thighs burn with pain. In the distance the Moon paints a gleaming stripe across the roiling sea. I am only dimly aware of my hand as it grazes the surface of the stone that braces me. Have the howling winds of this plateau smoothed it? It feels like taut silk beneath my fingertips.

Faintly I hear the steps of the Headsman. He holds His hand out to me.

...I have placed her inside the cave...

I take the small bundle that the Headsman is offering. My fingers can barely unknot the fabric. Within are shelled nuts, a wedge of bread, fruits.

...eat...

I devour it all greedily, gratefully.

The Headsman never eats.

...tonight you rest here...

I nod gratefully, for the very thought of having to venture back to the village overwhelms me. My exhaustion is excruciating.

The Headsman never slumbers.

My stomach filled, I recline on the luxurious stone and close my eyes. The surf lulls me. I feel like an infant in the arms of its Mother, Her rolling tide rocking me back and forth, back and forth...like the woman seated in the pithouse.

Though our surroundings are arid, a garden of stone, in the distance I hear an orchestra of crickets.

I do not dream.

The warmth of the sun upon my face draws me back to the land of the living. I sit up, groan.

The Headsman is nowhere to be seen. I stand and call for Him, softly at first, then at a volume to rival the pounding surf below. I climb and survey the area from many vantage points but see no trace. Am I being tested?

I return to our outcropping and I wait. I have courage enough to start homeward, but before I do, I must inspect the final place where the Headsman might be waiting.

With reluctant steps, I enter the cave. Once more I call for my master and the echo of my voice spurs violent sounds of movement. Startled, I stagger backwards. The firmly textured wall of the cave halts me. I feel the foul water that moistens the cave saturating my clothing. I squint to see but can discern little of my surroundings beyond mere black.

Something shifts in the darkness. Instinct causes me to look in the sound's direction.

I see.

I do not want to see.

She is sitting up in her casket. Her stiffening body is luminous within this grim cave. The shroud we had used to wrap her remains like a gift for the afterlife is now twisted and rent. One large section is draped over the lip of the wicker coffin like flung bedclothes. The woman herself—or what had once been a woman—is like a startled dreamer who has bolted up in her bed. Her hands molest the air around her and her headless trunk twitches as if trying to see.

A strange logy feeling comes over me. As my eyes grow accustomed to the gloom, I truly scrutinize the thing in the box. I study the halved neck; lumps of muscle, knots of bone, all held in place by the gluey clotted blood.

The whole image becomes a primordial volcano, spitting up waves of blood-lava and fledgling landscapes of tendon and of bone.

It is as if a new world is flooding out all around me. I see it with the eyes of my heart. It is a potent land whose laws are the bristling nerve, the pulsing red caverns and the stiff digits of bone.

Who will be the god of this grim, corporal world? What deity would dare send down creeds in the lawless wilderness of quivering skin and flowing blood?

She leaps!

Her escape from the casket is sloppy and awkward. Her hands swat the wicker box while her feet wobble over the cave's rutted floor. The thing staggers about in a series of blind, brutal rings. She is as a panicked moth trapped in a bell jar. Though she has no face, the headless thing turns to face me. Worse, I know that in some way she *sees* me. The dark blotches upon her breasts come to resemble eyes. Horror seizes me utterly. I collapse upon the jagged stones, yet I cannot look away.

I watch her climb the cavern walls, nimbly, like some ugly salamander. She skitters to the very summit of the cave. She contorts her body and presses her open neck against one of the stalactites. For one indescribable instant, this creature dons the entire cave as her crown. The tapered rock penetrates her throat and suddenly I can hear the cave's long-buried song. It comes to screeching life through the woman's flesh. Her pores open like the mouths of some heinous choir.

The chthonic music screams at me.

I stagger up and charge down the daylit passage.

I would flee the area entirely, but I discover a trio waiting for me on the plateau: the Headsman stands with Matthias by His side. The boy is holding the block before him, not to boast of his appointment as the Headsman's new Trust, but to show me that he understands his duty, that he reveres it.

Standing behind them is the woman from the pithouse. Her face is worse than words can convey. I turn away from her, but not from revulsion. Her visage is a sun at full glare. I am awed. I am awakened.

The headless cadaver comes bounding out of the cave. She flails about like a manic puppet.

Gracefully, placidly, the woman from the pithouse advances. She swipes her claw-like nails at the cadaver, wielding these natural weapons with swiftness and skill. With a single slice, she ends the corpse's mad enactment. The thing falls, goes still.

I feel I should speak yet I can find no words. The only sound is the pounding surf and the incessant wind that creates dust-devils all around us.

The headless cadaver begins to twitch, but only for an instant. Something is struggling to free itself from that lifeless husk. It finds the yoni forged by the woman's razor-like claws. It erupts from the flesh.

A shrike.

Despite the gore that greases the bird's plumage, I can sense the pristine shading of its feathers. It seems to carry celestial light in its down. The bird's eyes are the silver of burnished nails. The bird takes flight.

I see. I want so very deeply to see *more*. But what observes this richly shaded world is not my eyes, but my throat, my fingers, the soles of my feet. I am a vent for visionary power.

The bird begins to sing. And I hear the music of the

spheres. I somehow comprehend the wisdom of the song. It speaks of a knowledge deeper than the mind, a frenzied light that lies within the flesh and beyond it.

The song stirs my soul while it lulls my flesh. I am only dimly aware of dropping to my knees, of resting my head upon the smooth block that the Headsman's new Trust has set before me.

※

I watch my predecessor and I believe she feels no pain.

She is now a bird, floating, soaring, singing.

She is riding sublimated light, along with the bird that was the woman from the cave.

They are the light.

My name was once Matthias, but now I am simply the Headsman's Trust.

I turn my gaze once more earthward and I see the pair of headless bodies. Their bones awaiting repurposing. Soon I will carry them to the pithouse shelter of the horrible Woman who has already slipped away from the Headsman and myself.

She is vile.

She is a Saint.

She and the Headsman have freed these two souls from the tyranny of their heads.

Their thoughts have now become a shrieking music, a deathly birdsong that now makes these decapitated corpses flail.

These mangled forms frighten me. They are rising and moving all around me. I shut my eyes and I shiver.

Everywhere I hear the screaming shrikes. Everywhere is the unbearable sound of dead flesh dancing, dancing...

Chain of Empathy

I.

The first link in the chain of empathy that would eventually bind Berthe to an obscure and fiery plane was forged the instant she spied the blacksmith's nail that had been stabbed into the trunk of an oak tree.

She'd been taking advantage of the first temperate day since October by riding her bicycle, pressing her way across the sucking mud of the lanes near her parents' farm. Berthe was a free woman with no interest in suitors, and as a consequence she had no prospects of security, nor did she truly wish to have any. She had grown inured to simply mimicking the shiftless existence of her parents. She occupied the same narrow chamber where she'd been birthed. Her adult life had truly been little more than a protraction of her adolescence. There were the same daily chores to be accomplished, the same perfunctory conversations to be had around the supper table. Of late, Berthe began to find these rituals stifling. What had once brought comfort now caused her to inwardly cringe, whether it be her habitual laughter at her father's jokes or her singing ballads with her mother whenever the two of them hunched over their spindles to pull wool for the loom. Today, she yearned to feel something of her genuine roots.

It was as if there were two distinct souls dwelling in her

skin: one obvious; dutiful and calculatedly naïve and performatively virtuous; the other, a latent yet sharp yearning for something Berthe could never quite define. It constantly tested her, allowing her only a few stolen moments of contentment now and again before once again filling her mind with briars.

Berthe had been happy to allow her superficial self to steer her. Life was much steadier this way; the lulling pattern of chores and family and rest and church on Sundays. But her latent self was forever giving hints of itself, teasing her with not only its grand scope but also how inextricably bound to her it was. Berthe could feel it stirring at the base of her spine, at the back of her skull; an iceberg showing glimpses of its drowned base when the waters are tossed. Its influence upon her had become so strong that in her private diary Berthe had begun to refer to this second self as 'the Master.'

Today, as she pedalled over the mud, the Master felt nearer than it ever had before. When she spotted the oak with its strange nail, Berthe was convinced that it was the Master who'd led her to this spot.

The blacksmith's nail had appeared to Berthe peripherally at first, insinuating itself into her field of vision, faintly but persistently, the way haints are rumoured to appear to unlucky folk in these parts. She slowed her bike and turned her head to better study the jutting black thing. The nail (which she first mistook for a sailor's marlinspike, akin to her great-grandfather's, which still hung by the chimney to ward off Hearth-Eaters; angry spirits who are said to crawl down the chimneys of unprotected homes and devour all family ties) had been driven into the trunk.

Everything about the scene made Berthe morose. The oak was still weeks away from budding, so its naked limbs appeared arthritic and feeble. The way the nail had been plunged in suggested something sinister.

She stared intently for a time. Her shallow self knew that

it was best to leave things as one found them, but the presence of the Master was welling up inside her, filling her, washing away all the internal fences Berthe had always relied upon to compartmentalize her life. The Master was rapidly becoming her all.

Entranced, Berthe was able to watch with icy detachment as her physical body dismounted the bicycle, marched to the tree, and quickly pulled the nail free. It popped out with such ease that for a moment Berthe was shocked by this hidden reserve of might. Only after she'd deposited the chunky black peg into the pocket of her trousers and had begun to pedal away did it occur to her that the nail may have been there not to punish, but to keep something contained...

Something that had helped her pry the nail loose.

Something awful.

Berthe's stomach felt foul and she feared she might pass out. *'What have I done?'* she thought.

She pedalled as fast as her strained legs would allow but could not place what felt to be a safe distance between herself and the punctured oak. The urge to start sobbing was strong, but she fought it nobly. After the road had placed enough twists and valleys behind her, Berthe began to feel reasonably secure. She was homeward bound now and was excited by the notion of returning to that womb of familiar walls.

A sharp popping noise startled and momentarily confused her. The realization that it was the sound of her front tire being punctured registered only after her bicycle began to wobble and pedaling became all but impossible. She dismounted. Her heart sank as she studied the ruined wheel. Although she was no more than two kilometres from the family farm, Berthe felt like a castaway. She allowed herself a brief cry before wiping her cheeks, righting herself, and commencing to walk, dragging the useless bicycle through the clay.

Somewhere on this journey she began to sense—palpably, undeniably—a legion of perdu companions moving at her sides, her back. The sensation outwardly scared her, summoned gooseflesh and shudders. Yet inwardly, at some remote nerve-end where she imagined the Master might be enthroned, there burned an ember of excitement, of unspeakable pleasure. Were these haints or Hearth-Eaters, Berthe wondered? Whatever they were, they infused the breeze and the fields and the empty lanes with fullness, as though the Earth itself was ballooning up, swelling to the point of bursting.

Berthe reached a hand into the pocket of her mud-flecked trousers and squeezed the concealed nail, pressing it like a winemaker would a grape: in quest of its juice, its essence.

"May this nail ward off the stalking fey and all sprits foul," she muttered desperately.

But the ghost parade remained in-step with her until the main road met with a nameless lane that curved southward, in the opposite direction of her farm. The hopelessness Berthe had felt only a moment ago was suddenly replaced with a fresh, delicious sense of everything around her becoming larger and more textured. It enthused her, made her more daring. She now wanted to explore, to do something (no matter how small) that she had never done before.

She rolled her bicycle toward the nameless lane down which she'd never ventured. Titillated by the novelty of it all, she followed the compelling slope.

In all probability, what Berthe saw and felt while she crept along was purely romantic, but the sky did seem to darken with her every step, and the wind did pick up and cause the gnarly tree limbs to cluck like scolding tongues. In time Berthe would come to accept that many of these impressions could have all been in her mind, but she might never, even in throes of a crisis of faith, question herself once she reached the end of that lane and witnessed the gravehands labouring in the tiny cemetery.

Berthe had known the burial ground was here, or she'd heard tell of it at least. Her parents always referred to it as 'the pioneer cemetery' or 'the founders' graves.' And if the head-stones were any indication, these plots were very old indeed. The markers were pale and wind-smoothed, jutting up from the soil like rows of misshapen teeth. The fence of woven wire sagged and was brittle with rust. The grounds themselves were shamefully neglected.

Why then, in a place so obviously lapsed, would there today be a trio of gravehands, wholly engrossed in their labours?

The figures (Male? Female? Berthe could not exactly say) went unwaveringly about their task. One worked the land with a pitchfork, stabbing and turning the soil, their actions more akin to a gardener's than a gravedigger's. The other two walked silently in and out of the stout vault that had been built into a hillock at the rear of the grounds.

Berthe's grandfather had once told her that this vault had long ago been used to store the winter's dead, when the early villagers had to wait until the spring thaw before they could bury their loved ones. Until that time the cadavers would be wrapped in linen shrouds and piled inside the vault like cut logs in a woodpile. The account had given Berthe nightmares when she was small, ones in which she would find herself trapped inside a cabin whose walls were not logs, but shrouded corpses that wriggled and moaned inside their linen cocoons. But today, standing in the vicinity of the actual vault, whose doors of corroded iron sat open like the covers of a holy book on a pulpit, Berthe experienced a sensation beyond fear. It was something richer. (Later, Berthe would struggle to accurately name this sensation in her diary. The nearest word she could conjure to describe it was 'fascination.')

The two gravehands emerged from the vault's black interior. They carried a body between them. It resembled a great mealworm, until one of its arms slipped out of the ancient shroud, flaunting its humanness, its mortality. The fingernails were black, and the flesh was livid, with blotches of pooled fluids forming a multicoloured map on the surface. The gravehands lugged the corpse toward their partner with the pitchfork. The dead arm swung like a pendulum with their every step. Berthe wondered if the body was waving at her, perhaps even beckoning her.

Berthe's next motions were drowsily executed. Her head felt foggy. Pins and needles coursed through her arm as she once again gripped the blacksmith's nail and freed it, holding it up so the gravehands might see it. Though she had no idea the reason, it was very important for her to reveal what she had found.

The instant Berthe held out the blacksmith's nail to the moving shapes in the burial ground, a profound shift occurred. It passed through her like a wave, bringing wonder and dread in equal measure.

The shift, Berthe then came to see, was the Master liberating Itself from her skin.

For the Master suddenly stepped out from the shadowy trees. He spoke to her in a voice as plain as any man's she'd ever heard.

As to the exact nature of their exchange, Berthe could only remember faint traces. She was too fixated on trying to convince herself of what she was seeing. The Master was a protean thing, shifting in amazing ways whenever Berthe's analytical mind attempted to pinpoint just exactly what this apparition looked like. One moment the Master was a fit young man dressed in finery, the next, a stooped vagrant propped up by a pair of crutch-style sticks. Always though, a luminous sty gleamed in one of his eyes, like an ember in a stove.

The only aspect that remained fixed was his masculinity. He was a male soul, a counterpoint to her feminine flesh. When he spoke, his voice raised the hackles on the back of Berthe's neck and warmed between her legs. The Master told her that he had much more to teach her and that this was only the beginning. He promised her that this entire day, from her freeing of the nail to the gravehands to his whispered counsel, would be sewn up for her in a soft pouch of dreaming. This, the Master assured her, was the safest way, for it would place the truth at a necessary distance, enabling her to return to the ordinary world, where she must hide until she was ready to experience their full union.

II.

The Master fulfilled his promise. Berthe awoke to find herself in her own bed. It was late afternoon, and the day had grown blustery and grey. She rose and rushed to the barn where she found her bicycle resting against its pillar, both tires in perfect condition. The only indication that the encounter had been anything more than a midday dream was the blacksmith's nail, which remained in the pocket of her trousers. Though Berthe found this article of clothing clean and folded crisply inside her dresser drawer, as if new.

This was all the proof she required to purge doubt from her soul. Not once would she regret the oath sworn that day to the Master, in the watchful presence of the gravehands, while she stood on that nameless path.

As a reward for her allegiance, Berthe had been granted fulfillment of a desire she'd harboured for as long as she'd known about haunted places: to move without her body, to experience the world as a ghost does. She was told that such a feat would require a trio of tasks, which Berthe was only too eager to execute.

First, she slipped out of her room and travelled to the place where four roads met. Under the light of a full moon she temporarily buried the blacksmith's nail at the crossroads, along with a sprig of parsley and a phial of her monthly blood.

Next, she stole the money from the family coffers and sent away for a fine new diary from a bookbinder overseas. It took weeks to arrive, but when it did it surpassed her expectations. The vermilion cover had the stink and texture of genuine leather. Its spade-shaped clasps were burnished bronze. The first time she opened its covers Berthe hearkened back to the open vault in the founders' graveyard, which summoned a mad grin to her face. Properly weathering the journal was a matter of spritzing the leather covers with rubbing alcohol, then scouring the book's surface with a bundle of copper wire. She then painstakingly stained each page with soggy tannin leaves and the heat of a beeswax taper.

By the time the tome was ready for her third precious task, a harvest moon was brightening Berthe's bedroom window. On the appointed night she ignited a fresh candle, slaked her fountain pen with ink, and switched her writing tool from her dextral hand.

She began to write.

As to the nature of the message, Berthe had only dim intuitions. She willed herself to remain aloof, to allow the words to flow solely from the cold, airy appendage that had closed over her own and now guided it. She recalled the rotted arm dangling from the shroud and wondered if this hand had now closed over hers in order to guide her.

Day was nearly breaking by the time this phantom limb slithered back from wherever it had come. By the last guttering flits of the candle's stump Berthe scanned the stained pages. Upon them a new pledge had been offered, which, through written by her hand, Berthe knew had come from the Master. She vowed to whisper these words into her pillow the following night, which would allow her to come to him.

The next night her mouth struggled with the bizarre charm, and in the end she shed her body like worn clothing and drifted into the night.

The experience of caroming from treetop to treetop, of having the bats sensing her skinless presence with their sonar and accepting her as one of their own, of passing nearer to the moon than she'd ever thought possible; all these sensations were, for Berthe, beyond description, beyond feeling.

At midnight she again met the Master. He was in the founders' cemetery. His afflicted eye gleamed and winked at Berthe like a shoreline fire guiding her inland. She went to him, dazzled by the playful way he had reconfigured the brittle headstones, presumably just for her. Each marker had been lifted from the soil and made to balance with unnatural grace in a new structure, one that seemed to change depending on Berthe's vantage of it. From one angle the headstones were arranged like a great marble rose that bloomed from a stem of dense shadow. Yet a mere step to the left transformed them into a cloister, the kind Berthe had seen in books about the great cathedrals overseas.

It was while the gravestones held this latter formation that the Master regaled Berthe with revelations about the Kingdom that sat beneath this world. His voice ran across Berthe's ears like silk.

It was all too much for her. It was not nearly enough. She swore to do whatever was required to experience the hidden world he described. The Master proceeded to instruct her in whisper.

The chain of empathy that bound the two of them together grew stronger.

III.

Berthe was awoken by a persistent jabbing against her back. She opened her eyes to find herself lying, dressed but dishevelled, in a horse stable.

"Why you restin' in my pappy's hay, Berthe-girl?" The voice had the squeak of male adolescence and the tarry drawl of the region. It was an unharmonious mix.

Snapping upright, Berthe saw a rail-thin silhouette standing on the opposite side of the stall. The young man held a pitchfork. Was this one of the gravehands come to watch over her, she wondered?

No, this was the Abban boy. She must have ended up on their property. Berthe struggled to sift memory from dream. Clearly, she had spirited back to her body sometime in the wee hours, but how had she ended up in the Abbans' barn? The Master had warned that until she grew accustomed to moving out of body, things could easily go awry. She must have drifted back to her bedroom after the Master's lesson at the founders' graves, then somehow slept-walk out of the house, across the meadows, to here.

Berthe pulled herself to a standing position and sputtered a blend of apologies and ill-conceived explanations. Rushing from the barn, she turned back to see the Abban boy pointing a stubby finger toward her.

"...ain't right," he hollered as Berthe ran. He was a simpleton whose thoughts moved like poured molasses. Nevertheless, Berthe was panicked.

IV.

Time passed, moving in its cyclical way, but a cycle so vast it can give one the impression of forward movement, of progression. Berthe grew older and her folks grew frailer and died in quick succession. She tended to them in their ailing days as best she could, but her thoughts were constantly elsewhere; on honing the skills the Master continued to teach her nightly, on learning to sustain her awareness for longer periods while disincarnated, on caring and keeping safe the blacksmith's nail (which she now kept inside a mangled wooden pulpit, which she'd rescued when the local chapel had been struck by lightning and burned to charred ruins), and finally on doing her utmost to avoid the Abban boy and his kin at all cost.

Her nocturnal lessons with the Master advanced. He taught her not only how to travel, but also the vital properties of certain rare and toxic plants, which, once she inherited the farmhouse outright, Berthe dutifully planted and tended in the root cellar. She built a tidy little box-garden and filled it with deadly flora. One of her greatest pleasures became to survey the oleander, the starry mountain laurels, the regal purple blooms of monkshood, the plump baneberries, the full trumpets of datura that seemed ready to burst into song, and of course the fine and sacred belladonna.

Though grown and tended in their own unique beds, each plant maintained a hidden connection with its bedfellows. Berthe somehow simply knew this to be so. Joined like threads in a spider's web, together these toxic blooms formed a veil, formed *the* veil that distinguished one plane of being from another. And when the time was apt, this veil might lift for her. But for now, discretion was key.

Since the day he'd discovered Berthe in the stables, the Abban boy had grown increasingly obsessed with her. In the beginning this addiction had taken the form of clumsy flirtations, but when Berthe refused his advances the Abban boy grew embittered, spiteful. Rumours of witchcraft soon after began to circulate through the village, which forced Berthe to become intensely cautious, even during her most innocuous comings and goings. She kept her implements (nail, diary, ruined pulpit) secreted in a storage hatch above her father's old desk, removing them only under cover of darkness.

Her life as a spinster only increased local speculation about her innermost nature and raised questions as to exactly *how* her folks had passed away. Fortunately for Berthe, her neighbours' loathing was weaker than their fear of witches. In fact, only the Abban boy ever showed resolve enough to stand at the edge of her field where, in better times, her family's cattle had grazed. He'd lean on the frail wooden fence and stare at the house. The few times she'd glimpsed him doing this, the simpleton was concentrating so fiercely it was is if he could see through the stone walls of the farmhouse, through the flesh and bone of Berthe's brow, into her psyche.

It was after just such a fierce visitation from the Abban

boy that Berthe (who'd been spying on him from behind the frayed and yellowing cloth of her bedroom drapes) saw him produce a penknife from the chest pocket of his overalls and scratch something into her fencepost before he finally went tearing off down the road.

When she'd gone out to investigate, she found that a symbol had been crudely gouged into the wood. It was the kind of sign Berthe had grown up seeing, usually above the barn doors of superstitious farmers. It was a sigil of exorcising, of purification. Berthe knew that it was only a question of time before the Abban boy managed to convince enough of the locals that it was she that needed to be purified, purged.

All the pieces were falling into place. It could be made no plainer that the time had come for her final departure. This world had nothing to left to offer her. One by one its pleasures had lost their vigor, and its trials lost their joy when conquered. For years now, all the things with which Berthe felt empathy seemed to radiate from another world, or at least from a hidden sector of this world that few people ever sensed.

The time had come to pass through the veil.

Deep down it bothered her knowing that the Master had extended this invitation to Berthe at the very beginning and that she'd naively resisted it. There had always been some promise or glimmer of potential that kept her clinging to worldly life: her relationship with her parents, her duties on the farm, and so on.

Convincing oneself of not needing human company in order to make isolation more tolerable was one thing, willingly writing oneself out of the Book of Life was another thing entirely. Now Berthe felt prepared for a full and final departure.

Hurrying away from the marked fencepost, Berthe worried whether she had the gumption to see this through. But by the time she entered the kitchen, she was prepared to do whatever needed to be done.

V.

At twilight she opened the hatch above her father's old rolltop desk and retrieved her implements.

She'd cleared a space for herself within the root cellar.

Discerning all the scribbled entries she'd made with her wrong hand was a chore, particularly in flickering candlelight, but she spoke the impossible words and executed the gestures the Master had taught her. Then, with gloved hands, she plucked her box garden barren and ground toxic petal, berry and bud into a rich dust. She removed her gloves to prick her index finger, and then fed just enough blood to transform the powder into a paste.

All around her Circle, the darkness thickened, as if a crowd was gathering to bear witness and their shadows were stretching across Berthe's sacred space.

Then it came time for her to perform the final tasks, the ones she'd witnessed being done by others when travelling astrally with the Master, but she herself could never bring herself to do. Until now.

With unsteady hands she unfastened and removed her nightdress. The cellar's dirt floor felt clammy against her flesh as she stretched out before the charred pulpit.

She could sense him now, standing in the blackness just beyond the candleflame's reach. He was watching her, possibly encouraging her, or assessing her true worth. Would she see this through?

Perhaps to spite the Master, Berthe felt for the pouch and tugged its drawstring. The blacksmith's nail felt cold and heavy when it landed on her belly. She warmed it by rubbing it between her thumb and forefinger, then took up the mortar and pestle. She smeared the tip of the nail with the poisonous unguent before forcing it between her legs. Wincing, tears streaming down the sides of her reclined head, Berthe plunged the nail into her cleft until its poisoned tip punctured her maidenhead. The unguent seeped into her bloodstream, swam through her circulatory system until it found her heart and loosened her soul from this nest. As this process unfurled, the darkness rimming her Circle was banished by a strange milky light. The Master was now elsewhere, if he had ever truly been in the cellar at all.

Pain and toxicity freed Berthe from her body. She revelled in the dizzying spin of her liberated shade. Frantic as a Saint-Vitus Dance, her fleshless self scaled plane after plane.

The agony of gradual poisoning spore Berthe into a new level of existence.

Her psyche left her body twitching down there in the filth and the shadows. She was free, expanding outward, in every which way. She was moving across the night-time meadows and farms. The leaves of the trees looked like ivory carvings that gleamed in the blackness. Everything appeared softer, more malleable. Berthe had no direction in her flight, she was simply drinking in this fresh liberation.

But no form of existence can be eternally without boundaries, and after a time Berthe began to feel her fleshless self being tugged, like a hooked fish. Had her chain of empathy really been yet another form of tether?

No...He was beckoning her. She followed, toward the only place the Master could meet her.

The founders' graveyard sat bathed in a scintillant sheen; a glow akin to freshly jostled coals. Drifting nearer to it now, Berthe could see fully (for her entire spirt was now soaked with sight) that the vault in the knoll once more sat open, but its interior held none of the hopeless darkness she'd seen on that fine spring afternoon so many years ago. Tonight, the vault was alight, a roaring furnace. Smoke billowed out of the angled entrance like a black river flowing skyward. The vault mouth seethed with flames of crimson and orange and blue.

Berthe then saw him. He was standing on what she first took to be a platform of black marble, but the closer she went it became plain that the Master was waiting for her at the head of a long black stairway of shimmering black stone. The stairs cut a zig-zag path down deep into the Earth, into the sunken kingdom where the Master held dominion.

And she was going to be with him completely, at long last.

The Master opened his arms to her. He was a silhouette against the backdrop of flame.

Berthe had nearly reached him, when a second figure leapt out onto the crossroads.

Confusion warbled Berthe's flight. She became momentarily disoriented.

It was the opportunity the Abban boy had been praying for. Screaming a quote from Scripture, he swung at the air. Something glinted in his fist. Too late, Berthe discovered that it was a nail, newly forged by the Abban boy's father.

Berthe, still a novice at travelling without her body, did not know how to resist him.

He drove the nail into the trunk of an ash tree that grew by the crossroads' edge. Berthe found herself pinioned. The airy feeling that had enveloped her was pressed out. She was now smothered, stifled. The Abban boy then carved his cherished symbol of protection into the bark of the ash.

In an instant, the subterranean fire was extinguished, the vault door was shut and sealed. The Master was gone.

VI.

Berthe remained outside of her body, outside of time, but trapped. The nail rusted and the Abban family died out. Still, Berthe remained.

Her voiceless beckoning to the Master proved useless. Yet she remained.

There was nothing else for Berthe to do but strive to somehow touch that rare loner who might wander this forlorn path. Most passersby would perceive her Call as nothing more than a chill running down their spine, a symptom of daring to visit a haunted place.

She must be patient. Eventually one would come, one who is as she herself had been; the kind of person sensitive enough to perceive the plea of things unseen. The kind of person who might have empathy enough to pull out the nail and free her, the kind who is willing to forge a new link in the chain.

Three Knocks on a Buried Door

Never love thy neighbour. Were anyone ever to ask him for sage advice (which, in his forty-eight years on Earth, had yet to occur), that would be the hard-won wisdom Kolkamitza would offer: never, under any circumstances, love thy neighbour.

He himself had done so, had in fact *deeply* loved the woman who'd rented the upper storey of the house whose ground floor apartment had been his home for years. Her name had been Erin and she'd been several years his junior. She'd had a thin nose and barrel thighs and hair that had smelled of bergamot. Kolkamitza had courted her for two months, coupled with her for one, and for these efforts found himself rewarded with the unexpected role of executor after an aneurism had snuffed out Erin's life.

Her death had been sudden, yet she'd had the uncanny forethought to write a will within a week of her demise, one that left everything to Kolkamitza. Erin's prescience in this matter confirmed his suspicion that she had been, and perhaps still was in some form, a witch. But witch or not, Kolkamitza found himself as the unbidden owner of two settees, a sewing machine, sixty-three novels, a wardrobe stuffed with pencil skirts and wide-brimmed hats, cotton lingerie, a horn comb, five distinct nail buffers (she did not wear cosmetics), and a

219

jackdaw named Rheims whose home was a standing bronze cage.

To hear Kolkamitza tell it, this burden was a calamity that would have broken Job, but in truth the ordeal cost him only a single weekend of his life. The various charities he'd approached were grateful for the donations, and all unwanted leavings were simply bagged and covertly tossed into the dumpsters of the nearby plaza.

Rheims, however, remained Kolkamitza's charge. He was an unobtrusive creature who rarely cawed and never stirred loudly enough to wake him. Also, the bird's diet of insects and grain did not appreciably dent Kolkamitza's budget. (And it truly was his budget; Erin had possessed no money to leave him.)

In the end, having been saddled with belongings and bird was scarcely a hardship. The *true* burden came in the form of an inexplicable compulsion, a behavioural tic that began to chew on Kolkamitza's psyche day and night, abating only if he succumbed to its command. This compulsion was, of all things, a need to knock on strange doors.

This had originally been *her* habit, yet he seemed to have inherited it as he had her material goods. Kolkamitza had discovered this quirk about Erin on their first date, when he'd found himself standing awkwardly beside Erin as they'd called on what he'd assumed to have been Erin's friends or relations, only to discover after they'd responded to her rapping that they were all perfect strangers to one another. The first time this occurred had been mortifying. Kolkamitza had stood on the porch of some random townhouse, his face smoldering with humiliation while his lover rushed through introductions, explanations, questions. Love had allowed him to be fooled into this same scene many times afterwards, to the point where it had become a kind of game for him; waiting to see how long it would take before the resident or residents would shut and bolt their alien door.

It surprised him how rarely this had occurred. More often the occupants would answer Erin's genial questions and offer a few of their own. Mutual acquaintances would sometimes be sussed out, or common interests. More than once the pair of them had been invited in for coffee, even asked to stay for dinner. Kolkamitza had found these meetings interminable. He did not possess Erin's charm, nor her fascination with other people.

Initially Kolkamitza had assumed that Erin had dragged him along for those encounters to illustrate some point about people being inherently kind, or fundamentally alike, or some such.

But as time wore on, Erin had begun leading him further and further from the beaten paths of the city, into areas that he found unsettling, even menacing. He'd finally asked Erin how she had ever come to develop such a queer habit and was told, somewhat brusquely, that as a girl she had been obsessed with Drawing the Sortes. "On my seventh birthday, I flipped the Book open to *Matthew 7:7*. You know, '*Knock, and it shall be opened unto you.*' I'm still searching for the proper door."

Their last two visits had truly tested Kolkamitza's mettle. Each adventure had occurred on a Friday evening and ultimately led to a weekend of bewilderment and fear.

The penultimate visit had been to a plank cabin that sat by the rim of a quarry known colloquially as the Bone Cauldron, where pale stones cupped a pool of noxious water. When Erin had led him onto the cabin's sagging porch and rapped upon the flimsy excuse for a door, Kolkamitza was convinced that the whole ordeal was some grotesque joke. He'd been loath to experience the punchline.

The abode had consisted of a lone room. The window was a cut-out square over which plastic sheeting hung by wafer tape. This sheet pulsed noisily, like an infected lung. His surroundings seemed septic. The upper corners of the room were marred by patches of mould.

Erin either did not notice these details or was unfazed by them. Their visit had been brief, ending once the ugly little man who dwelt in the cabin had begun slipping from pidgin English into some demi-language. It was akin to the glossolalia one hears from the faithful while in fervor, but it had apparently communicated to Erin whatever it was she'd been seeking beyond that door.

Their final visit had been to a half-built house on a development lot. Erin had wandered around to the rear of the structure, where an ominous iron door had blocked their way. She'd rapped on it three times, which had been enough to push the imposing barrier back from its jamb. Inside the house they'd found, amidst the must and melancholy, an incongruously cozy scene: a parlour table that had been set for two. A tea service of newly polished silver shone defiantly against the gloom. A pair of china cups had been set upon the tabletop, presumably just for them. The oolong they'd held had been fresh, steaming.

Erin had gone right to one of the waiting chairs and was about to partake of the tea when Kolkamitza smacked the cup from her fingers. It had chinked against the marble floor but did not shatter. Eventually he'd convinced Erin to leave. They'd argued for the rest of the journey home. Kolkamitza had pressed her to confess to setting up the tea party beforehand, but Erin had been vehement that she'd never so much as laid eyes on that house until the two of them had been swept there by fate.

When Kolkamitza had told her that he refused to ever again knock on unfamiliar doors, she'd scolded him, saying that all things had their protocol, and in matters such as this, those of the liminal, things must always be met out in threes. She'd felt that two had now been completed. The third and most important discovery was yet to come.

"We have one last call to make before the cycle is complete," she'd told him. In less than a week she was dead. But her habit of knocking on strange doors lived on in Kolkamitza, who now found himself helplessly impelled to rap on closets, refrigerators, gates, crypts, cars, warehouse loading docks, houseboats, cupboards, hutches. He had yet to receive a proper response to his summons.

※

Morning was all but over before Kolkamitza took leave of his bed. Though he'd slept long and deeply, he felt unrested. Perhaps the emotional strain of last night's quests for strange doors had taken a greater toll than he'd realized. Midnight had found him among the tenements. It was a dangerous area to be skulking around in, but his exhilaration outweighed the risk. He'd rapped on dozens of ugly doors, and, upon knocking, would hunch like a garden gnome, hiding, waiting for some indication that his calling had been upon the right house, that he would be given some piece that was missing from inside himself. Much to his dismay, this did not occur.

Kolkamitza shuffled to the window. His first glimpse of the backyard revealed a very fine-looking Saturday. Summer had come 'round at last. He opened every window in the house before putting the coffee on.

Rheims was audibly restless before Kolkamitza had even removed the cage's night coverlet. Standing before the gibbet-like contraption, watching the bird flutter and flit, he was again arrested by the familiar temptation, the compulsion.

He reached to unlatch the cage, stopped short, and then, in tribute to Erin, gave the tiny arched gate a trio of slow knocks.

Rheims instantly went still. His wings taut at his sides, the jackdaw fell forward, landing against the papered base of his cage with a padded thump.

Kolkamitza gazed emptily at his fallen companion. He exhaled dramatically and fixed himself a mug of coffee, giving the kitchen table a measured *tap-tap-tap* before allowing himself to sit and drink.

His thoughts were an incomprehensible slurry. He fretted over whether he'd remembered to feed and water Rheims, concluding that he had. The bird must have perished from a broken heart, a longing for its mistress. Kolkamitza decided that the least he could do was give the creature a proper burial. He gulped down the dregs in his mug and got dressed.

Outside, the heat was sheer. The simple act of fetching the shovel from the tool shed had Kolkamitza sweating. Rheims was now reposing in a plastic grocery bag, which Kolkamitza rather unceremoniously carried to a random spot in the centre of the yard. He set down the bird in its crinkling shroud and proceeded to dig. The chore was taxing and the pit he wound up forging was slight. Kolkamitza set the jackdaw's bagged remains inside the hole to better gauge the worth of the grave. He decided to bore out a few more shovelfuls to ensure that Rheims would be safe from scavenging animals.

The shovel struck something solid. The kickback was severe, driving Kolkamitza's lower teeth into his tongue.

Stunned, pained, overcome with directionless fury, Kolkamitza stomped and swore before regaining his composure. Peering into the grave, he immediately spotted the culprit: a band of iron was poking up from the soil. Flipping the shovel, Kolkamitza proceeded to scrape and jab around the band in the hope of jimmying it loose, but the obstruction wouldn't budge. As he cleared away more of the earth he discovered that the band was of considerable length; some twelve to fourteen inches of it were now exposed.

It was Mystery enough to keep him engrossed. After investing far more energy than he should have on this fool's errand, Kolkamitza had managed to unearth a square frame, roughly two-feet by two-feet. The outline stood out from the base of the pit in bas relief. He sat on the edge of the hole, his chin resting on the end of the shovel handle. He studied it. Was it a lockbox? Thoughts of funds or incriminating evidence excited him momentarily but very quickly made him realize just how empty his life had become of late. To waste an entire day in pursuit of such a childish fantasy?

Kolkamitza reassured himself by reasoning that no time spent in a state of electric confusion was ever wasted. Just the opposite in fact.

He began to scour the metal frame in search of a latch or lock. Like some mad resurrection man, he scuttled about the grave, muddy fingers crawling over his nearly-exhumed prize.

There was nothing to be found. Clay still covered the surface of the square. Kolkamitza tried to clear it away but it clung tenaciously. The face of the square felt markedly less firm than the metal frame itself. In fact, it felt almost hollow. He wanted so very much to see the object in its entirety, wanted so very much to know.

Something inside of him parted, made him two selves instead of one. This shift occurred with such subtlety that it did not fully register with Kolkamitza. He only came to know that this second, deeper self had been roused when he reached out to grab his shovel. On the conscious level Kolkamitza was going to attempt to jimmy the frame open with the shovel's edge, but unconsciously his hand was resisting this instruction. It was instead curling into a fist and moving calmly above the muddy square.

Like an impartial witness to the workings of his own body, Kolkamitza watched as his hand knocked once, and again, and yet again.

The square gave way like a trapdoor. It fell inwards, further into the earth. Kolkamitza could hear the soft clatter as the bagged corpse of Rheims and several clumps of soil rained down into the passage. There then came the measured creaks as the forsaken door gently swayed back and forth on its long-dormant hinges.

Time stalled as Kolkamitza stared into the shaft. Knees bent like an anchorite, head as empty as the sky, he gazed wordlessly, unsure of how to feel. In one sense, he found the whole ordeal impossible, absurd; a notion that was compounded by the fact that the world around him was pressing on in blissful ignorance of his discovery. Children hollered and cackled in various yards, squirrels chittered and pounced within the overgrown hedges. But despite being surrounded by mundanity, Kolkamitza nonetheless felt himself at the hem of a deeper world.

From one of the neighbouring houses a mother squawked for her son to return home. The sound of this made Kolkamitza feel weirdly vulnerable. He was stricken with a fear of discovery. The muscles in his legs were achingly resistant to his attempt at rising, but once he was upright, Kolkamitza frantically peeled the sweaty shirt from his torso and laid it carefully across the pit, weighting it with little mounds of dirt. The fabric scarcely covered the hole, but it was concealment enough to confuse any spying neighbours.

He went inside the house, which was dim and cool, and thus provided a small measure of comfort. In the kitchen, he drew himself a glass of water and sat down. He badly needed to collect himself.

Was it truly so grand a thing, unearthing a hatch in the yard? Should such a discovery stir up so much anxiety and confusion?

He drained the water tumbler and managed to slow his breathing. He concluded that his discovery was not at all worth fretting over, for the simple reason that he had not truly discovered anything. Not yet. He'd unsealed a gate of some kind. But as to its nature and to where it may lead, these were truths yet to be realized.

And yet there was no denying that he had knocked, and fate had answered. Could this be the crucial third door that Erin had been seeking until the night she died, the one that would complete the cycle?

From the junk drawer Kolkamitza retrieved his flashlight. He was relieved to find that its batteries still had power. He grabbed and donned a fresh shirt from the hamper and marched back to the yard. After ensuring that the neighbouring windows were free of onlookers, he stripped his makeshift cover from the hatch. Part of him was expecting it to have vanished in his absence, but it not only remained, the pit seemed to have grown blacker and, paradoxically, more alluring.

He shone the light down and it immediately illuminated something fine, something intricate. At first Kolkamitza thought it might have been some sort of abstract pattern in the earth, but after scanning the beam about he realized that it was a Persian rug, a rich tapestry of scarlets and whites and complex arabesques. Squatting at the edges of the rug were a battered sofa, a rocking chair, and several wooden stools, poorly stacked.

'A bomb shelter? A repository?'

Kolkamitza couldn't resist reaching down with his free hand. The air below was cold, like a submerged spring. He rotated his wrist, swirling the chilly air. He wanted more, so much more. Fantasies about what else there may be to discover down there percolated in his mind and were immediately replaced by manic theories as to how he should proceed. Should he dig further? Daylight was depleting. Should he expedite the process by renting a backhoe?

Ludicrous.

A thin memory then flashed in Kolkamitza's mind, an image that could provide the simplest, most direct means of progress. It was stored in a corner of the tool shed. He'd not thought about it since the week he'd moved in. Had he glimpsed it earlier today when he'd fetched the shovel to dig the jackdaw's grave?

Racing to the shed, Kolkamitza was overjoyed to confirm that he had.

The tree swing had been left behind by the family who'd occupied the upper storey prior to Erin. Kolkamitza had pulled the swing down the very day they'd vacated. It had been his vengeance for all the loud, shrill summer afternoons he'd had to endure when the parents had let their son loose in the yard.

The swing's rope was comprised of thickly braided polyester. Kolkamitza was confident that it would support his weight. He unknotted the two lengths from the swing's plank, then tied them to one another to create the longest possible cord. This he bound to the trunk of the apple tree that grew close to the door in the earth. There was not enough rope for him to secure it around his waist, but, provided the drop wasn't greater than what it appeared to be, he could scale down using the hand-over-hand method.

Hunched by the rim of the hole, rope-in-fist, Kolkamitza hesitated. His reluctance was almost mystical; an intuition that somehow this descent would forge a rift in his life. This was a waymark. But whether this journey would lead to worse or better things he dared not guess.

Triple-winding the rope around his wrist, he pulled the makeshift towline taut and began his incremental repel. The neighbourhood's indigenous noises became muted, while the nerve-wracking creak and groan of the rope grinding into the tree trunk was amplified. Kolkamitza willed himself to stay focused. He was now eye-level with the lawn. He could see swarms of ants frantic in their obscured labours amidst the blades.

Drawing in a breath like a diver about to plunge into the deeps, he allowed the subterranean cold to swallow him.

All told the drop was roughly eight feet. The proximity of the ground along with the ribbon of daylight shining through the trapdoor assuaged some of Kolkamitza's trepidation. He told himself he would simply try to discover what the hatch was, then he would climb back to the surface. He would even phone the landlord and explain the saga to him in full. After all, he'd simply been trying to bury a cherished pet, when suddenly...

His boot soles hit bottom, creating a cavernous thud, even with the padding of the Persian rug to soften the drop. He pulled the flashlight from the pocket of his cargo pants and swung it about.

The room was large; roughly fifty feet by his estimation. But how could such a structure be possible? At this size, at least a portion of this wooden longhouse must sit directly under his home. Granted, his house had no basement, so such a thing *was* feasible, if far-fetched.

Moving the light above about, Kolkamitza took in more of what looked to be some form of storage unit. Furniture and crates lined the wood-slat walls, along with hulking forms made amorphous by fabric coverings. The air was musty and cool. The structure itself was like the hull of a ship, with its trussed roof and network of bulky support beams.

A light burst into view at the far end of the room. Though he only glimpsed it peripherally, the appearance of the bright orb caused Kolkamitza to gasp. His heart swelled, his testicles climbed upward.

He could see it plainly now: there was the silhouette of a man standing at the opposite end of the room. The figure's shape cunningly refused to be caught in Kolkamitza's flashlight. Kolkamitza stumbled backward, his trembling hand feeling about for the rope's end. Never had his desire to see the sun been so dire.

He began to pull himself toward the light. He looked back, certain that the figure was now charging toward him. How long had the apparition been down here, he wondered, just waiting, waiting for someone to open that buried door and set him free?

When Kolkamitza noticed that the man also looked to be scaling a rope toward the same bright square of daylight, he squinted to better accustom his eyes to the dimness. The ornate frame of a large mirror slowly became apparent. Once Kolkamitza had assured himself that what he had seen was nothing more than his own murky double reflected in that standing glass he laughed weakly. He lowered himself back down.

Something crinkled under his foot. Kolkamitza respectfully picked up the plastic bag that held Rheims and set it down on the arm of the musty sofa before crossing the room. He gave the cunning mirror an admiring once-over and noted more bric-a-brac, much of which was rather expensive-looking: silver candlesticks, a roll-top desk, a grandfather clock. Perhaps his landlord was an eccentric hoarder who had created this storage unit to conceal his compulsion.

Contented that any further investigation into this matter could be done on higher ground, Kolkamitza prepared to depart.

That's when Fate dangled another temptation before him; this one in the form of a pull-down staircase. The steps were collapsed in on one another like a nested serpent waiting to uncoil. Beneath the stairs was yet another door.

Kolkamitza wedged his wrist between the folded steps and rapped three times upon the rectangular door, which dutifully opened. The wooden stairs fell noisily into form. The obscene clattering sent Kolkamitza cowering behind the grandfather clock for fear of discovery. But discovery by what?

For a tense eternity, the room remained still. Its only soundtrack was Kolkamitza's frantic heartbeat. The storage room was now illuminated by a new light source, one that emanated from the opened hatch in the floor. It lured Kolkamitza as though he were a moth.

What stretched beneath this crude room of wood beams and clutter was not some grubby sub-basement, but a grand corridor whose floor was lavished with high-pile carpet and whose walls were panelled in walnut. The light, Kolkamitza now plainly saw, was radiating from a chandelier. Two or three landscape paintings brightened the dark wooden walls and there was an alabaster column standing directly across from the pull-down staircase. Upon it rested a vase of fresh chrysanthemums. Kolkamitza could smell their perfume.

How far down could this place go? How far indeed, for the room in which he stood was no mere storage bunker, it was an attic. And he had just discovered an access to the main house.

He carefully lowered a foot onto the uppermost step. He tried to make his descent silent, but even the slightest pressure caused the wooden stairs to creak or pop.

Now in the great hallway and ravenous for validation of what he was seeing, Kolkamitza pressed his palm to the wall. It was firm and cool. His perspiration formed a perfect hand-print on the walnut panel. He watched it dissolve.

A few paces ahead, a landing was visible, along with the pillars that flanked a great staircase. The only thing that diverted his attention from this majestic sight was the presence of a half-open door at the end of the hall.

To reach this door, he had to cross the open landing, which he did on tiptoe. He felt like a child playing some forbidden game. The landing overlooked a foyer of marble. A collection of coats hung from a standing tree. The foyer was lit by a chandelier that was easily three times the size of the one in the hall. The great staircase that connected these lavish storeys was spiral in design and was carpeted in what looked like animal pelts.

Kolkamitza turned his attention back to the door and peeked through its frame. The room it opened unto hosted a canopied bed, an armchair, and two dressers. There was also an uncovered picture window. Reassured by the stillness inside, he entered the room and shone his flashlight against the window glass.

"Do you come bearing my supper?"

The voice lurched out from the far end of the room, where a luxurious armchair was stationed before the window. The window frame was white, which made it luminous as fresh bones against its view of compact soil.

"I'm...I..." sputtered Kolkamitza.

How had he not noticed that there was someone in here with him? The figure was so plain to him now; seated in the armchair, its body dressed in a sloppy heap of silks. Kolkamitza squinted to discern the face but to no avail. He was about to fix his light upon it but was somehow unable. It was not fear that prevented him, but a queer sense of propriety. He simply knew that such an action was not appropriate, not in this house.

The figure in the chair turned its head and now appeared to be staring intently at the window. Kolkamitza followed this example. What he witnessed was a chthonic constellation; a firmament not of stars but of wriggling worms and thickly crooked tree roots and pale weeds as fine as nerves.

"I already told them that I do not care for what they're serving today. They sent me here. I've been informed that I enjoy the view." The figure's voice was awful; a wet, lurching sound, like porridge bubbling in a pot. Kolkamitza turned again to scrutinize the speaker. Its head, now in profile, remained frustratingly obscured. Was it wearing a stocking over its head in the manner of a thief? No, there was no mask. But something *was* insinuating itself between the figure's face and Kolkamitza's gaze, something hazy, a fine mist that was the colour of ground thyme. "Would you be good enough to inquire about my meal? There's little else I'm able to do for them here."

"Yes," Kolkamitza managed, bewildered, "yes, I will."

Creeping his way out of the room, Kolkamitza steeled himself for the figure in the chair to rise, perhaps even attack him. But the shape did not so much as flinch. Its attention was lost in the view of the land upon which Kolkamitza's house, and the civilized world, stood. Kolkamitza's eyes were drawn back to the large windows, where a plump grub was squirming flat against the pane, its white form flexing into a crescent-shape; a new moon rising in this buried nightscape.

Scared and speechless, Kolkamitza shuffled to the spiral staircase and made his way to what might be the main floor. The staircase bannister was smooth, as though well-worn by many hands. The foyer was colossal, gorgeous. This was a mansion. More than a mansion; a palace. He staggered about the cavernous room. How large was this place? He must be beneath one of his neighbour's houses at this point, perhaps beneath another street altogether. He wondered just how many regal structures like this one had been reposing beneath his feet without his knowledge.

There came the glassy sound of laughter from somewhere nearby.

Kolkamitza turned and, apropos for this journey, found himself facing a door. Its face was engraved with a bewildering pattern. The smell of wood-stain was heady. He eavesdropped as best he could to the conversations that rumbled beyond the door. Then he knocked three times.

The muted chatter dissipated. For several moments there were no sounds at all.

Kolkamitza strained to listen but his ears found only silence. Until a voice rang out, one bidding him to enter.

Jutting a finger toward the door's brass push-plate, Kolkamitza found that the most sheepish of touches was enough to push the swinging door back from the frame.

He found himself facing a dinner party, one so opulent and cliché in demeanour that Kolkamitza wondered if it was a parody.

"One of our guests lately declined their invitation," said someone with a reedy, almost musical voice. "You may occupy their setting."

Kolkamitza raised his hand. The finger he'd used to inadvertently open the dining hall door was still extended. One of the diners must have assumed he was pointing toward the ceiling.

"Yes, that's the one," said another guest. "Tucked away upstairs, the deluded creature."

"Sit," invited a third. "We'll be dining soon."

The feast hall was decorated in blue-and-black wallpaper and ivory mouldings. The floor was oiled wood that shone like a millpond beneath the various candles that guttered in their silver holders. The table was long, of a size one might see in a cafeteria, only much finer, much more lavishly set. There were china plates and silverware polished to a sparkling degree. The guests were all dressed regally. Kolkamitza wished to study them more closely but did not want to appear gauche. He opened his mouth to say something but found himself temporarily mute.

His bewilderment was so great that Kolkamitza did not even register that someone was approaching him from behind, even though they were pushing a serving trolley whose wheels were audibly parched for grease.

The figure stepped out from behind this cart and struck the small gong that hung by the dining hall entrance. The reverberations echoed through the great corridor and although the sound startled Kolkamitza, he did not flinch.

"This way," the servant said. A gloved hand was now at Kolkamitza's back and was pushing him into the room. This gesture was more seductive than forceful. The very idea of resisting somehow eluded Kolkamitza as he carefully squeezed himself between the rows of throne-like chairs and the gorgeously tall china hutches that lined the walls. These cabinets looked to be of the same walnut that panelled the upper hallway. Kolkamitza counted seven of them.

The vacancy was at the head of the great table. Kolkamitza was expecting the chair to be more comfortable than it was. It felt like cold concrete beneath him. One of the hutches loomed behind his seat, limiting his movements. The plate before him was chipped and the flatware was mismatched. His napkin was of purple silk. A quick inventory of the other settings revealed that each guest had a different coloured napkin. Kolkamitza dearly hoped this did not mean there would be party games.

The squeaking cart was wheeled into the room. A large silver cloche sat atop it. When the servant gripped the server lid handle, everyone reached for their napkin. Kolkamitza followed suit, but where he draped his across his lap, the others raised theirs to their faces. In perfect unison, all the guests blindfolded themselves. They then turned their masked eyes toward Kolkamitza. They resembled two rows of the condemned awaiting the firing squad.

The server—or was he the host? —lifted the cloche.

Kolkamitza spied a nest of pulsating lights. They were smallish and bunched together like luminous grapes. They were of a colour he could not identify. They flexed and twitched like beached fish.

There came the sound of creaking wood. Kolkamitza tried to rise but was forcefully seized by someone from behind. Had the creak been that of a hutch opening? Before he could even resist, his assailant had snatched the blindfold from the floor where it had fallen and swiftly bound it across his eyes.

"Still…" a voice whispered in his ear. He almost recognized it.

The dining hall was now awash in rattling, scrapes, shuffling.

Someone announced, "This will do. I found it in the Uppers. His, no doubt."

Hands were now pressing Kolkamitza firmly into that unforgiving chair. He then felt the pressure of the nylon rope he'd used to repel himself down here. It was now being used to lash his arms and his ankles to his seat.

"Be still…" repeated the voice at his ear. The speaker now wrapped their arm across his chest, their hand positioned above his heart. *"They're serving Fool's Fire...Eat..."*

He could feel something cold had been brought to his mouth. His lips were chilled by what felt like frost. Kolkamitza wanted to refuse but his jaw autonomously fell open. A fork was wrested between his teeth.

The delicacy on his tongue crackled, began to dissolve like candyfloss. It tasted like some bitter root.

With the offering now fully ingested, the crowd began to chitter and whisper amongst themselves. Kolkamitza asked what was happening. He heard a moan that was explicitly carnal, followed by footsteps clattering across that great marble foyer. These clacks grew fainter, more distant, soon becoming the slight groans of the ceiling above.

They were upstairs now, moving away, moving perhaps to the attic with its open hatch that led to the living world above.

Eventually there were no sounds at all.

"Hello?" croaked Kolkamitza. His voice bounced through the vacated hall like a stone skipping across still waters.

The hand was still at his chest. *"Shhhh..."* the voice purred, *"listen..."*

Kolkamitza strained. A new noise, one fluttery and crisp, flooded the dining hall. He then heard the familiar cawing of a jackdaw.

"Rheims?" he called in a broken voice.

"Thank you, darling..."

At last the hand was lifted from his chest. Kolkamitza could only listen to the telltale sounds of the woman crossing the foyer, scaling the spiral staircase, fading across the upper corridor with its fine walnut panelling.

All around him, the air was thinning, growing more and more scarce. Every heartbeat caused a flaring pain in his chest.

"Wait..." he muttered, but too late. His heart felt taut, like a fist within his chest. It began to slow. Wilting, resigned,

Kolkamitza counted off his heart's final beats, which were three in number.

Ten of Swords: Ruin

T he days had been thick with summer; with blades of sun and stifling heat and swarms of noisy, thirsty insects.

The eldest sister awoke first and was delighted to discover that this morning was the sort she and Celeste both held precious; a day when the sun stumbles a bit in its swagger, when it falls behind a drape of tin-grey clouds. A day when the swelter is pierced, when the trance of surf and shade and cicadas rattling in the greenery is threatened by the reminder that autumn is never far behind, that all things do pass.

This autumnal omen poured itself between the trees and columns of the great house like cold treacle. It might last only a handful of hours and may well be ignored by those who cannot grasp its meaning, its visions of harvests reaped and nights distending.

The sisters would not ignore this omen, they would welcome it. They had in fact been anticipating it, quietly hoping for that little oasis of breezes that would raise hackles instead of stirring dust. They'd been yearning for fog and billowing drapes and the muted lull that piles upon the world entire.

Desdemona stirred in her bed and knew intuitively that this was to be a day of secret things; of creeping about the great house on cat's paws and listening with bated breath and turning locks and pressing open long-shut doors.

Rain had been falling lazily for hours by the time Desdemona finally opened her eyes and stretched out the atrophy of youthful summers. She sat up and listened to the pattering upon the roof of their turret room. She was facing the mirrored backing of her dresser that stood against the far wall, but the morning's gloom prevented her from seeing her reflection. Nevertheless, Desdemona somehow sensed that she appeared unwholesome.

She turned down the sheets, moved to the curtains and peeked into the outer world. The lake that hemmed their property was brown and churning. The waves slapped down foamy against the great stones along the shore.

"Celeste, wake up," she said *sotto voce*, giving her sister's sleeping form a shake as she crossed the room.

Down the hall, the door to the parents' room sat open. Desdemona could see that their great bed had been crisply made and that Father's bag of things was no longer reposing on the circular table.

"Mother?" she called into the corridor, meekly, for she did not truly wish to be heard. When the only response she received was the rain's ongoing pattering Desdemona leaned back into the room. "It looks like they're gone again."

"Who's gone?" asked Celeste. Her mousy hair was splayed across the pillows like a great tangled net that had ensnared her slight face. She rubbed her eyes with the heels of her hands and yawned.

"Mother and Father. They've left. But don't be too sad. There's some good news, too. Listen. Do you hear the rain?"

The noise then became an agent for Celeste, who charged with the unbridled enthusiasm of Christmas morning. She bounded from the bed and hurriedly began to dress.

Desdemona did the same, but more discreetly. She slipped behind the Japanese shoji that Mother had given her for their thirteenth year together. It is well known that the most beautiful things need not come at a great cost, but lesser realised is that true beauty is something an object is not immediately born with, but is instead a quality that accretes after that object has travelled across great spans of miles, or of time, or both.

Besides this beautiful privacy screen of charred wood and moon-pale rice paper, Mother had presented her with other gifts as well: bottles, a palm-sized diary with a thin charcoal pencil, a rabbit's foot on a silver chain, a scroll that was revealed to be a sepia-toned chart detailing the lunar phases.

Worrying into a plain dress, Desdemona forced a brush through her hair and stepped out from behind the divider.

"You should do the same," she said, extending the brush to Celeste. "You look like Mr. Rochester's first wife."

Celeste huffed but complied. She scraped the brush across the mass of tangles, wincing with each pass. "Where should we start?"

"Start what?"

"Start looking. What else?"

Desdemona stared out again at the great yard, at the maelstrom of the lake. Something queer and greasy suddenly began to stir in the pit of her stomach. It was a very unpleasant sensation; not one of sickness, but of something foreboding, as though an invisible wall was trying to insinuate itself between her and something in her future. The sensation lasted merely a moment before fading.

"We need to eat first," said Desdemona.

"Why?" Celeste's voice curled with a disappointed whine.

A burst of lightning brightened the room with painful suddenness. The thunder that followed it was sonorous and seemed to shake the very foundation of the house.

"Because we are responsible women," Desdemona replied.

✖

Despite Celeste's request for a breakfast of mere butter and honey, Desdemona insisted that they eat the food Mother had left for them: hardboiled eggs and wedges of cheese and bowls of berries with cream. Their meal had been set upon the table in the great dining hall.

They ate at the long slab table, each sister positioned at one end.

"This is the head of the table, you know," Celeste proudly explained. "That makes me the leader, since Father isn't here."

"Father's not the leader. And don't put your elbows on the table."

"Who is then? Mother?"

Desdemona shrugged. "Maybe there isn't a leader."

For a spell they fed wordlessly, until Celeste finally confessed that she did not like the quiet.

"It reminds me of Mother's suppers."

"It's not one of those." Desdemona said firmly. She cleared her throat and changed both the tone and the subject of discussion. "So, what shall we look for today?"

Celeste thought hard on the question. "I want to explore Mother's things."

"No. That's not a good idea."

"Why not? Are you scared to?"

"Yes."

The frankness of Desdemona's answer caught Celeste off guard.

"But it's not like we'd get caught. Mother will probably be away for a while. Besides, even if she did catch us, we could just say it was your idea. She'd forgive you. You're her favourite."

"I'm not her favourite."

"She named you after someone she loved and lost. And Mother's told me that she and Father had expected you, that they'd tried really hard to get you here. I was an accident."

"Don't twist Mother's words," commanded Desdemona.

"She said you were a surprise. She never called you an accident. And why?"

Celeste's reply was low and mutilated.

"Why?" Desdemona repeated.

"Because there are no accidents." Celeste delivered this statement with a roll of her eyes, this rule of the house which Mother had drummed into them over the years. When she saw her sister rise and begin collecting the dishes, Celeste asked, "So can we?"

"Can we what?"

"Go through Mother's things!"

"No."

"But I had a feeling that we're supposed to," added Celeste.

"For real you had a feeling?"

Celeste nodded emphatically. Desdemona sighed.

"I won't wreck anything, I promise. And if we get caught I'll tell Mother you didn't know about it. Okay?"

"We can *look*, but that's all."

Celeste jumped from her chair.

At Desdemona's insistence, their pace slowed as they crossed the foyer and began their ascent of the staircase, which was spiralled like a vast fossil. Although they moved gingerly upon each step, the fine old wood groaned with their every movement. The daylight that illuminated the foyer through the high turret windows was dull and murky, touching the room with the atmosphere of late evening rather than morning.

They moved across the stair-head like stage play thieves; tiptoeing, their backs stooped.

Mother and Father's room seemed uncharacteristically small and musty. The tall windows were veiled in ivory sheers. The great house was old and draughty, Desdemona knew. But this knowledge hardly lessened the unnerving sight of the sheers billowing out from the panes like sheeted ghosts. Celeste seemed to take no notice of this effect. She was already at Mother's dresser.

The top drawer wobbled and squeaked as Celeste struggled to wrest it open. Fearing that it might slide out and injure her younger sister (or worse still, damage Mother's property), Desdemona assisted.

Items of silk and lace frothed up like sea-foam from the opened drawer, the sight of which immediately caused Desdemona to regret permitting this peculiar safari. But Celeste appeared unfazed. She plunged her smallish hands into the bundle and began to fish.

"What are you looking for?" Desdemona whispered.

"Why are you whispering?" cried Celeste before letting out a giggle.

"Just hurry please." Her anxieties had a basis. She had enjoyed similar explorations when she was an only child. In Father's drawers she'd discovered a brittle manila envelope filled with etchings...etchings that had jabbed hooks into her mind and had yet to release her; depictions of people conjoined in ways that made them resemble mongrels, things found only in the strangest fables. Desdemona prayed that her sister would be spared such an ordeal.

"Found it!" Celeste said triumphantly. Her hand emerged clutching a small crushed velvet pouch the colour of ground turmeric. Immediately she began to tug at the drawstring.

Desdemona clamped her hand over Celeste's. "That wasn't our agreement. I said you could *look*."

"But this is important! My feeling, remember? It was for all of us."

"What do you mean?"

"I mean we need to do some things 'cos we're all in this; you, Mother, Father...others."

Desdemona released her grip. "Which others?"

Celeste puckered her lips, which were conch-shell pink.

When no reply came Desdemona asked a second question: "What things do we need to do?"

244

"Wait. First!" Celeste moved to the great four-poster bed and began to shake the pouch violently. A shower of cards splayed across the bed. Desdemona stepped forward and looked upon the array of cards that covered the crisp duvet like vivid scales. Most of the cards were face down, showing only the uniform backing of a Flemish cross and lotus flowers. Some, however, had landed face up, creating a tapestry of celestial bodies, castle keeps, long-faced hermits, Queens, shadow beetles, coins, goblets of radiant wine.

"The one I need should be over...here," Celeste explained, passing her hand above one particular patch of the bed. In figure eights she moved her arm, until it suddenly halted as though something unseen had grabbed her thin wrist. Celeste slapped the back of one of the cards and turned it over. "That's it!"

The card's face depicted a figure (whether male or female, Desdemona could not tell) lying face-down on a bed of pale earth. A maroon cloak draped the figure's hips. Its head was turned to face a crepuscular sky. A battery of swords pinioned the body to the ground, having been plunged (wielded by whose hands, Desdemona did not wish to know) through limbs and trunk. Bright flags flapped from the handles of each sword, a different colour for each sword. The border of the card resembled brushed copper. The Latin words *Decem Gladiorum. Ruina* appeared in a thick black typeface.

Celeste snatched up the card and charged for the door.

"Wait! Where are you going with that?" cried Desdemona. She ran after her sister, but youth and determination allowed her to move with unnatural haste. "Celeste!" Her voice echoed through the empty foyer. Desdemona could see that the heavy double-doors of the house's main entrance had been pulled open. She bounded down the final curve of the staircase.

The gap between the doors was too slight for her to pass through. As she pressed the doors further apart Desdemona marvelled at her sister's strength.

Without, the morning was sodden and cool. The rain had already dwindled to a faint mist that swirled anywhere and everywhere. Desdemona's dress grew heavy and cold as fresh laundry. She called Celeste's name. Moving 'round to the rear of the house, Desdemona scanned the property in search of her sister. The sight of the empty pool caused her heart to plummet. Visions of Celeste charging blindly into the yard, her attention fixated solely on Mother's card in her hand, caused Desdemona to shudder. How easily she could have stumbled over the edge and landed headfirst in the concrete pit.

Her steps were sluggish with apprehension. She moved across the wet flagstones and, breath held, peeked over the rim of the pool.

The base of the pit was empty, but for shallow puddles of rainwater the colour of brandy, and mounds of last autumn's foliage.

A leftward glance proved the tennis court to be vacant. Had Celeste gone down to the lake? Desdemona called her sister's name again as she ran to the shore. It was all so dramatic, she thought; the roiling surf, her frantic cries, her flight from the great mansion on the hill...

Celeste was not among the stones and tide, which left only one place where she could be, the last place, the most obvious of places; her favourite.

Desdemona began the march to the family vault. It stood on the far side of the great gardens, in a shaded glen at the very edge of their property. Not once had she ever seen the vault free of shadows, and because of this, the atmosphere that surrounded the vault was perennially cool. The groundskeepers were lax in clearing away the leaves and branches and debris, which made the area littered, even somewhat dank. Desdemona felt that if the world entire had a cellar, its entrance would be that of her family's vault.

Celeste was there, hunched over a small patch of dirt at

the foot of the vault's steps. She was labouring intently over… something, all within the shadow and under the faceless gaze of a caryatid, who studied the child through a veil of rippled stone. Desdemona never had discovered who this sombre carved woman had been designed to commemorate.

"What are you doing?" asked Desdemona.

"This is how I'm supposed to do it," Celeste replied. "Bury it here, right beside the steps, under the Queen." She was using a sterling silver soup ladle as her shovel, dragging up scoopfuls of mud, forging a pocket.

"Is this the Queen?" Desdemona pointed to the caryatid.

"Of course."

"Has Father told you the story of the White Queen or is that also something you learned from your feeling?"

Celeste shrugged. "I never heard that story," she said.

Desdemona spent the next few moments watching her sister labour. The sound of the surf was at her back, a susurrus of distant voices.

"Where is it?" she asked when Celeste appeared to have completed her task.

The child produced 'Ruin' with her left hand.

"Wait!" Desdemona cried when she saw her sister lowering the card into the ground. "You can't actually bury it! Mother will find out."

"It's okay, really. She'd want this."

Desdemona sighed resignedly, and knelt beside her sister. The shadow of the Queen was a concentrated version of the rest of the world. Down here was eclipse-dark and cistern-cool. Desdemona reached out and helped her sister place the card in the pit. To not have a hand in the proceedings would have felt strangely improper.

"It has to be buried upside down," Celeste explained as she ladled on the first clumps of earth. When it was over she patted the fresh mound and asked her sister if they should say a prayer.

"I don't know any prayers," said Desdemona. Her sister's disappointment was clear. "We should get back to the house. We left an open door."

Celeste gathered the ladle and Desdemona gathered her and together they retreated to the great house. An uneasy feeling flourished when a queer, misplaced gust of wind passed over the sere land, bringing with it powerful, inexplicable scents: jasmine and sage, tar and the leaves of poorly-stored books. Like the persistent misting rains, this wind seemed to press in on them from every direction.

As they crossed the great yard, Desdemona noticed that the lake had now assumed the abyssal blue of winter midnights and that its surface shivered with countless tiny waves.

✳

Their retreat to the great house and the re-securing of the main doors brought Desdemona no relief. Though it was only a shade past midday she was already drained, yet there was still much to do: the foyer's marble floor required mopping to clear away the rain that had invaded through the open door, Mother's cards had to be replaced and all traces of their robbery erased, and then there was the matter of the remainder of the day and what to do with Celeste.

By the time these tasks were completed Celeste was complaining of hunger. Desdemona found them a platter of Mother's ham, along with two cups of cold tea. They had been laid upon a mahogany dining cart, which Celeste then insisted be wheeled into the dining hall. The cart's sides were carven with Old World images of the harvest: men slashing wheat with immense sickles, bent women shuffling down the crooked steps of a fruit cellar, bonfires, frothing cups of wine.

"Why did you draw the curtains?" Desdemona asked before serving the bounty.

"I want to pretend it's night-time. Look how dark it is!"

"Yes, I see how dark it is. I can barely see you sitting there, so let's open the drapes again, shall we?"

"Let's light the candles instead!"

Desdemona sighed.

"Please. *Please…*" Celeste's tiny hands were clasped like those of the devout.

"Just for a few minutes."

"I'll go get the matches!" cried Celeste.

"No, you will not. I will get the matches and I will light these candles. *You* will eat your lunch."

"You sound exactly like Mother."

Desdemona found her sister's observation oddly insulting. She slipped into the scullery and collected the matches and lighted the finger-thin tapers, and sat down and ate. Their meal nowhere near equalled the fullness of the harvest carvings on the serving cart, whose figures had now become faintly animated in the guttering candlelight.

Now sated, they spent a few silent moments watching the tapers spit hot wax onto the tablecloth. Desdemona set her empty teacup down onto its saucer. "We shouldn't have buried it. We had no right," she uttered. Her words lacked the full wind of conviction and thus travelled jerkily at half-sail.

"We did it, so that must mean we have the right."

"That's a very childish way of looking at things."

Celeste threw up her hands breezily. "The only things you shouldn't do are the things you can't do."

"It's that simple, is it?"

"I don't know. Maybe, maybe not. Is there any cake?"

Desdemona nodded. "It just so happens that Mother left a bit of slab cake in the parlour."

Celeste moved from her chair, from the dining hall. In her absence the room grew strangely brighter and far warmer. Desdemona looked sourly at the bands of golden light that brightened the edges of the heavy drapes. The dining hall had become a great oven, airtight and stifling. Today's drizzly respite was now being overcome. It was turning into the kind of day she detested; breathless and gnawingly still. Days like this enabled her to see the dust on the windowsill, hear the thick tongue-cluck of the grandfather clock on the landing. Days like this were awful because they squeezed her through the tedium of a day in the life of a young woman with no purpose.

"Aw, it's not working anymore," Celeste said mopily from the doorway.

Desdemona flinched. "You startled me," she confessed.

Celeste made a "tsk" noise with her tongue and said, "It doesn't look like night in here anymore. It's all bright and hot."

"The sun's back out," Desdemona said. She was looking at her sister, who stood in the archway of the dining hall, a small plate from Mother's tea set balanced on her chubby palms. A wedge of slab cake sat ringed in crumbs. Desdemona then noticed the manner in which Celeste's expression began to change. She had drawn her lips back and her cheeks blushed. It was the kind of face she'd seen the child make when she'd been embarrassed or been caught being mischievous.

"What?" Desdemona asked. Receiving no response, she turned back in her seat and followed her sister's gaze, to the heavy draperies that were now haloed in burning light. What she saw there stirred in her feelings that were far removed from Celeste's puckish amusement; hers were feelings of raw terror.

Staring out from the gap between the curtains was a lone eye, bulbous and milky with lifelessness and hanging too low on the withered cheek of the face. There may have been a hint of a nose, perhaps even hair, but little else to see. The mouth hung open like a cavern. Brilliant light shone through the flaking lips. Was this merely a mask hung upon the window frame? How else could the sun seem to radiating from inside the head itself?

But masks do not speak. What filled Desdemona's mind was a voice, as raspy as raked gravel, its tone overwhelmingly mournful. There were words, but only in the broadest sense; grunts of a nascent language, too new to fathom or too ancient to recall.

It came and it went.

For Celeste the apparition was a delicious thing, a miraculous thing, and its vanishing restored the room's heat and brightness.

For Desdemona the vision was an ordeal, one that ceased not with the return of the light but with a flood of darkness. She did not even feel her body sliding limp from the dining chair.

✖

Celeste roused Desdemona by using far too much water that was far too cold. Desdemona sat up on the dining hall floor, sputtering, coughing. She pushed the dripping hair from her face.

"I did it! I brought you back from beyond!"

"I only fainted, you fool," Desdemona gasped.

"Are you okay?"

"I...I think so. I'll be fine, just help me up."

Celeste did what she could to help her sister to the sitting room, where she stretched out on the plush settee.

"Can you unlace my boots?" she asked. "I didn't realise how muddy they are. I don't want to stain the furniture." After Celeste knotted the laces rather than loosen them, Desdemona simply wrenched the boots from her feet. She laid down until her senses felt relatively restored. "Celeste...what do you think that was?"

"What?"

"The face in the curtains."

When the only reply was silence, Desdemona propped

herself up on one elbow and gave her sister an interrogating gaze. The child was grinning, her delight verging on giddiness.

"You're not going to play this off as a joke, are you?"

"Well…not *exactly*," she returned.

"Then what *exactly* was it?"

Celeste shrugged her shoulders. "I dunno."

Desdemona sat up fully. "Celeste, you saw something. I know you did. It was written all over your face."

"I didn't *see* anything."

She reached out and gripped her sister's bicep, much too firmly. Celeste winced. "Are you responsible for this? Was this some kind of trick?"

"I didn't *do it*," cried Celeste, wrenching her arm free as she spoke. "And I didn't *see* anything either!"

"Then why were you grinning like a fool when you came back into the dining hall? Why were you staring at the window that way?"

"Because something told me to."

"Something told you to."

"Yes."

"When you say 'something,' do you mean one of your feelings?"

"Not really. It was a voice, a sad voice."

Desdemona reached for her sister, gently this time, but no less urgently. "I heard a voice too, but I couldn't understand what it said. Did you?"

"Of course I could, silly."

"What did it say?"

"It said for me to stop and listen and not be sad, because it couldn't come to me just yet, but that it would be with me again soon, as soon as it was brought all the way back."

The vertigo was rising once again. Desdemona had to shut her eyes and wait for the world to get back on its axis. She inhaled deeply and then asked, "Celeste, why did you look so happy then? Describe the voice to me."

"It just sounded funny."

"The voice sounded funny? Explain."

"Just funny, that's all. Like it was talking underwater. Can I have the rest of my cake now?"

"Hmm? Yes, fine. But not in the dining hall! Eat it in the kitchen, please. And when you're done I'd like you to amuse yourself for a while. I have some things of my own to do."

"What things?" asked Celeste.

"Personal things," she said.

The things to which Desdemona was referring were primarily sneaking back to the vault and digging up Mother's card, but the fainting spell had taken far more out of her than she'd first realised and Desdemona instead spent the remainder of the afternoon drifting in and out of sleep.

Celeste, thankfully, remained within earshot and amused herself with various games and songs. At one point she even joined her older sister in the sitting room where she proceeded to play solitaire. Desdemona was grateful that Celeste was able to keep herself occupied but the sight of her carefully laying out cards unnerved her just the same.

She was about to ask Celeste to check the grandfather clock on the stair-head to confirm the time when the sound from somewhere beyond the rear of the house became apparent to them both. At first, a gentle purling noise, but gradually swelling to a rumbling.

Celeste leapt to her feet. Familiarity led both sisters to conclude that this was the sound of a boat's motor.

Mother and Father had returned.

For the second time that day, Celeste went bounding through the large doors of the great house. Again, she managed to push back the great cedar barriers. She ran like a hare to where the water greeted the stones.

The motorboat was still far enough from shore that its passengers were little more than specks. By now Desdemona had followed her sister down to the stout dock where the motorboat stayed moored. Celeste was already at the end of the dock, down on her hands and knees. She was spreading crisp the length of white linen. A large wooden bowl was lying topside down near her blackened feet.

"Where's the water?" Celeste cried once she saw that Desdemona was arriving empty-handed. She huffed and, rising, said, "I'll do it. I have to do everything."

"No, I'll do it," said Desdemona, collecting the wooden bowl from the dock. "You stay here and watch for the boat."

Celeste was practically bouncing. "They're almost here!"

Desdemona turned and made her way up the hill and to the right, where the water well sat rotting among the weeds. Its shingled steeple covering hung crooked, held in place only by a lone tenacious nail. The rope that held the bucket was frazzled and dirty and thin. The less said of the state of the water bucket the better.

These blemishes notwithstanding, Desdemona maintained the actions as they'd been taught to her by Mother and Father. She took up the rope and dragged the bucket from its bed of greenery. She flung it down into the pit and waited for the plash. When it came Desdemona felt her shoulders slouch, for now she had to operate the horrible crank. Carefully she gripped the splintery handle and began to draw up the bucket. This evening's yield was meagre, which in one sense was a blessing, for it meant less strain on the ancient crank, but also ominous; a sign that the ancient well may finally be running dry.

She pulled the swinging bucket from the spool and poured out the water into the waiting bowl before returning the bucket to its nest among the plants Father had cultivated with great care.

Experience allowed her to carry the brimming bowl back to the dock without spilling a drop. The well water now in place upon the white linen, Desdemona joined her sister in watching the approaching boat.

It was now close enough for the sisters to see them; Mother and Father, she seated regally at the motorboat's bow, he usefully stationed before the boat's motor, manning the steering rod, guiding them toward shore. Desdemona saw the evening sun sparkle off Father's horn-rimmed glasses. He appeared to be wearing one of his oversized sweaters, or something equally out of season for June. Mother wore a dress of the same cut as hers, but Mother's was of a more luxuriant colour.

When the boat's motor was switched off, Desdemona knelt down upon the white linen, alongside Celeste, who was already in position.

It was obvious that Father had spotted them, for his face beamed with delight. He waved excitedly before taking up an oar to paddle them into the slip. Mother's hands remained folded upon her lap. She sat as still as a masthead until Father had moored the boat, stepped onto the stout dock, and offered her assistance.

Mother rose, then bent to retrieve a large wicker basket from the bottom of the boat. Clutching its handle with one hand, she took Father's with the other and stepped carefully onto the dock. The daughters remained stoic, Desdemona more so than Celeste, who was trembling. Little peeps of excitement slipped through her lips. Desdemona elbowed her for fear that Mother would hear. Father clearly heard but did not care. In fact, his face beamed with pride. He winked at the younger daughter, then quickly pressed a finger to his lips to save face.

The daughters held up the bowl between them. Desdemona averted her eyes as per the ritual, but she could see that Celeste did not.

Mother and Father in turn rinsed their hands, then smeared

a soaked fingertip over their foreheads and on the lids of their eyes. Father had to remove his glasses to complete this practice. Once Mother had walked her through the stages, Desdemona never once thought to question this ritual of arrival in any way. Celeste, however, when her time came to learn, grilled Mother (to no avail) then Father for every detail behind every step. Later that same night, while they were in their beds, Desdemona had interrogated Celeste to learn what she had learned. All Celeste had told her was that Father said this practice was a way of washing off the world.

Now suitably cleansed, Mother gestured for the girls to rise and together the quartet made their way up the stony walkway toward the house. Mother entered through the rear door. She was the only one to ever use this access. Once she had been subsumed by the great house, Father paused to embrace each sister. In particular he fawned over Celeste, which neither surprised nor pained Desdemona. That Celeste was Father's favourite was a fact often demonstrated.

"I can't say how pleased I am to see you both," he said. "You look so well and so present. Did we leave you with everything you needed this time?"

"We could use more cake," Celeste said.

"My dear Celeste, we both know that this old place could be packed to the rafters with sweets and you would still hanker for more," said Father. He winked and kissed the top of her head, then took both sisters by the hand and led them to the main entrance. At the double doors he stopped and spoke softly. "Mother has planned a Dumb Supper for tonight, so you both know what is required, yes?"

Desdemona said, "Yes, Father."

"These suppers are dumb all right," said Celeste.

"Hush!" ordered Desdemona.

Father raised his thick red hands and the girls grew instantly silent. "They do look a little silly, Celeste, I know. But is a thing only how it appears?"

"No."

"Correct. And we know, don't we, that, silly or not, Mother's Dumb Suppers are effective. So we shall all go inside and keep quiet and then tomorrow we shall talk and hike and do all kinds of things."

"You and Mother are spending the night?" cried Celeste delightedly.

"If that is acceptable to you."

"Of course it is!" she blurted.

Father was about to grip the iron handles of the doors when revelation struck Desdemona. Panic gripped her coldly.

"Father, wait!"

He gave Desdemona an inquisitive look.

"Who is tonight's fifth guest?" she asked.

"Your Mother hasn't told me. Why?"

Her experience in the dining hall came gushing out of her in a frenzied, desperate torrent. Father listened calmly, stoically. "If Mother's invitation to the Supper is an open one, we could be in danger, Father."

"Are you frightened?" he asked her.

"I am."

Father removed his glasses, and, with all the oily grace of an illusionist, produced a silk handkerchief from his breast pocket. He cleaned the lenses and returned the spectacles to the perch of his nose.

"I understand your concern. But some things are beyond our control. Fate is fate. You recall the fable of the Appointment in Samarra?"

"Oh! That's my favourite! Will you tell it to us? Please!" begged Celeste.

"Again?" asked Father.

Celeste clasped her hands together. "*Please!*"

Father gestured to the stone bench that stretched between the Grecian columns of flaking stone. They sat and he began to tell the tale.

"Once upon a time there lived a wealthy man in Baghdad. One fine morning this man sent his servant to the market-place to purchase provisions. A little while later the servant came tearing up the lane and into his master's palace. He was pale and trembling and he was empty-handed. 'What is the meaning of this?' cried the wealthy man. 'Where are my provisions? Where is the money I gave to you?'

"'Forgive me, Master,' the servant pleaded. 'I dropped your money and I made no purchase, for I have experienced something terrible!'

"'What is it, boy? Pray tell!'

"'I saw Death, Master. It was there, in the marketplace. I saw Death. It came in the form of a woman, all veiled in sheer black. She saw me and she howled at me and she made a threatening gesture with her awful hand! I fled, Master. I ran all the way back. But Death has found me. I beg your help, Master. I plead with you: loan me one of your horses so that I may flee my Fate.' 'But where shall you go?' asked the wealthy man. 'I shall travel all the way to Samarra. If I ride all night I should arrive there by daybreak.'

"The wealthy man loaned his servant a horse, and the servant drove his spurs into the creature's flanks and sped off.

"Aggravated that he must now fend for himself, the wealthy man travelled to the marketplace and there he found Death drifting amongst the throngs of people. He approached Her and said, 'Why did you threaten my man this morning?'

"Death looked at the wealthy man. 'I made no threat,' she said in a voice as cold and certain as a tombstone. 'My reaction was one of surprise. You see, I did not expect to find your servant here in the marketplace, for I have an appointment with him tomorrow in Samarra...'"

Celeste began to applaud, while Desdemona felt a tangled net of helplessness fall across her heart.

Father stood.

"I love, love, *love* that story!" said Celeste.

"What do you think it means, Celeste?" Father asked.

"That Death is a woman."

"That's one interpretation, yes. Desdemona, would you like to give your sister the moral of this story?"

"It means you cannot hide from Fate."

Father inhaled as though this statement were a draft from paradise. "Indeed," he said before rising. "Let us go in. Not a single word once we step through those doors, yes?"

The girls nodded and, mutely, followed Father inside.

✖

Celeste's game of pretending it was night-time was no longer required, for the dining hall was now a black sea, broken by two islands of candlelight. The tapers illuminated the sparse settings that had been laid out on the table: one for Father, Mother, each of the sisters, and the fifth guest, unnamed and unknown. When Desdemona discovered that her place card had been set next to the fifth guest's chair her panic was renewed. Fate or not, a second encounter with whatever had peered at her from behind the draperies was an experience she would give anything to avoid.

Mother emerged from the kitchen bearing cooked fish and potatoes and a bottle of white wine. The family seated themselves according to the place cards Mother had set for them. Seeing her serve the bounty was like watching a silent film; her motions dramatic, not for pageantry, but to ensure noiselessness. Mutely each received their portion and the Dumb Supper commenced by Mother's execution of a series of gestures, eleven in total: arrival, envelopment, accepting, beckoning, welcoming, benediction, assessment, attainment, communion, thanksgiving, and departure.

In between each gesture were spans of knives slicing meat, wine swallowed loudly (and, in the case of Celeste, with a sour expression and the jutting of a tongue), and scrutiny of the vacant chair beside Desdemona, the one spot at the table where the candlelight seemed unable to reach.

The meal stretched interminably, for every pop of wood, each lively hiss of the candle, any waxing shadow, resulted in an immediate halting of all action while Mother practically stood, her hand extended over the table, eyes wide as the dinner plates that decorated the table.

It was during one such tense interlude that the voice pulsated through the house. It chugged through the ancient, rust-laden plumbing. The pipes amplified what would have otherwise been a faint breeze of sound into a veritable rumble. Desdemona regarded it as something every bit as awful as the cries of one lost at sea.

Everyone in the family heard this sound. Desdemona turned to Mother. The expression on her face froze her.

Mother's mouth was a frozen scream. At first Desdemona thought this was a mask of rage and was directed at her, but instead it was a reaction of fear, the first time Mother had ever shown such an emotion.

Desdemona found herself incapable of looking to where Mother was staring. She could not bring herself to see it, not again. She was on the verge of crying out, of asking Mother what it was she was seeing, when Celeste lunged across the table in an attempt to silence her sister. Father slammed his hand down on the table. The thud and clatter broke the awful spell.

The tension was eventually broken after Mother sat back down and dabbed her tearful eyes with a napkin.

Father slid a dish down the table toward Celeste. It was covered with a lace doily, which the younger girl swiftly removed.

When she saw the dish filled with butter and honey, she beamed at Father and drew a heaping spoonful to her mouth.

By the time Mother executed the gestures of thanksgiving Desdemona was desperately tired. The vow of silence had to stretch until midnight, so Desdemona did not bother having to excuse herself.

Her bed felt marvellous beneath her, so cozy in the chilly evening that Desdemona felt weightless. She must have dozed off, for she didn't even realise Celeste had gone to bed until she heard "Psst! *Pssst!*" inside the darkened room.

Desdemona bolted up and shook her head.

"It's okay, we can talk again. It's past midnight. The wii-iiittching hour..." Celeste said, her fingers wiggling as she performed what she called her 'spooky hands.'

Desdemona could hear the rustle of sheets from across the room. She rolled over to see Celeste propped up on one arm.

"I wonder what life is like there," said Celeste in a raspy half-whisper.

"Where?"

"The place in Mother's cards. It looks so much more interesting than this world."

"Don't be childish. Those cards *are* from this world. They're just paintings."

"Well I know that! But where was the painter looking when they made those pictures do you think?"

Desdemona replied flatly, "They weren't looking anywhere. Except maybe their own imagination."

Celeste slumped back onto her mattress. Desdemona could just discern her silhouette staring up at the turret room's domed ceiling. "I wish somebody would paint pictures up there. That ceiling is too white. It's boring. I wish it had pictures like Mother's cards, pictures of towers and knights and gold cups."

"It's late. Go to sleep."

For a time the room's only score was the tranquil sound of a cool night breeze jostling the sheers. The air cascaded over Desdemona and she could smell the fresh perfume of the tide, of slaked earth. She was being lulled and she was thankful for it. All evening her anxiety (and no doubt her guilt) had been mounting over what they had done that day. Her fear was not over potentially being caught by Mother, but by how the little ritual seemed to have impacted Celeste. Being able to read her sister as well as she could, Desdemona knew that Celeste would awaken tomorrow and be every bit as fixated on the buried card as she had been today. The question now was, how to redirect her attention?

With the storm now fully passed, tomorrow would be unwaveringly bright, conducive to keeping Celeste outdoors and active. Mother would never discover what they had done because Desdemona had decided hours ago that once everyone in the house was asleep, she would sneak out to the vault and dig up the card. She'd hide it under her pillow until after Mother and Father left again. Then she would clean the card and secretly return it to the deck. After that it would just be a matter of keeping Celeste focused on other, less ephemeral things.

All would soon be righted. It was now just a matter of waiting for sleep to claim her family.

The breeze pressed through the room again, then again, as rhythmic as the nearby surf. Desdemona closed her eyes, but only to bask in the delicious calm. The quixotic tide managed to buoy her and to coax her, ever-so-gently, out to sea. Sometime during her voyage, the tide turned violent. Desdemona now felt her body being tossed and jerked. She opened her eyes and immediately squeezed them shut again. Gone was the soft darkness; it had been overtaken by keen light, and the genial night wind had been mangled into stifling gusts, like furnace blasts through the open windows.

"Wake up, Desi! Come see!" Celeste was at her bedside, clumsily grasping at her nightgown. "Come on!"

Abandoning her struggle, Celeste charged for the bedroom door. Desdemona had yet to sit up when she heard the rumble of her sister's frantic footsteps on the great staircase. She was about to call for her sister when she noticed that the door to

Mother and Father's chamber was shut. They must be sleeping still.

Desdemona's escape from the house was one of eagerness tempered by the genuine fear of waking Mother and Father. She moved through the sun-soaked foyer and the dining room, racing directly toward the scullery door at the rear of the house.

Her path to the family vault was sure. Celeste was standing in wait. Desdemona's sprint came to an abrupt halt when she saw what had become of the interred card.

The Tarot grave had erupted. No, not erupted...blossomed. The crude burial place had, overnight, become host to a nest of colourful roots. From this, a thick stalk had conquered the entanglement and had surged up. It now towered above the girls like an old growth tree. The bark was the same pattern of shimmering scales as the back of the card. Its boughs stretched every which way, jutting into the air at impossible angles. Several of these shoots conspired together, knitting themselves into a single, powerful appendage, one that grew long enough to reach the family vault and strong enough to rend its door. The once-imposing barrier of iron had been punctured by the colourful vine, which had then wound and rewound itself around the door's base, pulling it back from the stone frame like a peeled fruit rind.

For the first time, the sisters were afforded a view of the vault's interior, which had for so long been forbidden by Mother. The forced opening was low enough to the ground that Desdemona needed to crouch to spy the inside (a view she decidedly did not want), but it was the perfect vantage for Celeste. In fact, this new rip in the vault was a passage almost tailor-made for Celeste's slight body. Fearlessly, she moved toward the cave-like hole.

Desdemona grabbed her shoulders just in time. "No!" she commanded.

"But we're *supposed* to!" protested Celeste. "We have to

see inside!"

With a surge of strength that shocked her older sister, Celeste broke free and plunged herself headlong into the negative space beyond the iron door.

A millstone of impotence overwhelmed Desdemona. It caused her hands to tremble and her stomach to curdle and her thoughts to grow thin and malformed in her brain. She looked about her, at the fledgling day that was climbing above the woods, growing brighter and hotter. Somehow this made Desdemona feel all the more flustered.

"*Desi!*"

Celeste's voice escaped from the ruined tomb like a ghost's. It was amplified by the stone walls and was seemingly disembodied.

The younger sister's arm emerged through the crude opening. It was reaching for Desdemona. It looked so pale and delicate, like a doll's arm.

"You won't believe it in here! You have to come inside."

Desdemona bent at her hips with the intention of dragging her sister out from the forbidden vault, but what ensued was a violation. She felt herself being thrust forward, impelled as if by a potent gale, toward and through the jagged hole. Celeste did her part to aid in this process, gripping Desdemona's slender fingers and dragging her deeper inside.

The vault was a mere hint of a place, like the setting of a dream. It felt complete but lacked definition, detail. The daylight pressed in through the ruined door and then splayed out in a fan of sunbeams. Yet even this scant illumination was enough to confirm to Desdemona that this vault was far too slight to house even a single casket, let alone a string of corpses that reached back however far into the family's lineage.

Never having a head for specifics, Desdemona did not trouble herself with estimating the vault's exact dimensions. Instead she focused on the altar-like structure that stood in the centre of the chamber. It was a pair of wooden cubes, one set atop the other, askew. The surface of the wood was gouged, its finish worn and lustreless.

Upon this base there sat something veiled, something vague. To Desdemona's eye it was an unsightly lump masked in a swath of fine linen. Time had tempered its pristine whiteness to a mournful, grubby shade of grey. At once, two opposing drives took hold of Desdemona; one, the irrational wish to see what reposed beneath the veil, the other, profound repulsion toward the very idea of what might be concealed there.

Celeste clearly held no conflicted feelings, for she raced toward the concealed thing and, despite Desdemona's protests, tugged the veil free. She executed this move with all the flair of a stage illusionist.

What was it? A primitive drum, a clay pot forged in some ancient kiln? It was a halved sphere with a base of rosewood. A pelt of animal fur was stretched across the top and was held tautly in place by a web of thin leather straps. Dangling from this reeking mesh was an array of decorations: polished stones, bones the shape and colour of a waning moon, glass phials filled with sludgy fluids.

"What kind of coffin is this?" asked Celeste, her voice echoing against the stone walls.

"Don't touch it!" Desdemona said, but too late. Celeste was already on her tiptoes. She tapped on the pelt.

Something inside the bowl tapped back.

'The echo,' Desdemona told herself, 'only an echo...'

"Let's open it!" Celeste whispered. Her hands were clasped in excitement.

"Come away from there. Right now."

Celeste then acted with the rebelliousness that was her wont: her tiny hands clawed at the covered bowl. The cords that held the canvas snug must have been frail, for they snapped under the mild power of Celeste's tugging fingers.

She peeled the canvas back as though it was the rind of some ugly fruit. By now Desdemona was paralysed; her brain a cold lodestone inside her skull, her skin bristling with an anticipatory dread.

What had Celeste unveiled?

If the child's expression was any gauge, it was something cryptic, obscure.

Temptation flared inside Desdemona, and there were pangs of jealousy, too. It pulled her body like a magnetic force. She stepped up onto the dais and stared hard into the face of her sister. Celeste locked eyes with her for just an instant before turning her focus back to the wooden cauldron.

Desdemona followed her sister's example.

The bottom of the bowl was lined with a bed of ashes. Upon these ashes there lay a small sarcophagus, its surface vibrantly painted, its edges rounded. The face that stared up at the girls from the sarcophagus lid was jolly; cheeks rosy, a moon-like head crowned with lively-looking daisies.

"I didn't know they made coffins this tiny," Celeste breathlessly declared.

"It's not a coffin," Desdemona replied. She reached fearlessly into the hollow of the cauldron and removed the grinning lid. She set it down on a little ash dune. "It's a matryoshka, Russian nesting dolls."

"Just like Mother had when she was small like me!"

Desdemona nodded. "I always wanted one of these." Desdemona's tone was pained, sorrowful.

"Look! The next one's a man!" whispered Celeste. "Wait, I mean a king!"

Nestled within the slightly larger base of the first doll beamed the lid of the second: a man with wild eyes and woolly beard and a crown of yellow spikes. The king's mouth was open to an impossible degree, and in its cave-like gape there stood a golden ram with piercing eyes.

"Let's see the others!"

Thus began the sequence of unveilings. The king birthed a smaller shell that depicted a weighing scale with stars gleaming on its plates. From this, conjoined twins with distended heads and ossified frames. Deeper and deeper the girls went, each doll growing not only smaller but more gruesome. When Celeste uncovered the ninth, they could not even identify it as a human likeness. It was something shrivelled, crooked.

"Is that it?" Celeste asked.

"No," said Desdemona. "There's one more, I think."

"What are you waiting for? Open it!"

"I...I can't."

"I'll do it then!"

And before Desdemona could protest, Celeste had pulled herself up on the heavy bowl and reached down to fiddle with the tiny matryoshka. Her fingers pressed and twisted at it. Finally, the foetal lump split in two.

The halved doll emitted a noise; something near to a gasp, a keen wisp of breath. It froze Desdemona's blood in her veins. It was, to her mind, the single worst sound she had ever heard.

Until the deathly silence of the morning was shattered by an agonised scream. Another immediately followed. The cries came tearing across the land from somewhere near, somewhere beyond the family vault.

"We have to..." Desdemona began, but the words dissipated before she could even organise her thoughts completely. She looked at Celeste. The child's expression was a broken one. She was sobbing.

Another scream, this one nearer.

Desdemona craned her head and peered over her shoulder, through the open crypt door and up the path toward the lawn.

What she saw hollowed her, clawed out all the elements that kept her intact.

Father was tearing across the rear yard, racing down the slope toward the dock. He was dressed only in a pair of pyjama bottoms, which were saturated with crimson. His uncovered chest and arms were greasy with flowing blood. His face was bearded with a smear of that morning's shaving foam.

Desdemona cried out to him, but a fresh sight lodged her voice in her throat.

That sight was Mother. She too was racing across the lawn. But unlike Father, her journey was horridly graceful. She moved with all the speed and beauty of a shooting star. Still dressed in her billowing nightgown of soft whiteness, Mother glided after her husband.

Desdemona then noticed that Mother's feet were not touching the ground. She was like a puppeteer's prop, animated by a hidden network of pulleys and cords. Her head wobbled as though it was too heavy for her frame.

Mother held a pair of great knives in her fists. The one in her left hand (which was nearest to Desdemona and thus most plain to her shock-widened eyes) was narrow and dripping. The other, which Mother had raised above her bobbling head, was wide and chunky, nearer to a cleaver than a dagger.

On instinct, Desdemona snatched up Celeste and pressed the child's face into her shoulder. "Don't look," she muttered frantically into her sister's ear. "It's okay, shh, shhh. Just close your eyes."

But Desdemona was unable to follow her own instructions. She could but stare helplessly as Mother pounced upon Father and drove the blades into his prone body over and over again; chopping and plunging and slashing with impossible speed and savagery long after Father's screams had ceased.

Something in the damp, faint song of steel parting flesh managed to alter time, to slow it down to the protracted, inescapable torture of a nightmare. Desdemona couldn't guess as to how long she stood holding Celeste, listening to those noises that seemed to silence the wind. She stared in a *petit mal* trance at the rippling leaves of the great mountain ash that stood as a sentinel outside hers and Celeste's bedroom.

She remained transfixed on the sight until a sudden movement in her periphery forced her to look headlong at the sight of Mother, terrible Mother.

She was coming towards them now, skating on the hot morning air. Mother of Swords, her weapons still dripping from the fresh kill, advanced.

Her face was transitioning before Desdemona's very eyes. It was as if her flesh and the skull that braced it had become clay for eager and unseen hands. Muscles and arches and contours now existed for merely a blink before becoming hurriedly transfigured into some new and outlandish composition. Eyes sagged and then lifted. Lips that were plumped like those of a lover awaiting the union of a sacred kiss were suddenly pulled keen across the gums, giving Mother the appearance of an animal about to pounce on its quarry.

Desdemona ran; ran with a momentum she'd never before known. By now Celeste's insatiably curious nature had bested her ability to obey: she was staring out over Desdemona's shoulder, staring at What-Had-Been-Mother that was hunting them. Celeste began to scream and sob. Her little body quaked in Desdemona's arms, which seemed to double her weight. By the time the sisters stumbled into the rear entrance of the great house Desdemona's head was swimming.

Petrified that she might lose her grip on Celeste, Desdemona loped ahead, through the scullery and the kitchen where Mother's tea kettle sat wailing on the stove.

The spiral staircase was nearly insurmountable. Halfway up, Desdemona's legs gave out. She released Celeste with a whimper and shouted for her to run.

The Mother abomination came thundering into the foyer. She halted at the foot of the stairs, and for one magnificent moment Desdemona thought they might be safe.

She was studying the steps, assessing them like an animal seeing such a structure for the first time.

'Can this thing, whatever it is, even climb stairs?'

Desdemona wondered, or rather *wished.*

The creature threw itself prostrate on the foyer floor and plunged one of its swords into the bottom step. The second blade was stabbed into a higher stair. Using her weapons as braces, the Mother of Swords began to pull her twitching body up the stairs.

Desdemona shrieked and tore up the last few stairs. The terrible thunk-thunk-thunk sound of What-Had-Been-Mother stabbing the steps resounded through the great open foyer.

"This way, Desi! Over here!"

Celeste was in the master bedroom, her body half-concealed behind the ornate door. Desdemona dove through the open frame and kicked the door closed. She scrambled to her feet and leapt to one end of Mother's large dresser.

"Help me push!" she pleaded.

Celeste offered what little strength she possessed. Panic gave Desdemona strength enough for the two of them.

The dresser became a barricade, though Desdemona was wise enough to know that this was far from enough to protect them.

She flung the dresser's drawers open and rifled through Mother's belongings. She found the crushed velvet pouch, tugged its drawstring loose and shook the Tarot deck out onto the Persian rug. The sisters sifted through the scattered cards.

The thing was now just beyond the door. It was unleashing a rain of stabbing blows against it. The tips of its weapons poked through the wood, appearing like the silver beaks of some ravening flock. Desdemona knew it was only a matter of seconds before the barrier would be rent.

At last she found the card she was looking for. It had a sextet of gleaming golden wands clashing before a robust sun. Below the illustration, the card bore a single word of Latin text: *Victoria.*

She hopped over Celeste's hunched form and slapped the

card's face against the door.

The assault from What-Had-Been-Mother ceased instantly.

Bolstered by the effectiveness of her spell, Desdemona began to drag the card across the door, forming precise geometric patterns with great skill, just as Mother had tutored her to do.

From the landing there came the faint noise of slithering, of something slinking back down the grand staircase.

"Is it gone?" Celeste asked in an uncharacteristically small voice.

"I think so…but I'm not sure."

"What happened to Mother?" Celeste asked and immediately began to cry again.

Desdemona pulled her sister close and tried in vain to console her. The rapid, mumbled assurances had some effect, for Celeste's sobs eventually softened. In time the master bedroom's silence was only occasionally punctuated by Celeste inhaling sharply.

A form darkened the second storey window. Its shadow fell lean and crooked across the bedroom.

Celeste was the first to look out the window. Once again she started to scream. Though she harboured no desire to see, Desdemona felt her head turning to face the shape at the pane.

The entity was hovering on the other side of the glass. The swords were still gripped in its gory fists. It was smiling, smiling… By now the face had suffered so many contortions that its original traits were lost. It was now a mask, no longer human; the effigy of some chasmal entity that should not be witnessed in the world that lay outside of Dream.

"No!" Desdemona cried. The card still between her fingers, she leapt to the window and pressed the image of the Wands firmly against the glass.

The thing lost its grip on its weapons. Desdemona could

hear them clattering against the stone walkway so far below. She traced the protective designs on the window, then the other two windows that flanked it.

"Help me, Celeste!" she instructed as she opened the slat cupboard and began to wrestle free the cumbersome sets of storm shutters.

Forged from thick slabs of oak, the shutters were designed to protect the house's interior from the squalls of hurricanes, which, when the house was first built, had been very common on the island. Or so Father had told her. Each room had a double set of shutters; one external, one internal. Desdemona hoped that this single barrier and the strength of her magic would be enough to protect them until this most unnatural of storms passed.

Together the sisters secured all three windows, locking the shutters snugly with their latches of pig iron. Celeste was now more afraid than Desdemona had ever known her to be. Seeing Celeste this way upset her, but she hid these feelings and tried to convince her sister that this was just another form of 'playing night-time,' as she liked to do in the dining hall.

They huddled together in the gloom and listened to the sound of tapping, so incessant, endless. Mother had evidently scrabbled down to retrieve her dropped weapons, for the chamber was now filled with the hideous pulse of blades rapping upon the panes.

"Don't cry," Desdemona cooed, desperate to calm Celeste, "hush."

...taptap...tap

"She can't get in. We're safe in here."

...tap...

"We just have to wait."

...tap...taptap...tap...

"We'll wait until she goes away."

Celeste ran out of tears. She went silent. She slept.

...tap...tap...

"Can we go the scullery?" Celeste asked. Her voice was creaky. She was groggy and parched.

...*taptap* ...

"No. The rest of the house is unprotected. We're sealed in here. Just try to rest. It will be over soon."

"Will it?"

"It will."

...*tap*...*tap*...*tap* ...

The summer day began to unwind into the ember-and-shadow palette of dusk. Celeste was lying with her head on her sister's lap. The raspy shallowness of her breathing sounded grave to Desdemona's ear. She stroked her hair and struggled to stay alert.

...*tap* ...

"Celeste, do you remember when you called the stone statue 'Queen' and I asked you if Father had ever told you the story about the White Queen?"

She shook her head slightly against Desdemona's thigh.

"Oh, it was one of my favourites when I was small like you. It's called 'The Lovers.' Would you like to hear it?"

Desdemona looked down to see her sister nod once more.

"It was in another time; not the past, present or future, but a different time. There the disciples lived under the rule of the Black King. This Black King was benevolent but sad, sad because his nature confined him to the shadows. His loneliness soon became unbearable. So he went to the bank of a poisonous river, planning to drink a hearty swallow of the deadly water.

"But as the Black King was reaching a cupped hand into the river, his eyes were met with an impossible sight: reposing there, just beneath the surface of the poisonous river, was the most beautiful woman the King had ever seen. She was willowy and as pale as snow. She reached up and took his hand. He pulled the woman up from the river.

"She explained to the Black King that she had come to drown herself to alleviate her loneliness. The King confessed his reason for coming there, and the two fell deeply in love right there on the bank. Together they walked to the temple of the Hierophant so they could be married that very day.

"The Hierophant was delighted to perform the ceremony, but the moment he declared them the Black King and the White Queen, the Hierophant shocked everyone by uttering a magic spell that caused the White Queen to instantly vanish.

"The Black King was infuriated and ordered the Hierophant arrested. The guards dragged him into the royal dungeon and the Black King demanded a thorough search of the lands. But before the parties could even begin their hunt for the White Queen, winter fell heavy. Every corner of the kingdom was plagued with snow and wailing winds. The blizzard raged for so long that the kingdom began to run low on rations. Distraught and feeling helpless, the Black King ordered that the Hierophant be tortured until he confessed what he'd done with the White Queen.

"The Hierophant did not resist the torture chamber, but his confession was not believed by anyone. He claimed that he had cast the White Queen to a deep grave on the Moon. This sudden, unnatural winter was the result of the White Queen trying to dig her way out of her grave, which sent Moon dust down onto the Earth. The howling winds were her cries of distress. The Hierophant assured the Black King that this separation was necessary, that the Black King and the White Queen had to be apart so that they could eventually know the bliss of reunion.

"The Black King did not believe the Hierophant and decreed that he should be executed at dawn. The next morning, just as the royal executioner was about to deliver the fatal stroke, the Black King announced that he'd had a change of heart. He said he'd had a dream where the White Queen and he found one another again and that peace and happiness were restored in the land. So he decided to spare the life of the Hierophant and allow him to go free.

"Immediately upon showing mercy, the blizzard ceased. The sun broke through the dark clouds and began to shine across the kingdom, melting the snows. And then, the White Queen returned. She came rushing through the gates of the kingdom and she and the Black King knew the bliss of reunion.

"That is how time was born. Each year the Black King and the White Queen enjoy the heated summer of passion, the sorrowful autumn that precedes the White Queen's confinement in the Moon. And then, the joyful rebirth of spring."

Celeste was sleeping soundly. Desdemona felt herself wanting to doze as well. A great drift of sleep was piling up at the corners of her mind, filling her thoughts with visions of a lunar grave. It was on these thoughts that Desdemona willed her focus. Doing so helped her ignore the incessant tapping on the windows.

✻

It was silent when Desdemona woke; silent and bright, too bright in fact. The light spilled unrestrained into the master bedroom. Desdemona snuffled, grimaced against the sunbeams, and indulged in a deep stretch. She must have fallen asleep while cradling Celeste.

Only after she called for her sister did the panic begin to sink its claws into Desdemona's innards.

Celeste was gone.

The shutters on one of the large windows had been unlatched and opened. Desdemona could see the scratches and gory streaks left by Mother's swords. The view through the pane weakened her, nearly broke her.

Autumn had fallen over the island, and it was clear that this seasonal change had not been recent, for the leaves had long since lost their fiery colours and were now browned and desiccated, a dirty carpet stretching across the yellow lawn. The sky was cloudless and bright, but there was no warmth from the sun, even as Desdemona stood directly in its rays.

Questions flooded over her. She was driven to her knees under the weight of her own confusion and helplessness.

She scrabbled on all fours for the door and flung it open. Her mind only faintly registered the piled dust and the cobwebs that now marred Mother's once-pristine foyer. She raced down the spiral stairs, across the main floor, and finally out through the scullery door.

Damp winds lashed her the moment she stepped into the open world. The lake was choppy and was the colour of cheap tin. When she discovered that the motorboat was indeed no longer tethered to the dock, that it was gone (long gone no doubt), Desdemona began to pull her hair and plead with Fate, praying that the hand she'd been dealt was nowhere near as cruel as it now seemed.

But as she made her way to the dock to confirm that the motorboat had indeed ferried her sister away from the island, Desdemona literally stumbled upon an even crueller leaving: Father's corpse had been left to putrefy on the muddy slope of the lawn where the Mother of Swords had felled him. Time and the elements had transformed his handsome face to an unidentifiable mass of something like congealed roast drippings. The skin was as colourless as the mud on which the body lay. The nose had deflated and the eyeglasses sat askew over the empty eye sockets. The crows had visibly been supping on his eyes and the meat of his uncovered back. The blood, all that blood, had run out to slake the earth or had become indistinct russet stains on Father's pyjama bottoms.

In some final symbolic gesture, whose meaning Desdemona could not parse, the thing that had once been Mother had driven several long knives into Father's remains, pinning it to the ground.

Only after she'd begun to recoil in pity and disgust did Desdemona realise that Father's positioning was identical to the figure in the *Ruina* card. He was pinned to the soil by blades, his head was turned to face some mysterious expanse of unknown terrain (in this case, the lake and whatever lay beyond it), and then Desdemona saw them; the colourful scraps of fabric that Mother must have culled from her sewing room. They were tied to the hilts of the swords and now fluttered in the wind like the flags of some fallen kingdom.

She thought of the Tarot card, of Celeste's 'feeling' toward it, and a glimmer of hope brightened her soul. Could the child be hiding out there? Perhaps she had tried to put the matryoshkas back in place?

Desdemona turned on her heel and raced toward the family vault.

The crypt door was still an open passage, but the colourful vine that had hatched from the buried card had shrivelled and turned grey and now laid on the vault steps with the other dead foliage of autumn.

"Celeste!" Desdemona was pleading with the darkness in the tomb. The realisation that the Mother-thing might be waiting inside there did not occur to her until it was too late. She was inside the vault now. The various matryoshkas were nestled among the leaves and grit. The altar bowl was empty, as was the vault itself. Desdemona sank down onto the cold stone floor and curled into a foetal position and prayed with Fate to erase her. Her sobs bounced off the unfeeling stone walls and echoed back as if to mock her anguish.

Now almost catatonic, Desdemona was sprawled across the vault floor, staring emptily at the autumnal world outside.

She doubted her eyes when the first snowflake fell, but in time the flakes multiplied.

Desdemona pulled herself out of the crypt by her hands. When she reached the outside she rolled onto her back and stared up at the slate-tinted sky and allowed the snow, wet and weak as it was, to fall upon her.

The White Queen must be stirring in her lunar grave.

The vine from the Tarot card was pressed into Desdemona's back as if to somehow prod her, toward what she could not even fathom. She thought back to how this entire ordeal had started with the burial of the Ruin card, and how the Victory card had saved them…though only temporarily.

Inspiration seized her. She bolted up, stood, ran.

The lake had grown even rougher, for its pounding surf was almost deafening to Desdemona as she ran to the great house.

Up the stairs and back into the master bedroom. Mother's scattered cards were now coated with dust. She knelt down and rifled through them. Unlike before while she and Celeste had been stalked by their entity-possessed Mother, this time she did not know which card to look toward for guidance. She closed her eyes and began to assess each one by touch alone, hoping that Celeste's knack, which the child called simply 'feelings', was part of her makeup as well.

Finally, after enough attempts to cause Desdemona to believe this whole thing might just be an exercise in futility, she lifted a card that seemed heavier than the others. She laid it flat across her left palm and felt (or believed she felt) a strange warmth trickling through the inside of her arm.

She opened her eyes.

Sinum currus. The Chariot.

The card was laden with images of Cancer, the crab, and of the element of Water. A water sign somehow meant that this card could not buried in the earth. Should she carry the card to the lake? Could divination really be rooted in so simple an act as following an impulse (or a 'feeling') that felt appropriate? Surely there must be more to the Gift than this? But in her desperation Desdemona found solace in the minor gesture of holding the Chariot card tenderly against her breast while she made her way toward the water.

She froze mid-step the instant she saw the Sign.

The Chariot had been readied for her. It floated just above the surface of the lake, which was now unnaturally still, from maelstrom to millpond in a matter of moments. Autumn mist crawled leisurely across the water, giving Desdemona the impression that she was now among the clouds.

Willing her weak legs to carry her to the dock was a chore, and when this new proximity confirmed the nature of her Chariot, Desdemona began to cry.

Father's corpse now floated upon the water. It was laying facedown and its limbs had been reconfigured in a manner that would have been agonising in life and was indignant in death. The arms and legs were bent backwards and held still in rigor mortis. From the wrists and ankles several silken cords had been wound, forming a rudimentary boat. A pair of long and bloodied swords lay crisscrossed upon Father's back. These, Desdemona felt, could serve as her oars.

The wind blew low and eerily. It was no longer snowing. She stared at Father's remains, simultaneously entranced and repulsed by the sight. She knew what must be done.

"I...can't...I can't..."

Her protest was small, and a moment later she realised how insincere it was, for as soon as she heard Celeste's distant cry from somewhere out on the water, Desdemona submitted herself to her duty.

She climbed down onto the rotting Chariot, wincing at the feel of the soggy meat coming apart under her weight. Only Father's bones seemed to keep her from falling into the water. But these bones were raft enough. Desdemona took up the swords and pushed away from the dock.

The fog banks piled up all around her like drifting snow. Desdemona rowed herself far enough from the island that the sound of the surf disappeared. For a long span the only noise she heard was the rhythm of the blades slicing the unseen water, propelling her deeper into the unseen. But she did not lose faith, for every so often she could hear Celeste's unmistakable voice seeping in from this direction or that. Sometimes Desdemona would call out to her sister, but more often she would simply do her best to steer her morbid raft in Celeste's direction.

⁂

"Hush now, my dear girl," said August, the pellar. His voice was soothing. It was the kind of tone that Charles knew well from their long work together. "You are safe now, Celeste," August continued, "perfectly safe. The ugly spirit is gone. It can no longer harm you."

Charles moved alongside his partner and love. He placed his hand upon August's back, both to congratulate and comfort him after this draining exorcism.

"Can you hear us, Celeste?" Charles called into the dim parlour. "Please give us a sign if you can."

The flame inside the red signalman's lantern (the room's only light source) flared in response.

"Very good, Celeste," said August. "Rest now, sweet child. We thank you for speaking with us. We will call upon you again soon."

Charles extinguished the lantern once August had deposited the spirit bottle into a small pouch. They exited the chamber and made their way into the kitchen. Charles lit two cigarettes and handed one to August, who accepted it with a trembling hand.

Familiarity with his lover's post-séance condition had trained Charles well. He removed the tea towel from a plate of cheese, bread, and chocolate. He pushed the plate toward August.

"Eat," he said. "I'll get you some coffee."

The two men sat and talked until dawn, for even though August had successfully ensnared the ugly entity that had been plaguing the ghost girl who called herself Celeste, he still felt that this work was not yet completed.

"What's left to do?" Charles asked him.

August rubbed his face, sighed. "That first Sitting we did, the one right after I had the dream about Celeste and that awful spirit-possessed Mother travelling across the water from the spirit world, Celeste said something about a family vault on an island somewhere, that she and her sister had released something that had been stored inside that vault."

"The malevolent spirit?"

"It's possible. Once I banished the evil spirit, I saw a clear image of a woman standing behind Celeste, like a protector, a mother. Maybe whatever the girls freed from the vault possessed this woman and now the woman is free."

"Yes, but it's doubtful that the woman that Celeste referred to as Mother was her actual Mother," Charles said. "Remember, Celeste appeared consistently as a girl in an antiquated-looking dress, whereas the woman was wearing modern clothes."

August nodded. "I know. I don't believe she was Celeste's actual mother, even though from what Celeste has told us, she certainly filled the role. And there's something else I didn't fully comprehend until just now: when I was under and trying to purge that harmful spirit, the woman, Celeste's quote-unquote Mother, was helping me."

"Helping you how?"

"She knew the gestures, the words of purging."

"You think that in life this woman was a pellar?"

"Or a medium, a spiritualist. I think she became a caregiver to Celeste's spirit long after Celeste had died on Earth."

Charles sat back in his chair. The wood popped. "That's interesting...a very interesting observation indeed. But where does that leave us?"

"I have a theory," August said after a long pause. "It's a long shot, but it's the only way I can see truly putting this matter to rest."

"I'm listening."

"We dig through local history books, old maps, anything. I believe Celeste is a local spirit of place, a genius loci. So we look for a private island somewhere in the province; a private island with an old mansion and a family vault."

"You're right, that is a long shot," Charles returned. "But let's just say for the sake of argument that we find such an island, assuming of course that Celeste's messages and your visions haven't all been purely symbolic, what then? What's the next step?"

"We travel there. We bring the spirit bottle with us, then we secure it back inside the family vault."

"To what end?"

"Maybe doing so will put an end to what Celeste feels she started. Maybe she'll be able to go back home again. I believe she truly loves that house on the island. I think this woman was tending to Celeste and her sister and that haunted island. Maybe it was Mother who first bound that chaotic spirit in the family vault, but the spirit began to tempt Celeste, preying on her childish curiosity, urging her to free it from the vault. Perhaps if we right this error, Celeste will find the peace and happiness she knew on that island."

"Perhaps, but wouldn't it be better to urge her on? To send her to the realm of the dead?"

"Ordinarily I'd say yes, but in this case, I think Celeste has found her paradise on that island. It's a soft place; she can probably partake of the spirit realm and the material world in equal measure there. It was abandoned, except when Mother and Father made the trip to feed and communicate with them."

For a long span the only soundtrack was the ticking of the clock on the living room mantle. At last Charles spoke.

"Okay. We'll do it. We'll start the search. But right now sleep is what we both need."

✖

They searched; first through maps and websites and history books, then later upon rural highways and back roads. Every spare day they had, the pair would be traversing. They parked at countless beachfronts and fields so that August could stand and Sense. He carried the spirit bottle with him and would call out to Celeste, and then wander like a dowser in search of occulted waters.

In the springtime they came upon a thread of great promise: a cluster of tiny islands on a lake in a southwest corner of a peninsula. They booked a room at a grimy inn and rented an outboard motorboat, and at daybreak they struck out onto the water. The two of them sat under blankets, shivering against the frigid winds that pressed across the vacant lake. Charles steered the vessel while August did his utmost to activate his Sensing abilities.

At first the presence that August felt moving alongside their boat did not seem to fit their quest. The presence was arresting in its gruesomeness: the sight of a gaunt young woman floating upon a boat made of human remains. But August was well accustomed to the occasionally shocking and repulsive forms the spirits took in order to penetrate the chatter of the human mind, therefore he knew that this appearance likely had some underlying meaning.

That meaning came in the form of navigation. The ghostly woman was conveying to August images of an island, one with a great stone house and a family vault, even a dock for their boat. He urged Charles to follow the spectral guide.

August shouted directions with such urgency that Charles felt himself panicking. He did his best to steer them in the proper direction, but every inch they travelled seemed to bring them only further out. A seemingly endless sprawl of grey water stretched out before them. Charles began to worry about their safety. He eyed the jerry-can at his feet and prayed they'd have enough fuel to get back to the mainland.

"Shut the motor off!" August suddenly cried. He was practically standing.

Charles killed the engine and then sat listening to his heart thumping in his ears. He suddenly felt light-headed and light-hearted. A lump grew in his throat.

The island was there.

It seemed to have arisen from the depths like a lost continent. But it was real, utterly real. Nevertheless, Charles felt as though their vessel had somehow crossed a precious threshold where dreams had heft and matter was weightless. In this giddy, topsy-turvy bliss the pair of them glided toward the island's shore.

The great house was stunning. It was the stuff of August's boyhood love of haunted houses; almost archetypal in its perfection: majesty crumbling, sorrowful and beautiful at once; a monument to permanence that was somehow, paradoxically, slipping into oblivion. They had been blessed with a glimpse of the mansion in that rare moment between permanence and nothingness.

The tide pulled the boat to shore. Charles sculled them toward to the wooden dock and then moored them.

"Look at this," August whispered, indicating the upturned bowl and the dirty, soggy length of white linen upon the dock.

They explored the house; an experience that snatched both men's breath and voice.

At the end of a stout footpath they found the open stone vault. Intuition ordered Charles to collect the scattered matryoshkas. August secured the spirit bottle in the smallest doll and then the matryoshkas were reassembled and set inside the bowl.

It was while the two men were silently exiting the tomb that they saw her. She was smiling at them, her smoky form stood out in bas relief from the woodlands that surrounded them.

"Hello, dear Celeste," August said in a tearful voice.

✳

All seemed hopeless once Desdemona had lost the tether of Celeste's voice. Her sister silenced, Desdemona had resigned herself to merely floating upon the boundless water, surrounded by the fogs that masked the world from her. It felt like an eternity and she felt forsaken.

But then she heard the motorboat. Shock made her numb. Had Mother and Father somehow returned? Had the whole ugly ordeal been a nightmare? Desdemona scoured the mists. She heard voices: men's voices first, but then...

Then...

Celeste. She was no longer crying, she was elated, chatty. She had been restored somehow.

Desdemona took up the swords and rowed until her arms burned. She did her utmost to follow the voices.

Fate, she discovered, had moved her in a full circle. She found herself back at the island. A boat, not unlike Father's, was tethered to the dock.

It was only when she went to steer her raft toward this dock that Desdemona realised she was walking, or rather gliding. She crossed the lake and the lawn.

She found the family vault restored, down to the great iron door, which had been reattached and re-locked. The great house was a welcome sight, but it nonetheless seemed somehow altered. It was paler, blurred, like a poorly-snapped photograph in an old album.

Desdemona entered the house with an ease that unnerved her. She slid through the scullery and the foyer and up the spiral staircase. The house was tidy and visibly cared for.

There were voices down below.

She moved down to the dining hall. She found them:

Celeste and the two men who were laughing with her. The heavy curtains were drawn and the tapers sat burning in the candelabras. Celeste would never tire of playing night-time.

She uttered Celeste's name but found that her voice was distant and warbled. She moved around the long table, slipping behind the drapes.

Peering out through the opening between the curtains, she was delighted when Celeste turned her head and saw her, or so Desdemona thought, hoped. She hearkened back to the warm summer afternoon when she had seen some apparition, something indistinct, through these very curtains. Had she seen a premonition of herself that day?

She told Celeste to not be sad, that she couldn't be with her just now, but that she would be with her soon.

Just as soon as the men called her back to the great house.

The two men were staring intently at the tabletop. An adjustment of her perspective allowed Desdemona to see Mother's Tarot cards laid out in a King's Cross spread. She knew that the deck was missing Chariot and Ruin, but she watched intently as the men attempted to decipher her future, or perhaps her past.

Desdemona hoped that their reading would somehow spell out a way for her to fully return to the island. She was here but not quite here. Part of her still felt adrift on her chariot, inside that grey void.

Fate, which had so kindly kept her and Celeste together for so very long, had now driven a cold, painful wedge between them. Desdemona imagined herself as a pale queen in a distant grave. She clung to the hope of reunion.

Publication History

"Scold's Bridle: A Cruelty" is original to this collection.

"Chain of Empathy" is original to this collection.

"Banishments" was first published in *Looming Low*, edited by Justin Steele and Sam Cowan, Dim Shores, 2017.

"Fragile Masks" was first published in *The Mammoth Book of Halloween Stories*, edited by Stephen Jones, Skyhorse Publishing, 2018.

"Neithernor" was first published in *Aickman's Heirs*, edited by Simon Strantzas, Undertow Publications, 2015.

"Deep Eden" was first published in *The Mammoth Book of Cthulhu*, edited by Paula Guran, Running Press, 2016.

"The Patter of Tiny Feet" was first published in *Searchers After Horror*, edited by S.T. Joshi, Fedogan & Bremer, 2014.

"The Rasping Absence" first appeared in *Black Wings IV,* edited by S.T. Joshi, PS Publishing, 2015.

"After the Final" was first published in *The Grimscribe's Puppets,* edited by Joseph S. Pulver, Sr., Miskatonic River Press, 2013.

"The Sullied Pane" was first published in *Crooked Houses,* edited by Mark Beech, Egaeus Press, 2020.

"Crawlspace Oracle" was first published in *Mannequin: Tales of Wood Made Flesh,* edited by Justin Burnett, Silent Motorist Media, 2019.

"Cast Lots" was first published in *Nightmare's Realm,* edited by S.T. Joshi, Dark Regions Press, 2015.

"Notes on the Aztec Death Whistle" was first published in *Weird Fiction Review #10,* edited by John Pelan, Centipede Press, 2020.

"Headsman's Trust: A Murder Ballad" was first published in *Pluto in Furs: Tales of Diseased Desires and Seductive Horrors,* edited by Scott Dwyer, Plutonian Press, 2019.

"Three Knocks on a Buried Door" was first published in *Apostles of the Weird,* edited by S.T. Joshi, PS Publishing, 2020.

"Ten of Swords: Ruin" was first published in *Their Dark and Secret Alchemy,* edited by Robert Morgan, Sarob Press, 2019.

About the Author

Richard Gavin explores the realm where fear and the numinous converge. His eerie, nightmarish stories have garnered high critical praise, appear in several volumes of *Best New Horror* and *Year's Best Horror*, and have been collected in five previous books, including *Sylvan Dread: Tales of Pastoral Darkness* and *At Fear's Altar*. Along with fiction, Richard produces works of esotericism and meditations on the macabre, such as *The Benighted Path: Primeval Gnosis and the Monstrous Soul* and *The Moribund Portal: Spectral Resonance and the Numen of the Gallows*. He dwells in the North. Online presence: www.richardgavin.net